HUNGRY LOVE

HUNGRY LOVE

a novel

TOMIKO DIAZ

ST. ŌDE
Press

This is a work of fiction. While certain real persons, public figures, businesses, or places may be mentioned, all characters, dialogue, and events are products of the author's imagination or are used fictitiously. Any resemblance to actual persons, living or dead, beyond those clearly referenced in a fictional context, is coincidental and unintended.

Published by St. Ode Press
saintodepress.com

Library of Congress Cataloging-in-Publication Data
Name: Diaz, Tomiko, author
Title: Hungry Love
Identifiers: LCCN 2026907450 (print)
ISBN 979-8-9949662-0-4 (paperback)
Subjects: Romance fiction. | Romantic comedy fiction. | Chefs—Fiction.

Cover design by Boja
Book design by Timothy Halloran

Printed in the United States of America
10 9 8 7 6 5 4 3 2 1

First Edition

To the ones who feed us—in every way.

Music and food shape the world of this novel. When songs appear in the text, you're invited to listen along. If you'd like to press play—or preheat—the playlist and recipes await at the back of the book.

HUNGRY LOVE

PART ONE

CHAPTER 1

Climbing Without Ladders

THERE'S A KIND of hunger that looks like ambition and tastes like survival. At Pulse, it comes dressed in mood boards, curated cool, and the confidence to make it all look effortless. The work is real. The rest is just camouflage.

That's the theory, anyway. In practice, *my* survival looks more like this: the sidewalk doing that New York thing where walking's a team sport, and I'm the weak link. A tourist family forms a human barricade in front of me, debating directions to Central Park. Something squishes under my heel. Fruit, maybe, though unidentified organic matter feels a lot more honest. Someone behind me yells into his AirPods like all of Midtown is his therapist. And suddenly, I have the brief, irrational urge to flee to a remote village and churn my own butter.

When I finally reach my destination, I stop and crane my neck. The glass tower rises above me, so sleek it looks photoshopped onto the grimy, gum-polished sidewalk beneath it. It's not just a building. It's a mirror. A myth dressed in steel and glass—a skyscraper-sized dare. It's home to Pulse, where the espresso's free, but the expectations aren't.

I pull the strap of my tote higher onto my shoulder. Somewhere at the bottom, my Converse sulk like they've been benched in a pivotal playoff game because, for once, I'm wearing heels. Not towering stilettos, just enough lift to say *I'm serious* without seeming desperate. Because today matters. I have a chance to be seen not as someone who makes other people's visions look good, but as someone with a vision of her own.

In the building's glass, my reflection stares back. I smooth my blazer, arrange my expression into something that could be mistaken for confidence, and stand up straighter, but I still can't tell if I'm bracing for success or impact.

THE LOBBY IS chilled to a temperature best described as *you can't perspire if you can't feel your skin.*

In the elevator, the ride is like being reeled upward by a thread I can't see, but feel knotted under my ribcage. I doubt Darwin ever imagined a world where survival meant smiling through microaggressions and contouring your cheekbones like your life depended on it. But here we are. The modern working woman: evolving faster than our ancestors ever imagined, yet somehow still not fast enough. When the elevator doors hiss open, I release the breath I've been holding and step onto the fifteenth floor.

I'm greeted by a familiar sprawl of cubicles, an awkward landscape of half-walls and fluorescent lighting that somehow combines the worst parts of open concept *and* solitary confinement. A layout clearly designed by someone who's never tried to meet a deadline next to Greg from Sales and his daily tuna wrap.

The air smells faintly of expensive perfumes, microwaved quinoa, and anxiety. The espresso machine sputters in the staff break room. Heels click like metronomes against white marble floors in the corridors. Manicured nails clatter on keyboards. This is our orchestra of overachievers, performing their tight-smiled overture to capitalism, one Slack ping at a time. And like any orchestra, it needs patrons.

Pulse profits from the idea that women are too busy to curate their own best lives but will happily buy someone else's if it comes with flattering lighting and a swipe-up link. It's the brainchild of Marisol Von Phelps, lifestyle oracle and chief curator of want, supported by a "teensy" team of seventy-five. I help oversee the editorial department for print and online, which means I spend most of my time editing other people's words and managing the chaos of Pulse's food and other lifestyle content.

I duck into the staff kitchen long enough to air-fry a plate of tater tots—breakfast of champions—and start weaving my way back toward my desk. I try to slip past Valerie Thorne, our Executive Editor, former Paris bureau chief of *Elle*, rumored descendant of minor European royalty, and firm believer that dressing down is a moral failing. But her all-glass human terrarium of an office is the corner-office equivalent of a watchtower, and she's impossible to miss, leaning in the door frame like she's posing casual for one of our fashion editorials. Her silk sheath is cinched at the waist with a belt I'm 60% sure is vintage Hermès and 100% sure costs more than my rent.

Several staffers hover nearby, all clearly focused on the man she's flirting with. He's tall, broad-shouldered, every inch of his posture radiating ease and power.

It's not until he turns slightly—devastating profile, hair too artfully disheveled to be accidental—that my stomach does a swan dive into my heels.

Gavin Jones. The man I've spent eight years avoiding, and who has always treated me like a problem he hasn't decided how to solve.

I spin to retreat, hoping to slip away unseen.

"Ava," Valerie calls out.

I freeze.

I consider pretending I didn't hear her and bolting.

Instead, I turn.

And I walk straight into Gavin.

The plate jerks in my hand, and a few precious, ketchup-bright stars streak across his very white shirt, one landing like a comet right above the second button.

"Oh my God," I say automatically, stepping back. "Sorry. That was—You were—"

He looks down at the constellation, then lifts his eyes to mine. Something like recognition flickers there before it disappears.

"Still with the tater tots?"

My cheeks flare. "They're restorative."

Valerie steps in, lips pursed. "Gavin, I'm so sorry," she says, shooting me a look. "Ava's still learning to walk in heels."

I don't look at her. I can't. I merely extend my free hand toward him, mortified but determined to keep some kind of professionalism.

"Ava Diaz," I say, like we haven't shared eight years of holidays, and one extremely tense family cruise to Mexico.

He reaches out. His hand is warm and familiar in a way it shouldn't be.

"Gavin Jones," he replies, like I haven't known that name since the first time Jared brought me home, and Gavin looked at me like I wasn't nearly good enough for his baby brother.

Valerie's gaze flicks between us, interest sharpening. "Well," she says, placing her hand gently on his shoulder, "let's get you a shirt from wardrobe, Gavin."

FIFTEEN MINUTES LATER, I'm still wondering why Gavin Jones was in Valerie Thorne's office. *Corporate espionage? Feature profile?* Or maybe they're secretly merging into some kind of morally flexible power couple.

I stop to check in with Kiki, our production coordinator and one of my favorite humans on the planet. Kiki has this way of dressing like she's a walking protest sign against conformity. Today, it's a Kusama-inspired polka-dot blouse and a pair of men's plaid pants that might've once belonged to a very fashionable grandfather or a Wes Anderson movie extra. While others judge, I cheer quietly from the sidelines.

"You look… irritated," she says.

Today's pitch is the biggest of my career: *A Girl's Gotta Give*, a charity campaign I built from the ground up. Marisol has even flown in to hear it in person. It's not just the most ambitious thing I've ever created; it's the most *me*.

"Pitch got moved," I say. "To later today. Valerie wants more time to… channel the muses."

She furrows her brow and bites her bottom lip.

"What?"

"It's probably nothing."

"*Kiki*."

"Minion," she says, using the nickname we use for Valerie's assistant, Minerva, "asked to see the deck."

"To review?"

"That's what I thought, but she went into the conference room. With Valerie. And Marisol," she says, voice getting faster. "And our potential VC investor. The hot guy in the suit," she says all in one breath.

My stomach drops. *This can't be happening.*

I slip inside the conference room as quietly as I can, my hands shaking. Marisol gives me a brief smile before turning back to the presentation. Valerie barely glances over—she's in full performance mode—as I take a seat in the outer ring of chairs with the assistants. Not because I belong there. Because I don't trust myself not to do something unhinged if I sit any closer.

And then I see him. Again.

Gavin, in a new tater tot-free shirt. In *my* seat. Next to Marisol, legs casually crossed. Cool as a glacier and just as likely to crush someone without trying. The chill in his gaze as it meets mine isn't new. Still, it always stings. Apparently, he's the high-profile VC Valerie and Marisol have been courting.

I catch the other staff stealing glances at him like he's the Second Coming, if the Second Coming wore Tom Ford, went on silent retreats in Iceland, and had a face that made ovaries reconsider their retirement plans.

I force myself to look away and back toward the head of the room, where Valerie—hair in the kind of perfect high ponytail I've never once been able to replicate—stands beside the screen.

She starts the video I spent forty hours editing, and I see it.

My introduction, word for word. Even my punctuation. But

Valerie's name sits beneath it like it's always belonged there. The audacity is almost impressive. Almost.

Marisol and Gavin lean in as images flicker by: a boy in India blinking into the camera, a nurse steadying his arm for a vaccine. A mother in Alabama, clutching a paper grocery bag like it's oxygen. A classroom of Sudanese girls, their notebooks balanced on chipped desks, their faces lit up with hope.

They are the people we could be helping, if Pulse chose to.

The room is spellbound.

Our head of public relations wipes a tear from her eye as Valerie clicks off the presentation, and the lights come up. There's a brief moment of silence as everyone looks to Marisol for her reaction.

Marisol beams. Valerie beams. *Me?* My pulse pounds.

As the room bursts into applause, I press my hands into my thighs, willing my heartbeat to slow and my face to behave. Minerva looks to me for my reaction, a weird combination of guilt and pity crossing her face.

From across the room, Gavin's eyes flick once—quick, sharp—to Minerva's face, then to mine. It's like he's connecting dots he shouldn't even have access to, then his gaze tightens as if he senses the undertow, the part of me pulling away.

This was my chance to show Marisol how much I've evolved, and how much the company could evolve by doing more good in the world. Now it's Valerie's crowning achievement. I think of all the late hours spent helping her meet deadlines, all the stupid social posts I ghostwrote to shape her public image while mine remains unseen.

I come back into my body just as Marisol turns to Valerie.

"It's perfect, Valerie. Fabulous job."

More applause, each clap a reminder of all the dinners I abandoned, the weekends I forfeited. I'd dressed those sacrifices up as ambition, but now they stand exposed as the naïve bargains they were. I'd been so determined to climb the shiny career ladder in front of me, I didn't realize it was leaning against the wrong wall until I was already halfway up.

I catch Valerie's smile. Triumphant. Unbothered. And, for once, I see her actions clearly: this wasn't a slip or misunderstanding. It was a choice.

I've spent years swallowing things I shouldn't. But I'm done being hungry in a room full of people who keep eating.

CHAPTER 2

Your Fears Are Like Bullies

THE RULES WERE never written down, but I learned them fast: Be competent, but never threatening. Warm, but not soft. Stylish, but not loud. Be sleek. Be sharp. Be always, always available.

The real dream was culinary school. Making food with my hands instead of merely writing about other people making magic.

Some people meditate daily. Some people learn guitar chords they'll use at parties. I practiced pâte à choux, that tender, bouncy dough you coax into shape with a pastry bag, piping it into perfect, satiny mounds for cream puffs, and pretending I was the kind of person who could afford to do this for real. When my brain got loud, I'd slice an onion into perfect half-moons, a carrot into matchsticks—steady pressure, straight cuts—until my pulse matched the rhythm of the knife.

But dreams—and tuition—get expensive when there's no one left to split the bill.

If life had gone as planned, I would be pulling croissants out of an oven right now—not walking into Valerie Thorne's office with my stomach in knots. But I took the smart job. Just three years, I promised myself. Long enough to save up. Five years later, I'm still here. No savings. And, I rarely cook, unless warming oat milk in the microwave counts.

And the only thing Pulse has given me?

A seat at the table—as long as I'm not too loud and don't eat too much.

Fuck the rules.

Still, the second I approach Valerie's office, my heart jackhammers. As I push open the door and hover in her doorway, the old instincts line up: don't provoke, don't need, don't take up space.

She doesn't even bother looking up from her computer.

"You have three seconds," she says, thumbs flying across her phone now.

My eyes catch on the green smoothie perched on the edge of her desk, condensation dripping down the plastic like it's trying to escape.

It's not just Valerie sitting there anymore.

It's Laurie, from foster home number five. Ordering fifteen-year-old me to make her protein shakes every morning. Complete her chores. Write her book reports. As if she were doing me a favor by letting me exist in her house. Because otherwise, she'd tell her mom I was "a bad influence." And in foster care, "bad influence" didn't mean detention—it meant a trash bag and a new house.

It wasn't that I was happy with Laurie's family, but their home was decent compared to the others, and her mom cooked real food, not whatever unidentifiable protein product came out of cans in my other foster homes.

I force a breath. *Your fears are like bullies. Stand up to them, and they'll disappear.*

"You stole my pitch," I say, stepping closer.

She leans back in her chair, her silk sheath unruffled, her expression a mix of irritation and amusement. "Weren't you the one who said, 'The best ideas are always a team effort'?"

I slap a folder down on her desk with dramatic flair.

"Is that how it works? Well, here's a list of every time you've 'team efforted' your way into someone else's work."

"You brought props. That's new."

Heat crawls up my neck, but if I stop now, she wins.

I read the first page aloud.

"Number one: guilting me into covering Christmas week while you disappeared to Cabo. Number two," I continue, my voice climbing. "Taking credit for Pulse's new social strategy after it doubled traffic. You paraded around like you'd masterminded it while I worked in the background, editing hashtags."

"If this is your version of leverage, Ava, it's...adorable."

My hands tremble, but I flip to the last page. "Let's skip ahead. Number thirty-two: sleeping with Marisol's husband."

There's a tightening at the corners of her mouth, just enough to let me know I've hit bone.

"Ava," her voice full of manufactured patience. "I get that you're upset, but you really need to learn how to pick your battles. Marisol loved the campaign. Gavin Jones loved the campaign."

"That's not the point."

"What *is* the point you're trying to make? Because all I'm getting is proof that you don't have the polish Marisol expects from her executive team."

She stands and smooths her dress. "But you still have a job. If I were less generous, you wouldn't."

She breezes past me like we weren't mid-confrontation.

I follow her into the open office, where the rows of cubicles stretch before us like a maze designed to test my endurance.

"I quit."

The words land louder than I meant them to. Colleagues pop up from cubicles like meerkats.

The words hang there, loud and irreversible. Even I blink, like my mouth just went rogue. *Where did that come from?*

"Very funny," Valerie tosses over her shoulder. "Like you'd give up future Deputy Editor."

"I'm serious." The fear shows up in my voice like an uninvited plus-one, but I pretend I don't hear it.

A low gasp rolls across the floor like a glitch in the matrix, and the look on Valerie's face is priceless. *Kiki's face?* Even better: eyes wide, mouth half-open, a perfect *what-the-actual-fuck* moment.

"Ava, if you walk out that door, I'll make sure you never work in this city again."

That almost sounds like a blessing.

But then I catch the looks from my coworkers—the whispers, side-eyes— and doubts start popping off in my head like kernels in a microwave, each louder and hotter than the last: Economic downturn. Low deductible health insurance. Deputy Editor. Stability.

Kiki recognizes the doubt spiral. It's the look I get when I've declared I am going to eat gluten-free for two weeks, then someone sets a raspberry croissant before me. It's the look she's seen a million times when I've vowed to stand up to Valerie and then folded. Because deep down, I am still that teen girl weighing the cost of rocking the boat when the alternative is losing everything and everyone—again.

Kiki stands up so fast her chair screeches across the floor like it's trying to escape the impending disaster. She turns to our stunned coworkers, arms raised.

"Who's with us?!"

Nobody moves.

"Okay, wow. Love the solidarity," she mutters, and starts stuffing her life into her oversized purse: a Jane Austen figurine hugging Ruth Bader Ginsburg, five different colored highlighters, a lipstick she thought she lost in 2024, and—

"What do you think you're doing?!" Valerie shrieks. "You—whatever your name is—remove one more thing, and you're fired."

Kiki locks eyes with her, then slowly, deliberately, drops the company stapler into her bag.

"Great," Kiki says. "Now I don't have to come to the company picnic."

I notice her hands are shaking, just a little. And I realize, for the first time, that for all her confidence and enthusiasm, Kiki's not bulletproof. She's just brave.

I follow her lead, grab three dead succulents off my desk, and place them in a box with the last photo ever taken of me with Mom and Dad and another with Jared at the top of the Empire State Building, grinning ear to ear.

We walk through the sea of cubicles together, trying our best to look cool (we suck in our guts), calm (we grip each other's hands like we're about to jump off a cliff), praying we don't trip and ruin the moment, and the wild thing is, the floor doesn't open up.

It holds.

On the subway, I open my phone with my thumb hovering over the screen. Valerie should be there. Valerie is always there. But my notifications are blank.

For a second, it's so unexpected I almost laugh.

Silence. Tiny, improbable, perfect.

The subway car lurches, squealing against the tracks, and I clutch my cardboard box tighter against my chest, my weird bouquet of dead succulents bobbing with every bump.

For the first five stops, I'm riding on pure adrenaline. Bright, fizzy, electric.

I did it. I stood up for myself. I didn't shrink into someone else's version of me.

Across the aisle, an old woman with a neon-green scarf gives me a slow, approving nod, like she can smell my freedom. Or maybe she just likes dead plants. Hard to say.

I hug the box tighter, grinning into the overhead lights, already rehearsing how I'll tell Jared. He's always said I should bet on myself more.

Today, I placed the bet.

And it feels—good.

CHAPTER 3

The Thing About Love

THE RAIN IS washing the city clean, and I am seeing it anew.

Before today, I constantly noticed the trash heaps on every corner; the way strangers always seem two seconds away from snapping at a cab, a barista, or each other; couples arguing in public like it was their part-time job. I saw the sky as a perma-gloom, a dull grey filter that made even spring feel like a shrug.

Now, I see the young couple kissing on the sidewalk like they've got thirty seconds left before the world ends. The old couple holding hands across the table next to me, like they wish they never had to let go. I swear the clouds are trying to form the shape of a heart in a sky that looks at least three Pantone shades bluer than usual. Now that Valerie is behind me, I'm no longer stuck in survival mode, adapting to a world I never wanted to belong to. I'm part of this brave new world where quitting isn't failure; it's freedom, where breakdowns make space for breakthroughs.

I am sitting at a table near the window of Taj Mahal, our favorite Indian restaurant in Brooklyn. It's the kind with strings of fairy lights twinkling across the ceiling, a carnation-strewn altar to Vishnu and Ganesh and a dozen other gods for good measure, and the scent of cardamom and ginger that embraces you before the door even closes behind you. The sound of tandoori sizzling in the kitchen mingles with the soft hum of Bollywood music and the light rain tapping against the windowpane.

The waitstaff knows us by name. Raj always slips me extra mint chutney without asking. Sima insists we try whatever new dessert her aunt mailed from Mumbai this month. It's the kind of place that makes you feel like family, even if you're dripping rainwater onto their vinyl red booth seats. This is where Jared and I come whenever we have something to celebrate: promotions, birthdays, anniversaries, surviving a particularly aggressive flu season.

Today, I have two things to celebrate.

One: I finally grew a spine and quit the job that's been slowly leaching the color from my soul. Two: I'm finally ready to say yes to moving in with Jared—the decision he's been gently, cheerfully nudging me toward for months.

Now that Pulse isn't sucking my soul dry, it just makes sense: our books mingling, our records cohabiting, a shared spice rack. The beginnings of a life that's not just convenient, but chosen. With happy, spontaneous, carefree Jared. If it were up to him, we would already be married. Not such a wild notion, considering we've been together for eight years.

My phone buzzes, jolting me back to the present just as Raj drops off two glasses of champagne and a basket of naan—warm, pillowy, and smelling faintly of butter and garlic.

It's a text from Jared.

> JARED
>
> Whatcha daydreaming about?

I look up and see him through the window, crossing the street. The rain has stopped, and the sun is straight-up photobombing his arrival. He's movie-scene gorgeous today, and I wonder: *How did I get so lucky?*

As he enters the restaurant, he runs his left hand through his wavy blonde hair, oblivious to the effect it has on the women around him. Two weeks in London have done him good. He looks like a *GQ* model who moonlights as the tortured lead singer of an indie band.

He sees me, and his face lights up. But there's something else there, too. Something I can't quite name. As he nears, I can see that he looks nervous. *Or is he excited?*

After a long embrace and a deep kiss, he slides into the booth across from me. My heart is practically breakdancing in my chest. I want to blurt it all out: *I quit, I'm free, I'm ready to move in with you.* But I hold it in, just for a second longer, as Jared reaches across the table and holds my hands. *God, he isn't going to propose, is he? What would I say?* It's not like I don't want to marry him eventually. We've talked about kids. His hazel-green eyes, my Japanese-Mexican-Scottish-and-who-knows-what-else ancestry, his gentle optimism, my chaotic realism. It would all make adorable, emotionally well-regulated humans, right? *Maybe I* would *like him to propose.*

"I have something I need to tell you, Ava," he says, interrupting my daydream.

"I have something to tell you, too," I grin.

"You go first."

"No. You go first."

I can't hold back my news any longer. He can't either.

And then, we both blurt it out.

"I think I might be gay," he says.

"I'll move in with you," I say.

The words collide mid-air.

I blink.

Then I laugh because my brain short-circuits when too many things happen at once. Because this can't possibly be real. Because… *what*?

He blinks back at me.

"Why are you laughing?" he asks.

"I thought you said you think you might be gay."

"I did," he says gently. "I think I am."

The world slows.

"Although technically, I guess I'm bi."

"Technically?" I don't know what else to say.

I'm not laughing now. I am examining his face. He's dead serious.

He sees my stunned silence as his cue to explain, to keep me from slipping away inside myself.

"Well, when I asked you to move in, I think you knew that something was missing."

"Actually, I didn't." I thought he wanted to move in together because he was in love with me.

"Anyway," he continues. "You were right to want some time to think about it…"

My mind swirls. *How can he be gay? No, he said "bi." But how would he know that if he's only slept with me? Oh, God, he's only slept with me, right?*

"Ava, stop. I know what you're doing. Slow the thoughts down. Ask me whatever you're wondering in that beautiful head of yours."

"But we have sex. Really good sex. *Right*?"

"Great sex. It's not about that."

"Then what is it about?"

He exhales *and* rubs the back of his neck. "I don't know. Maybe it *is* about sex. Or intimacy? Look, I'm confused, too."

"Have you slept with a man?" The words feel strange in my mouth. I always thought the question would be *Have you slept with another woman?*

"No. God, no. I would *never* cheat on you."

God knows a million men have used that line when having an affair. But Jared? He's never lied to me. He's the most honest human I know, my best friend, *my person*. I trust him.

"Then how can you know?"

"I think I may have wondered before, but I thought I was just open-minded. Remember your theory?"

I remember years ago, telling him I agreed with The Kinsey Scale, the theory that says there's a spectrum of human sexual preference and that people are not just either gay or straight; it's more like a sliding scale. Not so black and white. Human nature rarely is.

He starts drawing on a napkin…with my lucky pen. I've been looking for that pen for weeks, but I don't say anything. Maybe the pen is not so lucky after all.

He draws a line across the napkin. On the far right, he scribbles the word "straight," and on the other end, the word "gay." In the middle, he writes "bi."

"You are here," he tells me as he writes '*YOU*' pretty close to 'straight'. "And, I *thought* I was here…" he gestures to a spot between 'bi' and 'straight,' then moves the pen over slightly to the left, closer to 'gay,' and writes the word '*ME*.' "But now I realize I am here."

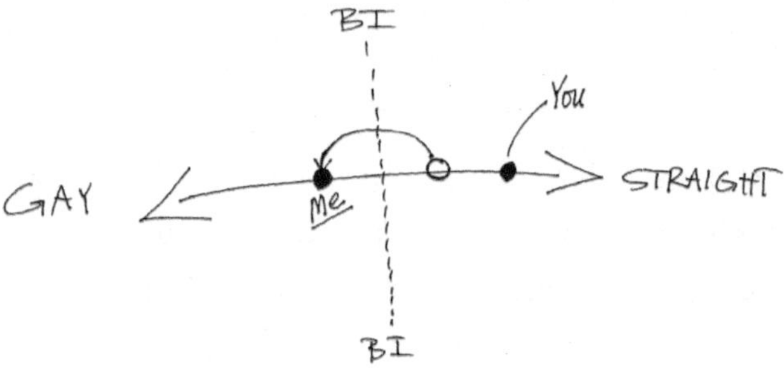

"How could things change so suddenly?" I ask. "Before you left, you asked me to move in with you."

"I met someone." He practically whispers.

The words couldn't hurt more if he shouted them. *It really doesn't matter what comes after these words.*

"Ava, did you hear me? I said…"

Oh, god, I have to hear those words again.

"I met someone," he repeats, this time louder. "Ava, please don't be hurt. This has nothing to do with you."

That's the most absurd thing he could say. And yet some part of me knows it's true. The tears begin. There is a spectrum of crying behavior, too, and at this moment, mine consists of the kind where tears delicately well up and slide out and down one's cheeks, but I can feel myself slipping dangerously down the sliding scale toward the shoulder-heaving-snot-flying-scrunched-up-ugly-face cry.

Raj approaches again, grinning, with our chicken tikka masala. His eyes meet mine, and with a frown, he turns right back around.

My mind is trying to make sense of everything Jared has told me. It's as if I had a vision board of us and our future together, and now he's swiftly rearranging the photos on it, tossing the ones of me aside and replacing them. He's bi. Or gay. He's confused. He's met someone. So many lines of thought, none of them connecting to the shape we used to be.

"Are you breaking up with me?"

"No," he answers quickly, then, after a pause, he says with less conviction: "I don't know what to do. I still love you, Ava."

"But you might love someone else, too," I say quietly.

"I honestly don't know," he drops his head in defeat.

"Have you…have you done anything with him?"

"I don't even know if he's gay. It might be one-sided."

"Like… a crush?"

He nods. "I thought it was just a deep friendship. Then it felt like what you and I had in the beginning, but stronger."

Ouch.

"I realized I was looking forward to his texts too much. I was rereading them. I was imagining what it would be like if…"

He doesn't finish the sentence, but I hear it anyway.

Silence expands between us like a balloon.

Until he pops it.

"What were you going to tell me?"

"I quit my job."

He blinks. "You what?"

"I quit Pulse. I walked out."

The news is not nearly as exciting as it was fifteen minutes ago.

"That job didn't deserve you," he says softly. "You'll find another."

I nod, though my throat is tight.

"And I gave notice on my apartment."

"Oh."

It lands like a paper airplane hitting a wall.

"You can get it back," he says automatically.

But you can't get me back.

"My landlord called me to gloat that he rented it for more than I was paying."

He winces. He hates hurting people. He doesn't even like hurting insects. He catches spiders in jars and walks them outside like tiny, entitled guests. Me? I *squash* them. I do feel bad doing it, but I squash them nonetheless. Maybe this is karma for all the spiders I've smooshed during this lifetime.

Jared excuses himself to the restroom.

I glance at the two glasses of champagne I ordered for our celebration, then down both of them.

I grab the napkin and get up to leave. It's not so much a souvenir but documentation. Of love. Of change. Of how sometimes, becoming yourself breaks someone else's heart.

CHAPTER 4

This is Where I Leave Me

It's been one week since Jared told me he thinks he might be gay. I told him I needed space to think, and I still haven't had the courage to tell anyone what's going on. Instead, I've been quietly unraveling inside my apartment, which now looks like a time capsule exploded. Open books are splayed on the coffee table as if they fainted mid-read. A sweater I meant to return three months ago has found its forever home draped over the back of a chair. Magazine piles are so high they give me hoarder cred. My three dead work succulents are now cozied up next to my houseplants—two Pothos and a Ficus named Tim—all of them in various stages of passive-aggressive death.

Two dozen moving boxes sit around the apartment, waiting to be filled.

Outside, a siren wails, rising and falling as it tries to weave through bumper-to-bumper traffic. Somewhere nearby, someone screams at their dog, or their partner, or the void. I've stopped trying to tell the difference.

This apartment was not supposed to be permanent. It's a one-bedroom with slanted hardwood floors, questionable plumbing, and a window that frames just enough of a maple tree to trick me into thinking I live somewhere beautiful. But it's mine, and it's a living vessel that holds my wall of photos of Mom and Dad and Jared and his family, my secondhand Turkish rug, which costs more to clean than it did to buy, and my mismatched collection of mugs with quirky feminist quotes.

This is the apartment I lucked into a year after college, after a decade of bouncing through foster homes and Craigslist chaos. It's the first place I ever chose for myself, and it felt like it belonged to just me. It's the place I got brave enough to try color therapy and painted an entire wall teal. I hated it and painted it back to a soft cream two weeks later, but the point was I could paint a wall. It's the place I returned to after every deadline. Every celebration. Every heartbreak.

Now, I have to give it up like a pair of shoes that no longer fit but still look good with everything.

Through the condensation on my windows, I can make out the outline of the maple tree outside. Its bare branches tap against the glass, like they're trying to get my attention, to tell me my apartment will not pack itself.

So, I order takeout.

Outside the restaurant, someone's yelling about garbage bins as I wait for Raj to bring me my chicken tikka masala. I munch on the complimentary naan and mint chutney he left me, pausing mid-chew when I hear a laugh.

My head jerks up, heart thudding before I even see him.

It's Jared.

Not in our booth, but at a table near the back.

Across from him is a man. Tall. Blonde. Crewneck sweater. He's said something that makes Jared laugh, that crinkles his eyes, bright enough that a couple at the next table turns to look.

My body moves before my brain does. I twist on the barstool, turning toward the window, pretending to study the street. Too late. Jared's eyes find mine.

Recognition flashes across his face.

He starts to rise.

His chair scrapes loudly against the tile.

Raj appears beside me, too cheerful, too loud. "Extra rice, just how you like it!"

I grab the takeout bag—my escape parachute—and turn to flee, but Jared is already there.

"Ava—"

"Don't. I can't."

The words come out sharper than I intend. People glance up. The blonde man half-stands, uncertain.

Jared freezes.

For a split second, it's just us.

Then someone behind me is asking about samosas and utensils, and the door is right there.

I push through it.

Outside, I clutch the warm to-go bag to my chest and walk as fast as I can, then the walk tips into a jog, as if I'm late to something urgent. Maybe my own emotional breakdown.

My phone buzzes in my pocket with calls from Jared. The vibrations feel like dozens of tiny, panicked heartbeats.

My sneakers slap the pavement like awkward applause for every awful choice I've made this week. A few tears fall just as the sky opens up, rain hitting hard and cold, and pedestrians glance away, afraid my heartbreak is contagious.

On the bright side, this is the most cardio I've done in years. Maybe the endorphins will cure the heartbreak. Maybe I'll lose those last stubborn ten pounds.

I glance down as the toe of my shoe catches on something. *Broken sidewalk cement? Exposed tree root? Karma?* Doesn't matter; it leads to the same thing. I stumble forward, flailing my arms with wind-up duck energy, straight into a man wearing a peacoat.

The impact launches my takeout container against his chest just as his hands catch me, keeping me from face-planting on the sidewalk. The vibrant red-orange sauce explodes across him.

"Oh my God," I gasp. "I just Jackson Pollocked your coat."

I glance up to see the face of my victim and good Samaritan, and immediately wish I hadn't.

Of all the people in a city of eight million, with my heart broken, makeup and now sweat dripping down my face, the universe doesn't just kick me when I'm down, it invites my emotionally constipated, almost-brother-in-law to spectate.

"Ava." His voice is robotic, as usual.

My mouth opens, then closes like I'm buffering.

He frowns at the red stain on his chest, then glances back up at me. "Is there a reason you're attacking me with condiments again?" he asks.

"Not a condiment," I say automatically. "It's chicken tikka masala. The best in the city. And it was an accident. Obviously."

I brace for a signature Gavin Eye Glare, but his expression shifts just slightly.

"You're crying."

I wipe my face with the back of my sleeve. Useless. I try my hardest to keep the tears in. My face twists in a mess of emotion—part grief, part hormonal chaos, part mid-level facial gymnastics. Gavin actually winces.

"You're shaking," he says, stepping closer, his hand reaching out to my shoulder, but he stops it a few inches away, and it hovers in the air awkwardly. Now he's buffering.

"I'm not shak—" But I am. My body is trembling from the cold and the adrenaline, and maybe the overwhelming sense of doom.

"You need to get out of this rain," he says, his tone leaving little room for argument.

"Not necessary. I'll be fine. My apartment is right here."

A rumble of thunder and a shock of lightning break the sky in two, and the rain becomes a thunderous downpour.

"Right," he mutters, already reaching past me to hold open my door.

Inside, I shiver as he helps me peel off my coat, then he shrugs off his soaked peacoat and hangs them both on the hooks by the door.

"I have some dry clothes," I say, nodding toward my bedroom. "Check the right side of the closet. Jared's stuff."

Gavin hesitates at the doorway, as if stepping into my bedroom will activate a booby trap.

I turn up the heat, then glance back, just in time to see him pulling his shirt over his head.

Oh.

He's shirtless, rummaging through my closet as if it's a tactical mission. He's not just Jared's older brother anymore. He's a half-naked man in my bedroom. A tattoo curls from his ribs to his back—a line of script in some elegant, unfamiliar language. *Hebrew? Arabic?*

I want to ask. I don't, but I do remind myself that I absolutely, definitively have never been attracted to Gavin.

I see him wince at the pile of clothes that has imploded on my bed.

"If I don't show up at your parents' anniversary party, it's because I couldn't find anything to wear," I call out.

When he returns in one of Jared's hoodies, I ask, "Why are you here?"

"I was in the neighborhood. Jared asked me to check on you. He was worried."

That's when the dam breaks. Not a cute, cinematic single tear. No. This is snot-dripping, shoulder-heaving, hyperventilating sobbing.

He blinks, alarmed, and looks wildly uncomfortable, like he just stepped into a puddle of feelings and isn't wearing boots.

Gavin is not one for public displays of affection. Back when Jared and I were together, he used to vanish from the room whenever we so much as held hands.

So, when he pulls a literal handkerchief—white, monogrammed, absurdly soft—from his pocket and hands it to me, I blink at it like I might have just ugly-cried my way into a Regency novel.

"Who even *has* handkerchiefs anymore?" I manage between gasps, collapsing at the table. "Are you secretly eighty?"

He shrugs. "They're practical."

He moves toward the kitchen. Opens cabinets without asking. Finds my teapot. Fills it. Boils water.

He sets down two mugs. No words. Just tea and his presence. And for now, that's enough.

I don't owe Gavin an explanation. But he is Jared's brother.

I search my purse for the napkin. Even now, I am irritated that my purse is always such a freaking mess. Jared used to joke that he needed a HAZMAT crew to find my keys. Out of the corner of my eye, I catch Gavin watching me, confused, concerned, as though he's observing some strange animal burrowing into his perfectly organized life.

The napkin is ink-smeared, as if I carried it across a wet battlefield. A message that would have to get to the other side, where it would make more sense. Maybe it will be my map back to understanding the order of things. I push it across the table toward Gavin.

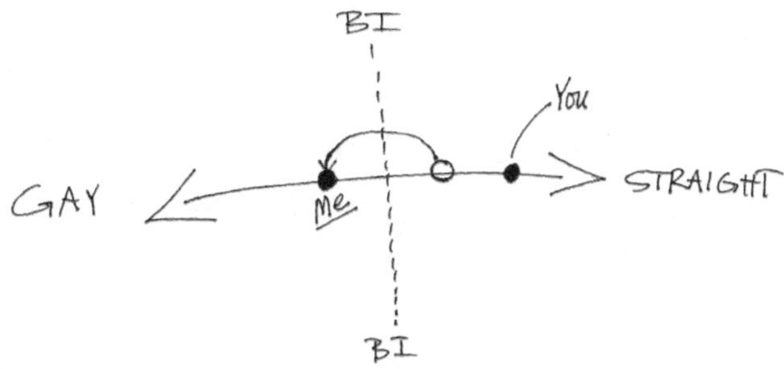

He studies it, then glances up at me with his grey-green eyes. I never noticed how similar they are to Jared's. He furrows his brow, glances back down at the napkin, and then back up at me.

"Wait. Are you coming out?" he asks, looking confused.

"What?"

"Are you trying to tell me that you're gay?" He pushes the napkin back at me.

Now I see the problem. The word 'ME' is between 'bi' and 'gay'.

"No. It's Jared's. He wrote that. He told me a week ago."

A lump rises in my throat. Saying it out loud still hurts.

He stares at the napkin again. Then at me.

He doesn't move. Doesn't reach out. But something in his expression softens. Like he just remembered I'm a person, not a problem.

"I see."

"You don't look surprised," I say.

"Maybe he'll change his mind. Remember when he quit anthropology to study photography?"

"Are you equating being gay with switching majors in college?" I'm being slightly mean, and I should stop, but …

He rubs the back of his neck—the same tell his brother has when he's stressed. "Forget I said that."

I stare at him for a long beat. He's trying. Failing a little. But trying.

And somehow, that's worse.

I take a sip of the tea. It scalds my tongue, but I welcome the sting. I'm not crying now, just watching Gavin across from me. He looks like he's trying to solve an equation where no one gets hurt.

Spoiler alert: Everyone gets hurt.

CHAPTER 5

Beautiful Wreckage

I ARRIVE FIRST at *Old Tree*, a bright red-and-pink sculpture on the High Line, the repurposed railroad tracks-turned-pedestrian parkway that weaves through the Meatpacking District and Chelsea. It will be one of the things I miss if I ever leave New York City. Neighbors came up with the idea. Instead of demolishing the abandoned structure, they rallied to transform it into something beautiful. I want to believe I can do the same with my life.

I have not felt strong enough to see Jared in person since our run-in at the restaurant, but we have texted about today. We both agreed: no big announcements. It's his parents' day—Patricia and Liam's anniversary—not ours. Our goal: hold hands. Smile easy. Keep our history intact. My goal: do not emotionally disintegrate in front of his family.

A ripple of attention moves through the crowd, the kind of collective pause that happens when someone magnetic approaches. I glance around, expecting Jared, but it's Gavin, cutting a striking figure in a tailored suit, catching the eye of every woman within range. As one of them stops him to chat, he catches my eye and counters my smile with a scowl. *Classic Gavin.*

Cari, Jared's younger sister, envelops me in a hug. She's radiant, as always, but there's an extra sparkle in her today, possibly powered by the cute guy on her arm. He's her age, maybe twenty-two, and grinning so wide you'd think he just won the lottery.

Cari is a self-professed romantic, the kind of person who believes in grand gestures and happily-ever-afters, and she wears that optimism like a badge of honor. It's one of the many things I've always loved about her.

"Hello, Ava," she says, admiring my outfit, a midnight blue jumpsuit that makes me look like I have my life together. "That jumpsuit should be illegal."

"Oh, this old thing? Arrived on my doorstep yesterday. Pretty sure Gavin got word to your mom that I threatened to bail on their anniversary if I couldn't find something to wear."

She glances down at my feet. "And, those are definitely not sneakers. What's gotten into you?"

"I thought your parents deserved a little glamour."

Gavin approaches like a cloud blotting out the sun. Cari envelops him in a hug, then steps back and loosens his tie.

"You're not at work, Gavin."

"What do you know about work, Little Sis?"

"I work. I happen to only work at things that don't feel like work." She turns to her beau. "Gavin, this is Max. Max, this is my bossy big brother, and this is the fabulous Ava."

Gavin shakes his head at his sister, his lips dangerously close to a smile.

"It's nice to meet you both," Max says as he extends his hand for Gavin to shake, then turns to me. "I've heard a lot about you, Ava. Read the original Substack, of course, and your work on Pulse."

"The interview with Ina Garten and *Hapa Nom Nom* was entertaining," adds Gavin. Or, at least that's what it sounds like. Hard to believe Gavin has read anything I've written.

Before I can ask him about that, Patricia and Liam approach, holding hands.

"Patricia," I say, leaning in to kiss her cheek. "Thank you for the jumpsuit. It's perfect."

She pulls back slightly. "The jumpsuit?" Her brows lift. "Oh! I may have mentioned to someone that midnight blue would look stunning on you."

I feel it before I see it—Gavin going very still beside me, like a man who has just been accidentally identified.

"I didn't send anything," she continues lightly. "Though I wish I could take credit."

I glance at Gavin just as his jaw tightens.

A second later, I feel a hand embrace mine. It's Jared. Standing so close I can feel his warmth. He smiles down at me, squeezing my hand a little harder. "You look amazing tonight."

His words feel better than they should.

"You, too."

It's true. He looks healthy, happy, and slightly mischievous. I almost forget that we pressed pause on us so he could figure out who he is when he isn't choosing me. It was my idea. Or at least I said it first. I'm not sure which is worse.

"OLIVIA!" CARI SHOUTS excitedly. We turn to see Olivia striding toward us in a dress that looks like it was commissioned by angels. Her beauty is effortless, luminous, her blonde hair cascading down one shoulder.

One of the most beautiful women in the city shows up for him, yet Gavin doesn't look the least bit excited.

Jared and I say our hellos to Olivia, then drift behind as Patricia and Liam envelop their future daughter-in-law.

Jared has a half smile dancing on his lips.

"What are you thinking about?"

"It's nothing," he says.

"After eight years together, I can tell. It's something."

"I'm not sure I should tell you."

"Puhleeeease. You tell me everything."

He hesitates.

"I kissed John."

All sound falls away. I know people are talking around me (I see their mouths moving), and cabs must be honking, and I see a plane fly overhead, but I don't hear any of it. He kissed someone who isn't me. His name is *John*. I feel a lump in my throat. My eyes grow hot and sting. And, as the sound comes rushing back, *damn it*, I can't stop the tears that come with it.

I know exactly why I'm crying. I just don't know how to stop. I was the one who wanted him to explore. *But two weeks later, and he's already kissed someone?*

I force fingernails into my palm to distract myself from crying.

"I'm sorry, Ava. I'm an idiot. I shouldn't have told you. You've been so encouraging, and we said we'd still be there for each other. I thought that meant… You're the first person I want to tell about everything ..."

I wipe my eyes on the back of my sleeve, leaving a lovely streak of mascara. "I'm fine. I'm fine."

Jared guides me to a bench.

Across the path, Gavin locks eyes with me just as his parents and Olivia catch up to him. He smoothly points to a sculpture, steering them away from us. He doesn't come over, and he makes sure no one else does either. He stands there, a steady point on the horizon I can aim my breathing at.

I dig into my pocket and pull out Gavin's handkerchief. Apparently, he has a habit of quietly giving me things before I know I need them. I had washed it and planned to return it tonight, but now he'll have to wait. As I wipe my tears, Jared puts his arm around my shoulder and pulls me close. His touch is comforting, but it doesn't hide the fact that I am losing my boyfriend and my best friend. I am not ready to lose him, so I take a deep breath and do what I always do: Be there for him.

"Tell me; I want to hear," I say.

"Are you sure?" he asks.

That version of me that wants to comfort him and put him first? I don't know whether to worship her or tell her to sit this one out.

"This is important to you, and we're there for each other when it comes to the important things."

I reach for his hand as he starts to talk.

"I wasn't even sure John was gay, but we sat next to each other at a dinner party and I could feel electricity the whole night … but I didn't think he was feeling the same thing ... he walked me home, and when we got to my door, he told me he couldn't stop thinking about me, and he just pulled me into him and kissed me." His words almost come out gushing.

The look on Jared's face is blissful. He looks alive. Like something inside him has finally exhaled, like he's found a piece of himself that was missing.

Could he already be in love?

Somewhere under the ache, there's a flicker of warmth. This is what I want for him—to feel joy, to feel true. Even if I'm not the person standing beside him when he does.

Before I know it, I am crying again, and I can't stop.

"Oh, God, Ava, I'm sorry …"

"I … I don't know what's wrong with me …"

"Nothing is wrong with you, Ava. You're perfect. This situation is far from perfect."

The words are coming out of my mouth before I can stop them.

"Jared, I wanted to be there for you. I thought I could, but I don't know how to be there while I'm losing you."

CHAPTER 6

The Art of Staying

WE TURN A corner to catch up to the family to tell them we're heading home early and... "SURPRISE!"

Assembled in front of an outdoor movie screen are all of Patricia and Liam's closest friends and family. Gorgeous floral pom-poms hang from the trees. Twinkling lights are draped everywhere, casting everything in that forgiving golden glow that makes people look softer than they are. There's a dessert bar filled with lush pastries, all of Patricia's favorites from her many travels, and one gigantic cotton candy machine for Liam.

I dab under my eyes with a wet napkin, hoping the damage is minimal—just a little smudged mascara and puffiness I can blame on allergies. Nothing that suggests I most likely lost my boyfriend and my best friend in the span of ten minutes.

After everyone greets each other, Gavin passes his parents two glasses of champagne, and the crowd hushes as Liam lifts his glass.

"To Patricia. My noon, my midnight, my talk, my song; before her, I thought love could not last forever. Now I know I was wrong."

A murmur ripples through the crowd. Patricia presses her fingers to her mouth, already crying, the way she does when she's happy. Liam reaches for her free hand, and she squeezes back, hard, like she's afraid he might disappear if she lets go.

Jared steps next to me. His shoulder brushes mine, light but steady, like he's anchoring himself—or maybe me.

We clink our glasses together.

The delicate chime rings out, sharp and bright in the warm night air.

Our last toast.

"Did you help plan the surprise?" I ask him, keeping my voice light, like my chest isn't caving in.

"Actually, it was all Gavin. I'm as surprised as they are."

Gavin—the family android—planned this?

I glance over at him. And—shockingly—he's smiling, his eyes on his parents as the movie screen flickers to life.

Vintage 8mm film begins to play, the projector whirring softly behind us. First: Patricia and Liam in the early days—grinning like kids in Liam's old VW Beetle, Patricia's hair whipping across her face as Liam tries to steer with one hand and hold the camera with the other.

Then come the photos: sunburned beach days, blurry late-night dinners, Patricia laughing so hard her head tips back out of frame.

Their wedding.

Then the kids—babies held up like trophies, sticky-faced birthdays, Cari, Jared, and Gavin climbing on Liam in the backyard like he's a jungle gym while Patricia films and laughs behind the camera.

Cari puts her arms around both our shoulders.

"One day we'll be doing this for you two," she chirps.

My stomach drops. *Sweet, sweet Cari.* I'll miss her so much.

A loose tear escapes me, rolling down my cheek before I realize I should wipe it away.

She notices.

"Ah, Ava's a happy crier, just like Mom."

If only she knew.

I laugh softly and excuse myself before the next tear can betray me.

I MADE IT through the rest of the celebration without ruining anything for Patricia or Liam. Which felt like its own Olympic sport: smiling at the right moments, laughing half a second after everyone else, blinking back tears every time Jared's arm brushed mine.

The last thing I wanted to do was share a ride home with Jared and spend the whole time wondering if he was thinking about John.

I step toward the curb to hail a cab—

A black town car pulls up before I can lift my hand.

I turn.

Gavin stands a few feet away, watching me.

"Need a ride?" he asks.

I hesitate, then nod. Anything that gets me home faster—somewhere I can unravel in peace—sounds perfect.

Gavin steps forward and opens the back door, as if this is the most ordinary thing in the world.

As I lean down to get in, the driver glances back through the window between our seats. A familiar face. His thick gray eyebrows lift in recognition.

"Miss Ava?"

"Ray? You remember me."

"Of course I do," he says. "Hard to forget the only person who ever smuggled me cupcakes from that bakery on Ninth."

"How are your grandkids?" I ask. "Last I heard, one of them was determined to become a dinosaur."

Ray chuckles. "Still is. The other one decided she's going to be an astronaut."

Gavin glances between us.

"You bribed him with cupcakes?"

"It wasn't a bribe," I say. "I didn't think Ray should have to sit outside smelling pastries all night while we were stuck inside that three-hour charity gala."

Gavin studies me for a moment, like he's recalculating something. His expression settles into the faintly disapproving look he seems to reserve just for me.

He closes the door with a solid click, sealing me inside the car's quiet bubble that smells faintly of leather.

A moment later, the other door opens, and he slides in beside me.

As Ray pulls out into traffic, I try not to notice how close Gavin and I are sitting to each other.

"Where's Olivia?" I ask, mostly to distract myself.

"She had to take a flight back to L.A. Just came in for the night."

"That was nice of her."

"It was."

Silence stretches between us as we both stare out opposite windows, the city slipping past.

Then—

"How are you?" he asks.

The question lands harder than it should, but in a bizarre twist of fate, Gavin is the only person I don't have to hide my feelings from tonight.

"Jared kissed a man."

Gavin's brow creases, and for a moment, it feels as if he's going to say something, but he doesn't.

He's difficult to read. Always has been.

I remember the first time I was introduced to him. He looked at me like I'd walked into the wrong room. As if he was shocked his charming, good-looking brother would bring someone like me home when he could have a smarter, prettier, more fashionable girl. Someone like Olivia.

Gavin was single for the first few years we dated, and at family functions, he avoided me like the plague. Once, at Thanksgiving dinner, he even moved a name card so he wouldn't have to sit next to me. I assumed he thought I couldn't hold an intelligent conversation, as if I might bore him so badly that he'd end up asleep in a plate full of stuffing.

When he and Olivia finally got engaged, the worst snub was not being invited to their posh engagement party.

Jared said Gavin and Olivia wanted a family-only event.

But when Jared arrived without me, he saw Olivia had all kinds of friends attending, and Cari had brought a date.

All night, people asked where I was.

Jared wasn't going to tell me. But when he got home, he was so upset, I knew something was wrong.

When I forced him to explain, he admitted that everyone had dates—except him.

When he confronted Gavin, he mumbled something about a miscommunication before disappearing for the rest of the night.

I tried not to make a big deal of it. I didn't want to come between two brothers. But I felt singled out. Like I wasn't good enough for Gavin and Olivia.

I glance over now and find him watching me.

I give him a weak smile.

“Thank you,” he says.

“For what?”

“For coming tonight.”

He pauses slightly, like the words might cost him something.

“It meant a lot… to my parents.”

It might be the most thoughtful sentence he’s ever spoken to me.

CHAPTER 7

Bad News for People Who Love Good News

THE JONESES' HOUSE has always been my safe haven. Tucked on a tree-lined street in Hoboken, it's the kind of home that feels lived in without ever looking messy, polished without ever feeling cold. It's where Jared grew up, where Patricia—who now styles flowers for Marisol and Pulse photo shoots—perfected her talent for turning any table into a still life. In the foyer, loose flowers spill out of a vase as if they grew there overnight, sunlight slants across polished wood, the faint smell of coffee and citrus permeates the air.

I've spent more holidays here than even my own family's house. And, I can already feel the ache of missing it.

Patricia pulls me in for a hug, firm and fragrant. "You look too thin. Are you eating?"

"Enough," I lie.

She pulls back, looking me up and down like she's trying to scan me for damage. "I heard Valerie's at her wits' end without you, by the way. Two writers ghosted her, one's threatening to move their column exclusively to Substack, and no one seems to understand how to meet a deadline without you standing over them with caffeine and consequence."

"Sounds about right."

"She now knows you're irreplaceable," she says, ushering me inside like she always does, like I still belong here.

The plan was simple: Jared and I would tell the family—together—at our first Sunday brunch of the month that we are breaking up. But Jared's flight from London is delayed, and "together" hasn't really been our strong suit lately.

So now it's just me, Gavin, Cari, Max, Liam, and Patricia, around the dining table with Mimosas, Eggs Benedict, and a centerpiece that is spectacularly Patricia.

"Jared's missing his favorite meal," Liam says.

"Speaking of Jared, I have something I need to tell you." I can barely look them in the eyes. "I'm not sure where to start. Jared and I planned to make this announcement together, but I can't hold it in any longer."

Gavin freezes mid-spoonful, brow furrowed. Cari jumps out of her seat and throws her arms around me.

"Oh-my-God! You're finally getting married! It's official: I have a sister!"

"Cari, I don't think she can breathe," Gavin warns. Cari steps back, practically giddy.

His voice is low, steady, the kind that cuts through chaos without needing to rise. For a second, I feel the strange comfort of it. He's not looking at me like I'm fragile, more like he's bracing the room for me. And it's ridiculous, but the steadiness in him makes something flicker in my chest before I look away.

Patricia is grinning ear to ear. "Oh, I can't tell you how happy this makes me, Ava."

Liam raises his glass. "To our Ava—we can actually say that now—and, of course, to Jared, my very fortunate son."

Gavin is staring at me with a *What is going on*? look, and I give him a shake of my head. Everyone is waiting for me to say something. Like maybe a 'thank you' for the sweet toast by Liam.

"I can't wait to hear about the proposal." Cari claps her hands together. "Every single romantic detail. But first ..." She picks up my hand, then looks confused. "Where's the ring?" My hand drops as she releases it. So does my stomach.

"Why don't we let Ava finish what she was saying?" Gavin says.

I take a big gulp of wine. The damn lump is still there, but I can feel it about to break loose. *Please don't cry. Please don't cry.* I take a deep breath and ...

"Jared and I are breaking up."

I recognize that look on their faces. They look like they've been punched in the gut. Patricia literally drops her fork onto her plate with a clang. Cari looks like she is going to cry, poor Max's eyes are wide, and Liam's brow is deeply furrowed.

"Are you sure?" Patricia asks quietly.

I'm silent but aware that a single tear escapes. Out of the corner of my eye, I see Gavin fidgeting. He looks pissed.

"I don't understand," Liam whispers.

"But you two get along so well," Cari says.

I wipe a tear from my cheek. "Honestly, I'm a little confused myself. It was initiated by something going on with Jared, but it's a mutual decision."

I pause to catch my breath.

"In case you're thinking it, he did not have an affair or anything like that. It's all a little complicated. I wish I could tell you more, but it's really up to Jared to tell you. You have all meant so much to me over the last eight years. You've really been the family I never had, and I . . ." The lump has escaped. There is no stopping the dam from bursting now. Tears spill from my eyes, and Patricia and Cari jump to my side to put their arms around me.

"This doesn't make any sense, Ava. You're the love of his life," Patricia says.

"Someone needs to talk some sense into him," adds Cari. "How long have you two been having trouble, Ava?"

Things would have been a lot easier if we weren't getting along. Like those couples you know that cheat on each other and bicker in front of their friends and family. As if they want someone to enact an intervention right there on the spot in the middle of whatever get-together. Instead, everyone resorts to whispering behind their backs: "God, why don't they just break up?" When "those" couples end a relationship, it makes perfect sense; the universe is put in order.

I can't answer Cari because I've officially crossed into hiccuping. Shoulder-heaving. DEFCON-1-level sobs.

"It has nothing to do with Ava," says Gavin.

We all turn.

"Jared's gay," he adds.

The room stills. My hiccups cease. Gavin drops his napkin, leaves the table, and then walks out of the house.

And just like that, my last meal with the Joneses is over.

CHAPTER 8

So Nice. So Smart. So What.

At arrivals, I hover near the baggage carousel like some half-lost suitcase no one's claimed yet. Jared doesn't know I'm here. After Gavin's spectacular brunch bomb, I couldn't text or call. I needed to tell him in person. To soften the blow, if that's even possible.

When he spots me, his grin is so easy, so *Jared*, it cracks something in me. He pulls me into a hug, kisses me, still warm, still familiar. For one stupid second, I almost believe nothing's changed.

Half an hour later, we're on our bench in the park, sandwiches between us, the city blurring around the edges.

"I have to tell you something," I say. "And you're not going to like it."

"You told my family we were breaking up?" he shrugs. "I kinda figured that might happen. I'm surprised Cari hasn't texted me yet."

"Yes," I say, careful. "I did tell them. And they didn't take it well. They were confused. Shocked." I pause. "Kinda like me."

He grimaces.

"The thing is, they started to bombard me with questions, a lot of them having to do with *why* we're breaking up. I didn't want to tell them, but it came out anyway."

"What came out?"

"They know everything."

"Ava," he says slowly, "we agreed I would tell them."

"I know we did. I tried, I really did, but they kept pressing and—"

"Damn it, Ava." His voice isn't loud, but it slices clean through the air. "I can't believe you would do that."

"Jared, I ..."

"How could you? It's a huge personal thing."

"I get that. But if you'd just let me explain—"

"You were right." He stands abruptly, the bench rocking slightly beneath me. "We need a clean break."

He inhales, unevenly—his tell. He's angry, but underneath that, he's hurt. I've known him long enough to hear the difference.

"Where are you going?" I ask.

"I'm pissed, Ava. If I stay, I'll say something I'll regret."

I watch him disappear down the street like some scene from a breakup montage, but there's no swelling music, no cinematic goodbye—just me, a half-eaten sandwich, and the cold, simple fact that this time, it's really over.

CHAPTER 9

Good News for People Who Love Bad News

I HAVE TRUDGED through three inches of snow, wind whipping my wet hair around my face, bits of icy rain stinging my eyes, all to get to a private New Year's Eve event at MoMA as Kiki's plus one.

Tonight, I will ring in the new year with truth. I will practice gracefully telling people that Jared and I have broken up. That Jared is exploring dating men. That my eight years with him have exploded in a poof of smoke.

The lobby hums with voices ricocheting off marble and heels striking the floor in bright, decisive clicks. Couples pose by the marble staircase, cheeks flushed, champagne already in hand. I check my reflection in the glass doors—frizzy hair, eyeliner hanging on for dear life—and think, *this is the face of someone barely holding it together in a room full of people thriving on togetherness.*

And then, Kiki appears. She's radiant, beaming, her dark curls bouncing like exclamation points. She's wearing something dramatic, of course: a vintage brown velvet cape over a silk dress with a neckline that defies physics, arms stacked with brass cuffs like she just wandered off a Fellini set in Athens. Just seeing her relaxes my shoulders.

She pulls me into a long hug.

"You've lost weight," I say.

"No more stress eating in response to Valerie does that," she quips, and I laugh for what feels like the first time in weeks.

Jared and I never developed a sitcom posse of friends, the ones who crowd into booths in bars and take annual group trips to Asheville. We always picked each other over the party invites. It felt *romantic* at the time. Now it just feels… *quiet.*

And Kiki? She's always been a work friend. Prosecco-on-deadline-day kind of friend. But I've missed her, and here she is. Hugging me in a sea of couples, holding the conversation like a lifeline. Maybe this is how real friendship starts.

She pulls back and studies my face. Not in the cursory, you-look-great way. In the what-happened way.

"You look… tired," she says, softer now. "And don't you dare say it's the weather."

Something in my chest gives. It's the kind of noticing Jared used to do.

"First, champagne," I say.

We weave into the party, canapés circulating like tiny sculptures on platters, cocktails and champagne sloshing over coupe rims, DJ Deadmau5 vibrating through my ribcage. Every few steps, someone stops Kiki to kiss the air beside her cheek or congratulate her on the turnout.

We grab two glasses off a passing tray and settle in a corner.

"You said in your text you had something to tell me," she says, half-shouting over the bass. "Should I brace myself?"

Jared and John have been pictured in photos in public—restaurants in Tribeca, a gallery opening in Chelsea, John's hand at the small of Jared's back like it's always belonged there—so I imagine some of our peers know, but Kiki will be the first friend I test my breakup script on.

"Jared thinks he's gay. Or bi. He hasn't exactly labeled it yet, and he really shouldn't have to, but there's a guy. His name's John. And I'm pretty sure he's in love with him."

I try to smile. It feels anatomical, not emotional.

"We're officially not together. And very officially not speaking."

Her jaw drops. "Fuck me. I really was not expecting that."

It's been a relief that nobody has said *I always thought he might be gay.* At least I wasn't the only one who didn't see it. Or at least that's what I'm choosing to believe.

"I'm so sorry. I really loved you two together."

"Me, too." I pause before adding, "I have mixed feelings, but the most important thing is that he's happy."

"But what about y—?" She's about to say something more, but winces. "Brace yourself. Gaggle, inbound."

I turn—and it's already too late.

"Ava!" Three glitter-drenched women start toward us in sparkly holiday dresses. Red. Green. Gold. We call them The Gaggle because they travel in formation and laugh like it's a competitive sport.

Kiki groans under her breath. "Do not engage," she says. They can smell vulnerability."

Before we can escape together, someone taps her shoulder.

"Kiki! The Atlas Mag photographer is asking for you—something about the lighting?"

She looks torn, eyes flicking between me and the sequins advancing toward us. "Two seconds," she tells me, squeezing my hand. "Don't let them narrate your life."

And then she's gone.

Before I can pretend not to have seen them and hide, they swoop down on me as a mutual acquaintance pulls Kiki away. Sparkly Red air kisses me on the cheek. Green and Gold hug me, one of them announcing, "We were just talking about you."

I was afraid of that.

"We heard about Jared. . . So crazy. . . It's hard to believe. . . You must be crushed. . . Devastated. . ."

I'm not sure who—Red, Green, Gold?—says what. I don't say anything back as I gather my thoughts, but Green—*or is it Red?*—leans in with a faux whisper.

"Don't you feel betrayed?"

"Betrayed?" I repeat flatly.

"I mean, obviously, he was having an affair on you." They nod in unison.

"Jared didn't have an affair."

"But he lied to you. Obviously."

"He has never lied to me. It's more complicated than that."

They stare at me like I'm speaking Swahili. They are not the kind of women who comprehend complexity. And my break-up with Jared, with the salacious bonus of Jared's coming out, is good news to them. Good news for people who love bad news. Suddenly, I feel protective of Jared.

"Well, sure, he *told* you that he didn't have an affair, but how could he not if he knows he's, uh, you know?"

"Gay or bi?" I ask.

"Exactly," one of them says, her confidence growing.

"I trust Jared," is all I say. *But I don't trust you.*

"But *should* you? Should you really trust him?"

That's when I hear him.

"There you are, Ava."

Gavin's voice—dry, low—cuts through the noise. The Gaggle turns as one, like a synchronized flock of predators, catching the scent of a better meal.

He stands just behind me, impossibly composed, tux crisp, expression unreadable, extraordinarily handsome. "Sorry to interrupt," he says to them, polite but final. "I need to steal her for a moment."

Red actually fans herself. "Well, we certainly won't stop you."

"Didn't think you would," he replies, without even a glance, and gently guides me by my elbow.

When we're clear of them, I say, "You didn't have to do that."

"I know," he says. "But you looked like you could use an extraction."

I huff a laugh. "You make it sound like a hostage situation."

He glances down at me. "Wasn't it?"

I glance back at the Gaggle, who are still staring after him like he's the after-party. "Now they'll think I'm sleeping with you."

He shrugs. "Let them think what they want. They will anyway."

It's maddening, the calm in him. Like he's been built with some internal ballast I'll never have.

Before I can reply, he disappears into the crowd.

THERE IS NOTHING quite like a room full of people on New Year's Eve, exceptionally well-dressed, happily coupled people, to make one feel utterly alone. To make matters worse, I see the trays of champagne being passed around and singletons trying to pair off. I check my phone. It's almost midnight. Only a few minutes until the start of a new year. *Good*, I think. I can't wait to put this one behind me.

Kiki reappears with two new glasses of champagne. "There you are! You're not trying to leave, are you?"

"It's not like I have anyone to kiss."

"*Pffffft.* That's what champagne is for. And, you don't want to start the New Year running away." She grabs me by the elbow and pulls me in close. "Plus, I forgot to ask if you've found a place to live or a job yet?"

I shake my head. "I got my landlord to give me a slight extension, but no jobs." I pause, unsure whether I should even mention anything else, but decide to share anyway. "Patricia mentioned Gavin might need a live-in chef for the summer."

Kiki perks up. "Gavin. Jared's hot brother?"

I nod cautiously.

"Tall, wavy brown hair, Ryan Gosling-like half-smirk, dresses like David Beckham?"

"I think David Beckham is a bit of a stretch."

"He just needs a woman's touch."

"He has Olivia," I remind her.

"*Pffttt.*"

"Okay, maybe we've had one too many glasses of champagne?"

"I'll take the job if you won't," she says in between sips.

"You don't cook."

"I made mac and cheese last night."

"In the—"

"Microwave."

"Powdered cheese packet?"

"Obviously."

I describe my go-to mac and cheese recipe adapted from Martha Stewart's: garlicky white roux, gruyere and sharp white cheddar, al dente gemelli pasta, freshly ground nutmeg, and green peppercorns, topped with homemade sourdough breadcrumbs. It takes two hours to make.

"That isn't mac & cheese. That's a long-term commitment," Kiki declares. "You'd better take the job! He's a handsome, wealthy single male. His summer home is probably a mansion in—?"

"On," I correct her. "Remote Orcas Island. It's between Seattle and Vancouver, only reachable by boat or seaplane."

Kiki's eyes sharpen in a way I recognize. Plotting.

"Don't," I warn.

She grins into her champagne. "I'm just saying. New year. New decisions."

Before I can say more, Kiki spots something over my shoulder and goes still.

"Stay right here," she says, already backing away.

"Kiki—"

But she's gone, swallowed by sequins and tuxedos.

I turn back toward the crowd just as someone steps into my peripheral vision and I take a reflexive sip of champagne at the exact wrong moment.

And then Kiki is back—triumphant, one hand wrapped around Gavin's sleeve like she's landed a prize at a carnival.

I practically choke. Champagne sprays in an undignified arc down the front of his tux.

"Oh my God—"

He looks down at himself, then back at me, infuriatingly calm.

"Ava," he says mildly, pulling a handkerchief from his pocket, "is this going to become a habit?"

"If you keep materializing without warning," I cough, still recovering, "then yes. Possibly. I mean—no."

Kiki beams between us like she's just solved climate change.

"I'll give you two some time to chat," she says, already scanning the room again.

"Kiki," I hiss.

She raises one finger. "One second." And vanishes again.

"Kiki said you were interested in the chef job," he says, as the music dips and the DJ's voice booms overhead.

"TEN ..."

"I—your mom mentioned it, but—"

"NINE ..."

"She'll take it," Kiki shouts. *And... she's back.* She reappears at Gavin's shoulder, breathless. "You will. You absolutely will."

"Okay, Kiki is drunk," I say, wiping some champagne off his lapel that he missed. "And I totally understand if—"

"Babe, it's almost time!" Olivia's voice slices through the crowd. She's approaching, glossy and perfect, in a black silk dress she wears like a second skin.

Gavin's eyes are still on me.

"FOUR ... THREE ..."

"The job's yours if you want it," he says.

"TWO ..." He doesn't look away.

He leans slightly closer, and I can feel his breath on my neck, his voice low but clear.

"Happy New Year, Ava."

"ONE!"

Confetti bursts overhead. There's color, noise, and the world briefly unhinged. Around us, people kiss, and embrace and cheer, and Olivia's laughter cuts through the din as she loops her arms around Gavin's neck and kisses him—hard.

The music swells. The year turns.

And I wonder if saying yes to Gavin will be the biggest mistake of my life or the first right thing I've done in ages.

PART TWO

ORCAS ISLAND

CHAPTER 10

New Landings

I LEFT THE City without saying goodbye to Jared. It felt like ripping out a stitch on a wound that hadn't closed—clean, decisive, and guaranteed to leave a scar—but it was the only way I could fathom leaving.

Outside the cab window, New York had already started to curdle. It was one of those hot summer mornings when the whole city smells like warm garbage and fermented fruit. A man in a suit was screaming at a hot dog vendor. A woman in heels was weeping silently into her phone. A pigeon flew headfirst into a Pret-A-Manger window, and no one even blinked.

At the airport, things only got worse. Overpriced salads wilting in plastic, way too many people at every terminal gate, more than one of them coughing into the air without covering their mouth, as if we've given up on the basic etiquette of civilization and hadn't just lived through a global pandemic. On the plane, the couple next to me spent the entire six-hour flight negotiating their prenup. No whispering, just full-volume, passive-aggressive warfare at 30,000 feet.

By the end of the flight, I felt scraped raw, like the city had taken one last layer of skin just to remember me by.

I LAND IN Seattle, then take a shuttle to a private airport on Lake Union, where I catch a second plane. It's smaller than I expected, a five-seater seaplane that, when its engine is turned on, sounds like it's held together by hope and duct tape. I put on the headphones handed to me while the pilot, Derek, dons aviators, flips a series of seemingly random tiny switches, and speaks into his radio while we prepare for takeoff.

The plane, essentially a skinny floating minivan with wings, rises smoothly over the mainland. Below us, the Salish Sea gleams like mercury, dotted with dozens of forested islands outlined by craggy coastline, and with every mile we journey, New York City starts to feel like a story I made up.

The tight band of anxiety that's been wrapped around my chest—since quitting Pulse, since Jared's confession, since saying yes to the *last* man I should have said yes to—begins to loosen.

As we arc toward an archipelago clumped in the shape of a heart, Derek gestures down to one of the smallest islands.

"That's Shaw. Population 382," he says. The little island looks like a secret someone tried to keep, with thick forests spilling to rocky shores, and only a few roads winding like loose threads through the trees.

"That's Friday Harbor, the big city of the San Juans," he says, pointing to another island. From up here, Friday Harbor looks like a tiny watercolor of coastal life. Fishing boats and yachts cluster in a horseshoe bay, docks stretching into the sound, and colorfully painted buildings fill a village surrounding a ferry dock.

"And over there: Orcas Island."

I nod, feeling a quiet awe, as I take it in. Patricia once told me that Orcas Island is half the size of Nantucket but wilder, with endless miles of wind-carved wilderness and coastline, and more solitude. Liam's great-grandfather was brought over to work the lime kilns in the late 1800s, she said, but when that work was done, he couldn't bring himself to leave the natural beauty of the island, nurtured for centuries by indigenous tribes. He became one of the first white settlers, falling in love with and marrying a fisherman's daughter who was of mixed Lhaq'temish descent. When the kids were little, Liam and Patricia returned here each summer, chasing tides and childhoods. After the grandparents passed, Gavin inherited the land and has spent a decade coaxing the old family home back to life, board by board.

In all the years I've known Jared, Gavin has never once invited us to visit him here.

As we descend, the island unfolds like a secret. The marina is tucked into a crescent-shaped bay, framed by weathered cliffs and old-growth forests of cedar, fir, and hemlock. It looks like a place people go to fall off the grid or fall in love. Maybe both.

Derek lands us on the water with barely a jolt, then jumps out and reaches out a tanned forearm to help me onto the dock.

He retrieves my luggage from beneath the plane's cargo area, handing it to me with a boyish grin. He's handsome enough that any red-blooded hetero woman in her right mind would notice and flirt back, but I'm not in my right mind.

"It was nice meeting you, Ava." He reaches out to shake my hand. "See you in a few months. Unless you can't tear yourself away."

I'm not quite sure what to say. There is no way this is a permanent solution to my current problems.

"Happens more than you'd think," he explains, reading my mind.

He hops back into the plane, and I watch it take off, shrinking to a speck and then disappearing into the sky.

Leaving just me, some gulls, and my impractical collection of luggage: my mom's beat-up old roller I've had since I was twelve, a giant duct-taped cardboard box, and my dad's old duffel bag.

The air smells like salt, pine, and the kind of clean that can't be bottled and sold. I inhale and feel something in my chest expand. For the first time in weeks, I don't feel displaced. I just feel ... here.

A WHITE TWO-STORY hotel sits atop a hill that rises above the harbor as if it's standing guard. Its copper roof is patina'd a sea-glass green, and its wraparound verandas make it feel like it was built for long summers, leisuring bayside with family. The kind of place where fairytales begin. Or horror stories, depending on the angle.

I pull out my phone on reflex and try to summon an Uber. One bar. Then none. The screen refreshes with: *No cars available within 100 miles.* Then I lose reception.

I hold the phone in the air and wander toward the road, arm outstretched like I'm searching for divine intervention.

A bald eagle soars overhead. I half expect it to judge me.

From somewhere on the other side of the dock, a voice calls out. "That's useless around here."

I turn and find a bearded man in waders at the shoreline, pulling a crab trap from a dinghy. His face is carved by weather and time, and he has the unbothered energy of someone who's never rushed for anything in his life.

"No reliable signal for a mile," he says.

"I was trying to get an Uber."

"I see." The man squints at me like I just said *I was summoning a Pegasus*. "What's an Uber?"

There it is. The sentence that perfectly captures the island and possibly the next three months of my life.

"It's a ride share."

"No Uber. No ride shares. There's usually a taxi, but Terry's on vacation. Your thumb will work, though." He makes the universal sign for hitchhiking.

For a second, I wonder if I'm about to hitchhike for the first time in my life.

And then I see him.

Leaning against an old green Land Rover Defender, halfway up the ridge above the dock.

Gavin.

I don't know how long he's been watching. Long enough, probably.

He's wearing jeans. Actual jeans. Beat-up boots. A soft brown T-shirt fitted enough that it's clear the man has shoulders, biceps, and not an ounce of fat on him. No blazer, no city armor. Just ... him. In the wild. His arms crossed. His expression unreadable.

He straightens, pushes off the fender, and starts walking toward me like he's got nowhere else to be, like this is just a normal Tuesday.

My pulse kicks. I didn't prepare for this part.

His boots crunch over the gravel. The sun turns his hair into some annoyingly cinematic shade of molasses.

"Welcome to the island," he says, stopping a few feet from me.

"Wasn't sure if I'd landed in the right place or a witness protection program. You've got a real *no sudden movements* vibe going."

Gavin huffs a laugh. "Well, we try not to startle the wildlife. That includes each other."

He narrows his eyes at my luggage.

"Let me guess. All the shoes you've ever owned and the contents of your entire apartment?"

I roll my eyes.

He lifts the box and immediately makes a sound like he's been punched in the kidneys. "Are you smuggling bricks? Is there cast iron in here?"

I hesitate.

"… Yes."

His brow lifts. "That explains the hernia."

"Cooking supplies and my mom's favorite pan," I say, quieter this time. "It's… sentimental."

He stops. Looks at me for a beat longer than I'm comfortable with. Then just nods once, as if he gets it. Or is pretending to.

I'm not sure which would be worse.

We load the rest in silence. I keep glancing at the water, the empty dock, the birds swirling above us.

This is it. The reset. The weird job. The eccentric remote island. The ex's brother.

On the flight from New York, I questioned everything. Accepting this offer felt like career sabotage with a side of emotional masochism.

But now … now the air is clearer and my heart is quieter.

And, it's only for three months. Now it feels less like running away and more like running toward something.

Am I really doing this?

I slide into the passenger seat, and Gavin closes my door with a solid, satisfying thunk as if answering me.

As he starts the engine, I catch a glimpse of his profile in this new context. The man not in a suit or across a conference table, but in the driver's seat of whatever this next chapter is.

If this goes sideways, he'll be the one to witness it all.

And somehow, that might be the most terrifying part.

CHAPTER 11

Honor System

WE PULL ONTO the one road that loops around the island like a lazy lasso. Green pastures roll out on either side of us, dotted with woolly sheep and newborn lambs that bounce like they've had too much caffeine. Wildflowers scatter themselves in every available space. Poppies, foxglove, Queen Anne's lace, something pink I can't name but desperately want to Pinterest later.

Gavin drives one-handed, like he's traveled this route a thousand times. The windows are down, and the smell of salt air and cedar keeps finding its way into my lungs like a slow-release sedative.

We turn down a road actually named Enchanted Forest Lane. So picture perfect it's ridiculous. There are no billboards. No honking. Not even a streetlight. Just the occasional cow or longhorn chewing on grass.

Further down the road, we pass an old weathered barn, one with a hand-painted wooden sign that reads: *Fresh Eggs, Cash Only, Honor System.*

Of course it is.

"You okay over there?" Gavin asks, eyes on the road.

"I'm fine," I say too fast.

Which means I'm absolutely not fine. His voice reminds me that I'm a walking Reddit board of rising panic: *How do you behave when your ex's brother becomes your boss? How do you start over after losing your job, your apartment, and your almost-fiancé to a man named John?*

Gavin never seems pressured to make small talk, which annoys me. I hate that he's always so good at silence. At stillness. Like he has nothing to prove and knows it. Meanwhile, I'm trying not to narrate my internal spiral out loud.

As we take a curve, the forest opens up, revealing another rocky shoreline, so stunning I momentarily forget to be anxious. The water glints silver-blue, and along the low-tide edge, a row of blue herons stands so still they look like statues.

I say nothing. I don't trust my voice not to tremble with awe, and I've already used up my day's quota of awe and vulnerability.

Gavin glances over anyway. "It's stunning the first time, but it never stops growing on you."

"I'm not here long enough for anything to grow on me," I reply.

"I've heard that before."

"Let me guess. They stayed?"

"Every time."

I roll my eyes. "Well, don't start rooting for me."

He doesn't answer, but I feel his gaze flicker over to me again before returning to the road like he's taking stock. Like he knows something I don't.

"What did you do before becoming a VC?" I ask.

"I was the lead singer of a rock band."

I burst out laughing. "That's very funny," I say, trying to imagine stoic Gavin on stage, guitar in hand.

His mouth tightens like he's already regretting hiring me. Then he brakes abruptly.

"Did we hit something?"

"Nope. Just giving the locals the right of way."

A small family of deer—mom, a buck, and two fuzzy fawns—ambles across the road.

I sit in silence, watching them disappear into the underbrush, and feel something in my ribcage shift.

Gavin's arm is still outstretched in front of me, like he was instinctively blocking me from impact, but he doesn't move it right away.

When I finally glance over, he's already looking at me, and suddenly the car feels way too small.

I clear my throat and fumble for something neutral. "That's the most Pacific Northwest thing I've ever seen."

"You didn't grow up with deer?"

"No. I grew up with cockroaches and chain-link fences."

He doesn't joke back, and now I wish I hadn't said it.

But then he says, softly, "Well, you're not there anymore."

I nod once and focus my gaze out the window like there's something urgent happening in a patch of poppies.

In the distance, the sun is beginning to dip, brushing everything in gold, and the trees go from towering to cathedral-like.

Gavin slows down to make another turn. "I forgot to ask. Are you allergic to Mohair?"

"I'm sorry—what?"

"We have three Angora goats. They're mostly harmless, unless you try to do yoga near them."

"Noted."

"I told them you were coming."

"The goats?"

He smirks. "Yeah. They're excited."

Gavin Jones *smiles*—and it's the kind of smile that gets stored in a mental folder titled *Do Not Revisit While Lonely or Tipsy.*

I cross my arms and look away.

Because this isn't the time. Or the place. Or the anything.

Because Gavin is off-limits.

Because Jared.

Because Olivia.

Because reasons.

But still ... my pulse has opinions. And I'm not sure if it's the view or the man beside me, but something tells me this summer may be a lot harder—and a lot more confusing—than I ever imagined.

WE TURN ONTO a private driveway and travel through a dense forest patch and switchback roads rimmed with sword ferns, and then through pockets of golden grass that slope toward the sea. Moss blankets rocks. The light is different here, less showy, more secretive. And those trees. I've never seen anything like them. They twist up from earth and rock like they've been fighting for centuries to touch the sun. Their bark peels in spirals, cinnamon-red and startling, revealing green underneath, as if someone had hand-painted them and forgotten to finish.

"What are those?" I ask.

"Madronas. My grandmother used to make a cider from the berries and tea from the bark whenever I had an upset stomach."

"They're gorgeous," I say quietly.

I spot more pale foxglove along the road, delicate but poisonous, he tells me, and wild huckleberries tangled with salal. It's the kind of flora that hasn't been planned or planted. It doesn't perform for you. It just ... is.

I catch my first real glimpse of the house. It's smaller than I imagined, and older. No pretentious facade, no oversized windows begging for attention. Just dark wood and a front structure that seems to have grown there from the ground up.

Gavin opens my door, his chivalry on autopilot.

I step out, inhaling damp cedar, as three Angora goats appear around the bend in the hill—white and absurdly magical, like tiny cloud creatures. One bleats at me, loudly, and I laugh.

"So, you weren't joking."

Gavin smirks and shrugs. "They came with the land."

Two smaller structures sit behind the house, half-tucked between a grove of olive trees and low flowering bushes.

"The guesthouse, and… an unfinished studio."

"Are those solar panels on top?"

"They can run completely off grid."

"For the zombie apocalypse."

"Exactly," he nods. "Both were built without disturbing the wild growth or any old-growth trees."

Wildness. That's what I couldn't name until now. This place hasn't been tamed, just gently stewarded. Like someone knew the land had a soul and tried not to trample it.

"Is this the original house?" I ask, still staring.

"My great-grandfather built the original structure, his homestead house, in the late 1800s. Everyone thought I should tear it down to make way for something new."

"Why didn't you?"

"Because he built it from trees he felled right here. I didn't want to erase the roots. I preferred to add on rather than tear down."

I feel myself warming to him again—annoying, broody, unapproachable Gavin Jones—who happens to sound like someone who believes in family and trees and legacy.

"You were supposed to stay in the guesthouse," he adds as we step toward the porch. "But the plumber ghosted me."

"Seriously?"

"Plumbers are in high demand on these islands. We're also on a septic system, which complicates matters."

"So, what happens when I flush the toilet?"

"Probably nothing catastrophic. Probably."

I raise a brow. He almost smiles. Almost.

"Anyway," he says, "you'll be in my mom's room. Inside the house."

"With you?"

"Not *with* me." He makes a face. "Just... in proximity." There's a long pause. "I'm headed off island tomorrow," he adds too casually. "Olivia has a benefit gala in L.A."

Of course, she's still in the picture. Olivia Hanson. America's favorite morning anchor.

"You won't need to cook until the next day. You'll have the place to yourself to get settled."

He opens the door. I expect starkness, maybe steel. But instead, it's warm. Lived-in. Earthy tones layered with books that look like they've actually been read, and sharp modern art. But also, softness: the right kind of pillows, worn leather, a throw blanket tossed without aesthetic calculation.

“I pictured something more... James Bond villain chic,” I admit.

“Italian marble? Underground lair?” he asks.

“At least a martini fridge and a remote-controlled fireplace.”

He smirks. “Sorry to disappoint.”

I trace the curve of a small carved sandstone elephant. There’s a baby one carved inside the mother’s belly, a delicate, hidden detail you’d miss unless you knew to look.

Just like this place of Gavin’s.

On an end table, there’s a photo of a young Gavin pushing a younger Jared on a bike. Jared’s excited. Gavin’s focused. I blink against the sudden prick of tears. This was almost my family photo.

“You look tired,” he says. “Let me show you to your room.” He doesn’t ask. He just pivots.

We head down a hallway until he stops at a room at the far end.

“My room and office are that way,” he says, gesturing in the opposite direction. “So, we won’t run into each other much.”

Light spills into the room from a small garden patio, and light from a skylight dapples the floor. A copper tub sits under a rain showerhead, separated from the bedroom by only a pane of glass.

I trail my fingers across the hammered tub.

“Olivia hated all the dents,” Gavin says. “Mom said they gave it character.”

“If things are too perfect, they evoke less emotion.”

He glances sideways. “Mom said almost the exact same thing.”

He points to a weathered black secretary’s desk. “That was my great-grandmother’s. Four generations old. Cari, Jared, and I used to hide toys in it. Three generations of women in our family have hidden love letters in its secret compartments.”

“It looks like it remembers everything,” I say. “I kind of love that.”

“Olivia doesn’t think it works with the modern interior.”

"And yet, here it is."

He shrugs. "Some things are worth keeping."

"The room's too nice, Gavin. Don't you have anything smaller?"

"Afraid not."

He hesitates. I'm staring at the wall above the bed.

"Is that…?"

It's a cluster of photographs by Jared. And in the center—me.

I step closer to the photo. The image is shadowy, intimate. I'm wearing Jared's button-up shirt. Drinking a cappuccino. My smile is sleep-mussed, radiant.

That morning. Our first morning. He captured me as if I were art.

Gavin clears his throat. "I didn't know. I've never really... looked."

We both know he has. Maybe not closely. But enough. I wonder if he'll take it down. I wonder if I want him to.

"I need to run an errand," he says. "How about I show you the kitchen when I get back?"

I nod, and he leaves, the door clicking shut behind him.

And just like that, I'm alone in a room surrounded by relics of a family I used to think might become mine.

I lie back on the bed, the sun-soaked mattress presses into my back like a hand trying to comfort me. The ceiling skylight is darkening, and I can still smell the lilac from outside. Still feel the echo of Gavin's voice when he said he didn't want to erase the roots.

Neither do I.

CHAPTER 12

Grief, Properly Punctuated

I WAKE TO the sound of music, something classical, floating in from the central part of the house. Gavin must be back. I splash water on my face, pinch my cheeks for color, and go looking for him.

I pause in the dining room. A grid of art takes up an entire wall. Each piece is a simple antique card about eight inches tall, featuring a single ornate character, hand-painted in bold black brushstrokes. I study the symbols, their shapes elegant but indecipherable. They remind me of something I can't quite put my finger on.

Gavin steps up next to me but says nothing.

"What language is this?" I ask.

"Sanskrit. Mom collected them on a trip to India and framed them for me when I needed art for this wall."

I study the brushstrokes again. "Do you know what they say?"

"Not all of them."

I glance at him, but he's still facing the wall. Whatever's behind that answer, he's clearly not wanting to talk about it.

After a beat, he clears his throat. "Want to see the kitchen?"

Gavin's kitchen is beautiful in the way some people are beautiful without trying.

The thick granite countertops are a soft ash-veined white, cool to the touch. A wall of walnut cabinets stretches along one side, hiding smart storage, and there's an eight-burner professional Viking range that looks like it could fuel a spaceship.

I pull open a few drawers. Everything is pristine. The knives—glistening Wüsthofs—are arranged like artifacts.

There's no clutter. No flour dust. No trace of anyone ever rushing through a weeknight dinner or improvising a sauce.

It's the kind of kitchen designed for someone who wants to feel like they would cook, but probably never does.

"It might not be up to your standards," he says.

"You do realize I lived in a one-bedroom apartment smaller than this kitchen?"

"Didn't know that," he frowns.

There's a pause. I think he feels as awkward as I do.

I open the fridge and wince. It's practically empty. "Eat much?"

"I meant to grocery shop."

He gestures to a small table near the window. We sit. He pours water. I pull out my notebook, but I hesitate before flipping it open.

"Just dinners, right? That's what I'm here for?"

He nods. "Dinners only. Mostly when Olivia is here. I tend to eat on the go when she's not around, and I'm not a breakfast person."

"You eat *something,* though."

"Coffee."

"And?"

"Cream. That's dairy. That counts, right?"

I smile despite myself. "Sure. If you're trying to build muscle tone in your ... spleen."

"Olivia has mentioned I could stand to tone up. She may have used the term 'six-pack abs.'"

"Do you want six-pack abs?"

"What makes you think I don't already have them?" he says, the corner of his mouth lifting.

I reflexively look down, then quickly force my eyes back up, but not fast enough to miss the way his T-shirt clings when he leans back. I'm guessing there's a six-pack situation happening under there, and unfortunately, I've noticed.

"Seriously, unless all I have to do is drink a six-pack to get them, then no, I don't care."

I laugh before I can stop myself. A real laugh, and I'm surprised how good it feels.

He merely lifts his glass and takes a sip, his eyes still on me. There's something unreadable in his expression.

"Any food preferences?"

"I'm not vegan. I'm not keto. Definitely not raw." He shrugs. "Honestly, I'm not picky about food, but I'm also not naturally attracted to salad as a meal."

"You Jones boys. Carnivores. Olivia said something about cholesterol and getting healthier?"

"Olivia has ... strong opinions."

"Right."

I pretend to write something down to avoid his eyes. I wonder if he's cataloging my flaws. My uneven eyes. My barely there eyelashes. My not-Olivia-ness.

"You don't have to overdo it," he says, voice low. "I know this situation isn't exactly ideal for you. And, I don't expect you to be cheerful for me. Whatever you need to feel, please feel."

I blink. The directness surprises me.

"No one's ever told me that before."

He tilts his head. "Really?"

"Yeah, I've felt moments that remind me of when my parents died. I mean, it's a different kind of loss and letting go, but still, most people like other people's grief packaged neatly. Punctuated with jokes, and thank you cards for their crappy casseroles."

"Not necessary," he says, then hesitates. "Are you handling all of this okay?"

I look down at the notebook still open in front of me.

"Not really," I say. "But I'm here. And I want to be. So that has to count for something."

He nods slowly, then leans back in his chair.

His gaze lingers on me a second longer than I expect. It's steady, unblinking. Not invasive, just... focused. Like he's actually paying attention.

I look away before I start reading into things that aren't there.

The silence that follows isn't strained. It stretches, then settles.

For the first time since I arrived, I don't feel like I have to perform. I don't have to apologize for how I look or what I'm feeling or how slowly I'm stitching myself back together.

We sit like that for a while. Not as strangers, exactly. But not as anything else yet.

Just two people in a kitchen, feeling a lot, but not saying all of it.

And for now, that's enough.

CHAPTER 13

What Feels Right

THE BIKE IS a clunky cruiser with a wicker basket on the front and a bell that sounds like a child's toy. I found it in the shed behind Gavin's house before he left to join Olivia in LA. He gave me one raised eyebrow when I asked if I could use it.

"Be careful," he said. "The brakes are... optimistic."

I took that as a yes.

Now I am coasting down Enchanted Forest Lane with the wind in my hair, the basket rattling with a water bottle, a notebook, and a bag full of cherries from the farm stand I just passed. There was no vendor, just a wooden table, a hand-painted sign that read *Pay what feels right,* and a coffee tin with a slot on top for bills.

I left ten dollars and a note that said *Thank you for growing joy.*

I pass a tiny two-room schoolhouse—white clapboard with a bright red door—and then Girl Meets Dirt, which turns out not to be a local gossip rag, but a charming little shop that sells award-winning shrubs, preserves, and wine with labels that look like they were designed by woodland fairies with impeccable taste.

Somewhere to my left, I hear the rustle of leaves, followed by the sudden, high-pitched gobble of what can only be described as small-winged dinosaurs in feather boas.

Turkeys.

Wild, unapologetic, vaguely vengeful turkeys.

Patricia warned me that they own parts of the island. She's seen them stop traffic at the ferry landing, stalk toddlers, and once—very aggressively—chase a tourist back into his Tesla Cybertruck.

This particular flock stares at me as I pedal by, unimpressed.

"Good morning, your majesties," I mutter.

One flares its tail in response.

I round a curve, and suddenly, the trees thin. Eastsound Bay comes into view, the water so calm it looks like glass, sailboats bobbing next to mooring buoys. In the middle of the bay, a small rocky knoll edged with tidepools rises out of the water. A single windswept evergreen clings to its crown, surrounded by low, salt-hardy shrubs. At low tide, a slender sandbar stretches out from the shore, serving as a natural bridge for someone to cross.

Main Street unspools in front of me like a postcard. Just before the road dips into town, I pass The Outlook, a storybook inn with a past that reads like a historical fiction montage. Founded by settlers in 1888, reborn as a hippie commune in the '60s, and now a hideaway coveted by honeymooners and wedding photographers in equal measure. Down the street, Brown Bear Baking has a line out the door for their version of Croque-monsieur, and across from it, the White Horse Pub leans casually on the corner like it's just waiting to pour someone a pint and tell them an island secret.

I slow down to take in the white wooden Episcopal church on

the shoreside and its stained-glass windows. It's from another time, its black steeple stoic against the cloudy sky as it stands watch over the sound. After that, there's Darvill's, a real old-fashioned independent bookstore, adorned with hanging pots of bright orange weeping begonias and windows filled with staff picks and clever chalkboard quotes.

Across the street, wedged between Gavin's two-story Venture Haus building and an old two-story brick building that houses the coffee shop Gavin warned me about, I spot it. An empty lot, half-eclipsed by vines and a sagging fence. Maybe it's the way the light hits the ginkgo tree in front, throwing golden shade across a mess of dry earth and stubborn weeds, but it makes me pause.

There's no reason for me to stop.

But I do.

Because something about the place feels ... abandoned. In a way that I understand.

I walk the bike to the edge of the fence, then duck through a gap in it, barely wide enough for me and my canvas tote. The soil is hard and cracked, scattered with wild nasturtiums, patches of rosemary, and a few brave herbs doing their best to look like they're gonna make it. Pear, pomegranate, and apple trees reach their spindly arms toward the sky—neglected but alive.

Tucked in the back of the lot, half-hidden by tangled morning glory and lilac bushes, is a large glass greenhouse, the kind referred to as a l'orangerie. It looks like it wandered out of a French fairytale.

The l'orangerie isn't grand. Like the island, it's modest but charming. The walls are paneled in glass, their iron frames streaked with salt and time. Moss curls around the stone foundation, and one of the hinges sighs when I nudge the door open.

Inside, the air is warmer. Earthier. It smells like damp citrus peel and wild thyme.

The citrus trees—one lemon, a sad little lime, one heroic blood orange—aren't thriving exactly, but they're surviving. Their leaves are waxy and curled at the edges, and someone once strung fairy lights through the rafters that still blink stubbornly to life when I flip the old switch. There's a long wooden table lying on its side, dusty, but sturdy, like it's been waiting for someone to remember it's still useful.

Back outside, near the base of the ginkgo tree, a patch of mint stops me mid-step. I kneel, and the scent hits before my fingers even touch it. Bright and green and heartbreakingly familiar.

Suddenly, I'm six. Barefoot in the neighborhood community garden, overflowing with mint and thyme. Dad picking tomatoes like they were heirlooms and gold rolled into one. *"If you can, pick them when they're warm,"* he always said. *"That's when they're sweetest."*

We'd walk the half-block home together, him balancing a box of tomatoes and other vegetables, me clutching the soft, speckled mint like it was treasure. Inside, Mom would be waiting, humming as she chopped, turning whatever we brought into something that smelled like comfort and tasted like home.

I blink hard against the memory and will back the sting of tears.

When I look up, I can see straight across Eastsound Bay. I hadn't noticed it when I whizzed by, but at the church's feet, tucked into a garden in front of the sea, is a labyrinth. A grass and stone spiral of intention, laid by the hands of the community decades ago. Cari told me that locals say you walk it when you don't know what you need but know something has to change.

I haven't walked it yet.

But I will.

I don't know how long I stand there, but eventually, my stomach grumbles loud enough to nudge me back into motion. I brush off my jeans, sneak one last look at the fruit trees, and head to the café next door. It looks tired, a little lopsided, with a flickering "Open" sign in the window that feels like a dare.

Inside, a woman in her sixties, her hair in a loose grey chignon, speaks animatedly to a man in his fifties as he sweeps the floor. Her accent is rich and musical. Middle Eastern, maybe Turkish? There are no customers. The woman smiles pleasantly at me, and I order a scone and a latte from her. Then, I sit at a table waiting for both.

She disappears behind the counter, and I sit near the window, admiring the ginkgo tree.

A moment later, she returns with the scone and a latte in a heavy ceramic mug. I see her watching me out of the corner of her eye as she wipes down a table next to me.

I take a bite. It's so dry that I choke on the crumbs. I quickly grab the latte and take a gulp. I can't help it, even with the woman watching, I scrunch up my face from the bitterness.

There are several factors that can make espresso bitter, including using inferior coffee beans, excessive water flow through the espresso maker, or an incorrect grind size. I have a feeling that multiple reasons might be contributing to this one being undrinkable. Gavin was not exaggerating when he warned me it's the worst coffee and scone he's ever tasted.

To my surprise, the woman sits down in front of me, exasperated. I look up from my mug at her. She is the opposite of many women I knew in New York, who are meticulously manicured, with all their hard edges, tucked and pinned, and polished. She's soft and round, wearing a flowing tunic over gauzy harem pants. Her face is etched with lines that make me wonder about the things she's experienced to earn them.

"It *eeess* terrible. I know. I know." She throws up her hands. "You look like a woman who would tell me the truth. You have an honest face. What is wrong with the scone?"

"I mean—it's not—"

"Do not lie. I want to hear it."

"Okay. It's dry. Did the chef forget the butter, or maybe add too much baking soda?"

"Or, probably both! No matter what he does, they come out like that. Terrible. I never understood why Americans like scones."

"If you don't like scones, why do you sell them?"

"My husband. God rest his soul. It, *this,*" she gestures to the café, "was his dream. To have a café, a place for locals to come every day and share a memory … So far, the only memories we've shared are ones we would all like to forget."

I want to distract her from her negative spiral. I shift in my seat. "I'm Ava."

"Isabel," she says, reaching across to squeeze my hand. "You're not from here."

"No, I'm not. I'm working as the summer chef for the CEO of Venture Haus."

"Ah. That one." Her eyes twinkle. "Very handsome. Lucky me, I get to see him every day."

"Every day?"

"He stops by every morning for a scone and a coffee on his way to his office."

"Are you sure you're not mistaking him for someone else?"

"What woman would forget that face?"

That's interesting. Gavin, who claims to hate Isabel's coffee and scones, buys one of each every day from her?

"Do you run this place yourself?"

"My husband, Ahmet, passed six months ago. I haven't even had time for a memorial. This place keeps me too busy."

"I'm sorry."

She nods, not brushing it away. "He was kind. And proud. Even made that little garden outside. Always said food should come from the earth, not a box."

My heart catches.

"The garden next door?" I ask, trying to sound casual.

"He tended to it, but I'm not patient enough for gardening."

"Would you mind if I tried?" I ask. "To bring it back?" I am not sure where that came from.

She gives me a long look. "It belongs to the landlord."

"Do you know who that is?"

She gives me a wry smile. "I do. Meet me here tomorrow at 5 pm, and I'll introduce you."

I'm halfway to leaving when I turn back. "You ever think about cooking the food Ahmet loved? To remember him by."

Her face stills. For a second, I think she might cry.

"I haven't had time."

"Well," I say, slowly. "I'm coming tomorrow, and I think we should cook for him. What was his favorite?"

She meets my gaze. Her chin wobbles, then steadies.

"Shish kebab."

"I just happen to know a great recipe for shish kebab," I tell her.

She smiles. "And, I will teach you how to cook something that will make you forget that awful scone forever."

CHAPTER 14

Power of the Pidé

THIS MORNING, ISABEL texted, and I surprised myself by replying, before I could overthink it:

ISABEL

Would it be all right if I invited a few of Ahmet's favorite islanders?

AVA

I'd love that

By late afternoon, we're cooking for Isabel, for Ahmet, for the people who loved him best—and, if I'm being honest, maybe for me, too.

I wash my hands and slip on the apron Isabel hands me. It's flour-streaked, worn thin in the middle, and probably older than me.

Behind us, flames lick up the wood-fired oven, and I now see an open door in the kitchen that leads to the garden.

"What are we making?" I ask.

"Pidé," she says with reverence. "Flatbread from my childhood. My Ahmet used to say, *if you can make good dough, you'll never go hungry.*"

She sprinkles flour on the counter and shows me how to stretch the ball of dough. Not too thin, not too fast. It resists at first, but then, it gives a little.

I try to mimic Isabel, but my piece stretches unevenly. One end tears. I press too hard. The shape warps.

"Wait—" Isabel stops me gently, placing her hands over mine. "Not so much pressure. Let it guide you."

I exhale, try again. Slower this time.

Together, we press it into something vaguely canoe-shaped to cradle the good stuff. The second one comes out better. Not perfect, but closer. My shoulders relax a little.

The prepared fillings—spiced lamb, sautéed onion, feta—smell like something worth believing in. We lay them onto the base, then brush the edges with egg before sliding the pidé into the oven.

I've brought my own offerings to cook. I roast red peppers until their skins blister and curl. Blend them with walnuts, Aleppo pepper, and pomegranate molasses I made from the fruit I picked yesterday. All of it, now: muhammara.

I soak bulgur, chop parsley, mint, scallions, and tomatoes, then let the tabbouleh wake up in lemon and salt. The rice pilaf simmers with toasted vermicelli, filling the kitchen with its rich, nutty scent.

Chicken kebabs hiss on the grill, marinated overnight in yogurt, garlic, onion, and spices. For the first time in ages, I feel my body remembering something my mind had almost abandoned. There's a rhythm that happens when I cook, and I can feel it returning to me.

Isabel watches me. "Your mother taught you?"

I nod. "And a few professional chefs. But mostly her."

My throat tightens. I haven't cooked like this since her. But I don't say that out loud. I just add more salt.

As I finish the food, Isabel moves through the garden, lighting candles, her linen dress fluttering in the sea breeze. Andréia, a local flower farmer and sound healer (everyone has at least two jobs on the island), drops off beautiful wild bouquets to help us with our decorations. Batu, Isabel's impossibly strong Turkish nephew, clears a space. Then he and a friend haul the old table out from the l'orangerie like it weighs no more than a broomstick.

I'm introduced to Tara, a petite woman with an asymmetrical bob and a septum ring. She's the local who helped turn a weathered boat shed into The Barnacle, which Cari insists is the most enchanting bar on the West Coast. Tonight, she's setting up an outdoor bar in the garden for us, laying out bottles, cut citrus, and shrubs. It's not formal, but it feels sacred.

As the guests begin to arrive, I remember that Patricia said the island favors the accomplished and the unconventional, often in the same body—and tonight's no exception.

There are Sara and Duke, owners of the local bookstore. Sara—half-Japanese like me—greets me with a smile so open it feels like an embrace. Duke, just as welcoming, wraps me in a hug that smells faintly of cedar and the gunpowder he uses to make works of art. The town calls them the Duke and Duchess, and I immediately understand why.

Lee, the baker at Brown Bear Baking, arrives with his handsome husband, David, and a warm loaf of their Mission Fig & Apricot hearth bread for me. I haven't even taken the first bite before deciding we're lifelong friends.

Then comes Melissa, an ex-cop who now teaches Pilates. She's tall, broad-shouldered, the kind of woman who could pin you with a stare or realign your spine—or probably both. She offers me a nod, all business and bone-deep kindness. It's like being assessed and welcomed at the same time.

Martha and Joe follow. Neighbors in their seventies, Isabel tells me. Martha has the energy of someone who once drank champagne with Georgia O'Keeffe. Pixie haircut, paint-smudged fingers, cornflower blue eyes. Joe has the kind of charm that sneaks up on you. You'd never guess he made a fortune, or that he's been quietly giving it away for years.

They settle in as if this is something they've always done—breaking bread, lighting candles, and remembering someone by the food he loved.

And then, the last guest steps through the garden gate.

Gavin. A bottle of Narince Turkish White in one hand. Sleeves rolled to his forearms. The late sun slides across his shoulders, catching in his hair, softening what I remember as hard, unyielding edges.

I see Tara's eyebrow lift as she watches him out of the corner of her eye. Melissa gives him a quick once-over before turning back to her wine. He's not just handsome. He's the kind of beautiful that feels almost dangerous, like standing too close to the sea during a storm.

This is not the Gavin I knew in New York. The one too busy, too aloof to linger anywhere.

Here, in this garden, with candlelight and the scent of citrus and soft laughter, he looks … at home.

I blink. The abandoned garden. The l'orangerie. The café.

He's the landlord.

And he's watching me as I carry out the salad—mint, pink radicchio, fennel, blood orange, raspberry vinaigrette—and nods, just once.

I take the last open seat, next to him, preparing to ask about the garden, if it's okay that I tend to it. But before I can say a word, he leans in slightly, his voice low.

"Isabel said you want to work in the garden." A pause. "It's yours as long as you want it. It suits you."

He doesn't look at me when he says it. But it lands all the same.

WHEN EVERYONE HAS a drink, Isabel stands with a glass of wine in her hand, her fingers trembling just enough to make me ache for her.

She clears her throat. "Ahmet used to say, '*When I die, don't just bury me. I want you to feed people. Let the flavors remember me better than I was.*'"

A pause, soft and full.

"I never held a memorial," she says, her voice catching. "I didn't know how. But tonight … with Ava's help … I cooked for him. And I remembered."

She sets a plate at an empty seat, tenderly, like she's placing it into someone's waiting hands.

No one speaks. But the silence feels like something being honored. Maybe even healed.

POMEGRANATE SEEDS GLINT like rubies in the candlelight as we pass food like memories between us.

The dishes are warm, flavorful, and honest. There's the sharing of bread, island stories, and laughter.

I glance around the table and wipe a tear, a happy one.

When I look up, Gavin is watching me.

Just for a moment, we're two people who see something at the same time, and neither knows what to say.

He glances away, but not before something passes between us. Recognition, maybe? Or understanding.

Once we finish dessert, Gavin raises his glass. Everyone follows.

"To Ahmet," he says, then turning to me, he adds: "And the people who make us hungry for life."

We clink. We sip.

The making of food didn't come easily tonight. That's the point.

But something's blooming here—slowly, wildly, maybe even in the right direction.

CHAPTER 15

Food to Die For

It's been three days since the garden dinner at Isabel's. Three days since we shared a table strung with fairy lights, overflowing with muhammara, shish kebabs, and laughter that felt easy. Three days since Gavin started eating dinner at his office.

I tell myself it's a coincidence that he's busy. That it has nothing to do with the way his eyes met mine in the garden, or how we both had to look away.

But something has shifted. And apparently, we've both decided to pretend it hasn't.

In response, I decided to cook something delicious tonight. Not because I want anyone to join me, but because I need to make something that takes my mind off Jared and now Gavin, too.

Food is memory for me, and most of my recipes are knotted up with Jared—dishes I perfected because he loved them. But this one isn't his.

Jambalaya. From a GQ article I clipped before I even met him, titled "The Impressive Bachelor Dinner." Back when I thought I'd be the kind of woman who lived alone by choice, maybe with a rescue mutt named Jane or Elizabeth or Bennet, and a record player that actually worked.

I pull the worn recipe card from my binder—grease-stained, smudged with time—and get to work.

When it's comfort you want, I've found you can never go wrong with jambalaya, cold beer, and masa cornbread made with real butter, maple syrup, and my secret ingredient. Still, I'm not planning to serve it to anyone. Especially not to Gavin.

But around six-thirty, just as I'm pulling the cornbread from the oven, I hear the front door open.

Gavin steps into the kitchen and pauses.

The room is a war zone: dishes in the sink, tomato paste smeared on the counter, me wearing half of what I chopped. It's chaos. Jared used to tease me about this. He was the kind of person who could make a five-course meal and leave the kitchen looking like it had been staged for Architectural Digest. If we were painters, I was Basquiat to his Mondrian.

Gavin raises one eyebrow. "What happened in here?"

"I'm cooking."

"Are you sure? Because it looks like something exploded."

"Art is messy."

He takes a long look around, then—without another word—grabs a beer from the fridge. He doesn't leave, though. He leans against the counter like he's considering something.

I take a breath and casually slide a steaming bowl of jambalaya toward him.

"I need feedback."

He eyes it like I just handed him a baby opossum.

"I'm not looking for company," I add quickly. "Just notes."

He sits.

I try not to show how relieved I am.

I slide a thick piece of warm, crusty cornbread beside his bowl and pour his beer into a glass.

"I'm surprised," he says.

"What were you expecting?"

"A plate of raw kale and a single almond."

"I'm impressed you know what kale is."

He smirks. Takes a bite of the jambalaya. Then the cornbread.

I wipe down the counter, but I'm observing him, pretending not to. He doesn't say anything, but something in his posture shifts. He's wearing a suit, but I can still see his shoulders drop, like something unspools a little.

"How's Olivia?" I ask, more casually than I feel.

"She and Quinn get in next week," he says.

There's something tight around his mouth when he says it. I get the sense he has mixed feelings about Olivia's arrival, and before I can stop myself, I wonder what could possibly be wrong with their perfect, curated life.

Then he coughs. Once. Then again.

His eyes go wide. He grips his throat.

"Gavin?"

He's not coughing anymore. He's choking.

I leap up and run behind him, my hands shaking as I wrap them around his middle and thrust upward—hard. I'm not even sure I'm doing it right, but I can't think. My heart is sprinting. He grabs my arms, shoving them away, reaching for a pen on the counter.

He scrawls one word across my hand:

Peanuts?

My stomach drops.

The secret cornbread ingredient. One-eighth cup of peanut oil.

I fumble for my phone to call 911 as he yanks at his briefcase. He's digging, pulling out what looks like an EpiPen, but it slips from his grip.

I stare at it. My breath catches.

He points to his thigh.

I drop to my knees, pull down the fabric of his pants, and stab. The pen clicks, and I flinch.

"Hold … ten seconds…" he murmurs.

I whisper to myself. "One … two …"

He's still gasping. His skin is waxy, pale. My stomach twists.

Then the room tilts.

I feel it coming—the way the edges blur, the ground drops, the air thins. My hands are still on his leg, but everything else feels far away.

And then—

Black.

When I come to, I partially lift my lids, still drowsy, and take in my environment through my lashes. My vision is soft, the edges of everything smudged. The beeping of machines is gentle and distant. A white curtain ripples faintly from someone walking past. A familiar, unwelcome scent hits me: disinfectant and plastic and lemon-scented sterility. It takes only a second for my body to recognize my surroundings, even before my mind catches up.

Hospital.

A slow unease curls in my stomach.

A memory flashes: me, age twelve, nestled against my father in a hospital bed. His skin too pale, his hand warm but unmoving in mine. There were wires and monitors and a nurse who spoke in a voice meant for grown-ups. Mom wasn't there. Because she never made it to the hospital. They said the crash had taken her instantly.

I close my eyes and shake the memory loose, as best I can.

When I open them, I spot a figure slumped in the chair by the window, and my pulse calms.

Jared.

The last time I woke up in a hospital, he and Patricia were there, flanking my bed like slightly overbearing angels, after I broke my wrist falling down a slick subway staircase, late to meet the family for dinner.

But something's off.

The man in the chair is wearing a suit. Jared never wears suits unless there's a seating chart or a eulogy involved.

I squint harder.

It's not Jared.

It's Gavin.

Sleeping, his limbs folded awkwardly, in a molded plastic chair, chin tucked to his chest. His tie is askew, and his hair looks like it's been through something traumatic. There's stubble on his jaw and tension in his shoulders, even in sleep.

He stirs, rubs his eyes with a closed fist like a boy waking from a too-short nap, and straightens in the chair. When his eyes meet mine, something softens.

"You're awake," he says, voice low and rough.

"Apparently." I try to sit up but give up halfway. "I feel like I drank a bottle of tequila and fell off a roller coaster."

"You hit your head when you fainted. Mild concussion. They wanted to keep you under observation."

"Fainted ..." I wince. "Right. The cornbread. Oh my God, Gavin—I could've killed you."

"You got the EpiPen in me before you passed out."

I exhale slowly. "I'm so sorry. I totally understand if you want to fire me."

"I don't." He leans back a little, watching me. "That meal was worth it."

"Worth dying for?"

"*Almost* dying for," he shrugs.

I roll my eyes, but my mouth quirks. His presence is strangely calming—steadfast and unshiny, the kind of comfort that sneaks up on you.

A male nurse enters the room with a clipboard in hand, wearing an unfazed expression.

"Mr. and Mrs. Jones? We're all set to discharge you."

I sit up straighter. "Oh—no, we're not—"

But Gavin stands and takes the clipboard from the nurse's hands like it's the most natural thing in the world.

"Thank you," he says, signing without hesitation. The nurse beams and exits.

I blink at him.

"Gavin. Why do they think we're married?"

He shrugs. "Technicality."

"You forged a legal relationship so you could spend the night?"

He gives me a not-quite-smile. "You didn't look like you should wake up alone."

I stare at him. And my heart does something annoying.

Before I can say anything else, his phone buzzes in his pocket. He checks the screen and silently passes it to me.

"It's Jared."

My throat tightens.

I take the phone.

"Ava?" Jared's voice is gentle, concerned. "Are you okay? Gavin called and told us what happened."

"I'm fine," I say softly. "They're discharging me now. Gavin's been here."

"I wish I could've been." He exhales, voice tight. "I hate the thought of you being hurt and me not knowing. I know it's not my place anymore, but caring about you doesn't just... stop."

"I know," I whisper. "Thank you."

He's quiet for a moment. Then: "I spoke to Gavin. He told me it was him. That he was the one who told the family about me being gay. Not you."

I close my eyes.

"I'm sorry I blamed you. I should've trusted you. And I shouldn't have said what I said."

I nod, even though he can't see me. "It's okay."

"No. It's not. You deserve better."

I swallow against the lump forming in my throat.

"I can't believe you left New York without telling me," he adds.

"I left because I didn't know how to stay," I tell him.

That familiar ache surfaces again.

"I don't think seeing each other or talking is a good idea. It makes it so hard to let go, to move on," I confess.

"I understand," he says quietly. "I just ... couldn't *not* call when I heard."

"I'm glad you did," I say. "But I should go now."

There's a long pause. I know what we would've said once, in this little pocket of silence. But that language doesn't belong to us anymore.

So instead, I say, "Take care."

Then I hang up.

I sit still for a long moment, staring at the screen.

One tear escapes, and I swipe it away quickly. I hand the phone back to Gavin, who's watching me with an expression I can't quite name—concern, maybe, but something gentler underneath it.

"Would you like me to call the nurse?"

"It's not that kind of pain."

He doesn't say anything else. He just sits beside me, silent, steady, and fully there.

And somehow, that's enough.

CHAPTER 16

Nico

I'M COVERED IN sweat and streaked with dirt, but for the first time, the empty lot is starting to resemble a real garden.

When I arrived this morning, there were bags of fertilizer, gravel, and bark and the weathered wood table in the l'orangerie—once slumped on its side—was propped up and sanded smooth, its grain coaxed back to life. I hope Isabel didn't spend too much or work Batu to the bone, but I'm grateful. All of it feels like possibility.

I spend hours clearing, digging, and weeding until my fingers throb. I plant lavender, mint, cilantro, and a brave little artichoke bush I rescued from a permaculture homestead in Deer Harbor, one of the island's five hamlets.

I'm bent over a stubborn clump of weeds when the crunch of footsteps on gravel makes me glance up.

Melissa appears first, her hair pulled into a no-nonsense ponytail. She carries a canvas tote full of pruning shears and twine.

"Reinforcements have arrived," she calls, pushing open the gate with her hip.

Behind her are Sara and Andréia, both waving like we've known each other for years instead of a single dinner party.

"We figured you could use some help," Andréia says, already eyeing the flowerbeds.

"You're saints," I tell them as I brush dirt from my knees and greet them with a hug.

In no time, we've divided up the tasks. Melissa moves straight to the fruit trees, her height a quiet superpower as she navigates the higher branches with ease. Sara commandeers the glass panels of the l'orangerie, power washing them until sunlight streaks through in golden ribbons.

Andréia kneels at the flower beds, her hands deft and knowing as she tucks in nasturtiums, borage, bachelor buttons, and violet pansies alongside dahlias and peonies. "This will be beautiful," she says, her soft Portuguese lilt warm, threading through the buzz of bees. "Edible flowers for salads and for beauty."

The air grows fragrant with mint and lavender, the sweetness of peonies mingling with the loamy scent of freshly turned earth. As we work, laughter weaves between us, light and surprising.

We're smoothing the last stretch of the new path when a bag of gravel I'm hauling suddenly slips out of my grasp. It's heavier than I thought, and I yelp in protest. As I drag it, it snags on a root, jerks sideways, and slips from my grasp again with a thud, sending a puff of earthy dust into the air.

"That bag's winning, you know."

A male voice—low, warm, edged with amusement—drifts over my shoulder.

A man leans against the gate, one hand hooked lazily in his back pocket.

His dark hair is a little wild, a lock falling into his eyes before he runs his hands through it to tame it. There's a quiet confidence to him, and it's alluring.

"I was rooting for you," he says, stepping forward. "But your technique is questionable."

"Questionable?" I echo, narrowing my eyes even as my lips twitch.

"Maybe more leverage, less brute force?" He steps closer and grips the bag, lifting it with an ease that makes me both grateful and mildly irritated.

"Fine," I say, brushing at the dirt streaking my palms. "You win. I was struggling."

"Don't worry. I won't tell anyone." There's the faintest glimmer in his eyes as he deposits the bag exactly where I'd been aiming for.

"You always wander around town assisting damsels in distress?" I ask, unable to stop myself.

He glances up at me. "You don't strike me as the helpless type."

"That's very feminist of you."

He shrugs, brushing the hair from his face again.

Andréia murmurs something to Sara, and they exchange a look. Melissa's eyebrows lift ever so slightly, the corner of her mouth curving like she's already planning to tease me later.

"Live on island or vacationing?" I ask.

"I'm here for the Doe Bay music residency."

"Sounds impressive."

"It is… me, not so much," he says, and the faintest grin appears. "Basically means I play music loudly enough to annoy the neighbors in exchange for a very cool cabin, studio time, and free food."

"Nico!" a voice calls from the sidewalk. Two guys are waving, one with a guitar slung across his back, the other balancing a drumstick between his fingers like he was born with it.

"That's my cue."

"Nice to meet you, Nico. I'm Ava."

Nico brushes the dirt off his hands and extends his right one. We shake and hold each other's gaze.

"See you around, Ava. You know where to find me."

Before I can answer him, he's already jogging down the path, his friends greeting him with mock applause.

I realize that the girls have all stopped to stare after him, too.

"*Mmm*," Andréia murmurs. "That smile is dangerous."

"Dangerous?" I ask, reaching for my gloves.

"Absolutely," Melissa adds.

Sara lets out a slight hum. "Oooh, that one. The baristas at the bookstore are in love with him."

"And, isn't it convenient he's here for the summer just like you?" Melissa adds.

"Okay, okay," I say quickly, pulling my gloves back on.

Melissa smirks. "What? We're not saying summer romance or anything."

"Yet," adds Sara.

But as I return to the garden work, I can't help the small, traitorous smile tugging at my lips.

CHAPTER 17

Cravings

BY THE TIME I walk back into the house, my spine is wrecked. My nails are jet black. There's a twig sticking out of my braid like it grew there.

The breeze that started as a whisper mid-afternoon is now pushing at the trees, tapping branches against the windows. There's a storm coming, maybe. But inside, for once, I feel calm. And I realize that for the first time in longer than I can remember, I didn't think of Jared once. Not while planting. Not while pruning. Not while talking to a cute guy who may or may not have been flirting with me.

Gavin looks up from his laptop and takes in my dirt-smudged face, the state of my overalls, and whatever mess is happening in my hair.

"What happened to you?"

"Your garden happened to me."

He arches a brow. "Uh-huh. By the way, Olivia's plans changed. She's coming in tomorrow instead of tonight."

"Perfect," I say, as I search the fridge. "Have you had dessert yet?"

"Not one that would keep me from eating another."

"Then sit tight. I have just the thing."

Fifteen minutes later, I reappear, clean and damp-haired in a soft cotton tee and loose drawstring shorts—what I'd normally wear after a shower and no plans to see anyone. But the way Gavin's gaze catches, flickers down my legs and back up again, feels like a touch I can feel. My skin prickles where his gaze lands. I grab two ramekins from the fridge to hide the heat blooming across my face.

"Is that... crème brûlée?" he asks.

"Vanilla cardamom," I nod, setting the dishes and a torch on the counter. "Our little secret. Olivia texted her list of foods to avoid this week, and sugar was at the top."

"Can I use the torch?"

"Men and fire," I laugh as I hand it to him. I sprinkle fine sugar over the custards with slow precision as a gust of wind whistles through the chimney flue. "Go for it."

The second he flicks the torch on, the kitchen lights flicker. Once. Then again. And then—*poof.*

Darkness folds over us, thick and immediate. Outside, the wind groans through the trees, sending a rhythmic creak down the old porch beams.

I freeze. "Did we do that?"

"Nope," Gavin says, unbothered, his focus still on torching the sugar that's beginning to bubble. "Power's probably out on half the island. Happens every time a tree sneezes near a power line."

"You're joking."

"Dead serious. Welcome to Orcas Island. Where power outages are part of the charm."

The only light left is the small blue flame licking at the sugar and its faint halo cast across his face. The sugar begins to melt and sizzle, blistering into amber.

There's something oddly mesmerizing about it. About him. The way he leans in, steady and assured, sleeves pushed up, forearms flexed just enough to be distracting. Not that I'm paying attention to that. It's just ... scientifically observable.

And then there's the light. The flame flickers gold across his face, catching in the arch of his cheekbone, shadowing the curve of his mouth in a way that makes it feel illegal to look directly at him, which I am not doing. Obviously.

God. I need to get a grip.

It's the lighting. And the sugar. And probably the power outage. This is just one of those strange, cozy apocalypse moments when your body forgets to follow the rules because everything feels like a movie, and your brain is the last to get the memo.

"And this is... frequent?" I ask to keep from staring.

"Frequent enough that I keep candles in every drawer."

"And Olivia's okay with that?"

He reaches down, opens a drawer with his free hand, and produces a handful of squat beeswax candles. Without missing a beat, he tilts the torch and lights them one by one. The flames dance along the wicks, then settle into a gentle pulse, and I become aware of the quiet between us.

"She tolerates it," he says after a pause, eyes back on the brûlées. "Not exactly her idea of luxury living."

Something in his voice is easy, but there's a small shift. I notice it because I'm watching and listening to him too closely.

"She likes things predictable," he adds. "Controllable. The island ... doesn't always cooperate with her."

The flickering light makes the room feel warm and drowsy and oddly intimate.

"I guess this means no Netflix?" I ask, trying to change the mood.

"Afraid not. But you've got crème brûlée, candlelight, and my undivided attention."

He says it casually, but something in me stirs at the words.

He finishes torching the dessert, then lifts one ramekin, tilts his head to inspect the glassy top, like a jeweler studying a gem.

"You're actually good at that," I say.

"Mom taught me a lot in the kitchen," he replies, setting the ramekin down with care. "Including the birds and the bees."

"Wait. That talk happened over cooking?"

He nods. "Cupcakes. I was fourteen. She said some girls—especially cheerleaders I couldn't stop staring at during rugby games—might look sweet on the outside, but underneath all the frosting and sprinkles, they were mostly preservatives and artificial flavoring."

I burst out laughing. "That's... disturbingly accurate."

"She had a metaphor for everything. And she always knew when something was on my mind. Cooking made it easier for me to talk. Less eye contact, more stirring."

He trails off for a moment, then says, "I always thought I'd marry someone like her."

Something about the way he says it makes me still. I try to picture Olivia baking cupcakes, and I fail.

"What about your mom?" he asks gently. "Did you two ever... have the talk?"

"She died when I was twelve," I say. "We never got there."

His gaze softens. "I'm sorry."

"I still miss her, but having your family around, especially your mom, has helped me over the years. I really don't know what I'll do without them."

Gavin studies me, and his voice drops. "If it came down to it, I'm certain everyone in my family would pick you over me."

I huff a small laugh. "That's a very nice thing to say."

He doesn't look away. The air stretches between us. His knee brushes against mine under the table. The contact is small but seismic. I could shift. But I don't.

Gavin doesn't move either. He keeps his knee in place. Solid. Warm. Unapologetic. It's the kind of contact that, in daylight, might feel loaded, but in the candlelit hush of the kitchen, it's something else entirely. Something we can pretend isn't happening, as long as we don't acknowledge it.

I turn to my crème brûlée and crack the shell with the back of my spoon. I glance up to hand Gavin a spoon to do the same and realize he's been watching me.

The tiny sound of sugar cracking feels indecently loud.

I take a bite. Creamy, warm, familiar. He leans in slightly, tapping his spoon against his ramekin like he's winding up to say something, but still deciding if he should.

His shell-like top splinters like glass, and he takes a bite, moaning his pleasure.

"Wow. Decadent."

And even though I know better, I lean toward the glow. I want to see that look again—the one people make when something is so much better than they expected.

"What's Olivia working on this week?" I ask.

His mouth twitches, as if he knows I'm trying to distract myself.

"She's interviewing the founders of The Love Lab who live on the island."

"Oh?" I arch a brow, picturing Olivia in one of her perfectly tailored pantsuits, interrogating the relationship power couple, Julie and John Gottman. We once did a feature on them at Pulse.

"Let me guess. Something thought-provoking, like 'Are situationships ruining our moral fabric or just our group chats?'"

He laughs. "Close. One-night stands."

"Classic Olivia." I swirl my spoon in the custard. "The Gottmans say lasting love is built on emotional safety, shared meaning, the deep stuff. Like, fight fair, stay curious about each other, make each other feel seen."

He tilts his head. "Isn't that... kind of the point?"

"Totally," I say. "But Esther Perel, whom your fiancée has had on her show multiple times, would argue that desire thrives on space, mystery, tension. She might say you can't eroticize someone who's also reminding you to buy oat milk."

"Can't you have both?" he asks, watching me now.

"That's what the Gottmans think. And they've got four decades of research and a marital batting average that rivals baseball legends."

"So you're team Gottman?"

"If I ever get back in the game? Yeah. I want the good fight. The deep knowing. Not just a sexy stranger I don't have to do taxes with."

"She asked me how many one-night stands I've had," he says, almost sheepish.

"Did you answer?"

He taps his spoon again. "Nope. Dodged like a pro. Have you ever had one?"

"Wow. Just... going for it, huh?"

He shrugs.

I hesitate, then: "No. I haven't."

He tilts his head, like I just said I'd never eaten pizza. "Never?"

"I met your brother when I was twenty, and we were together for eight years. I'd only had one boyfriend before that."

His expression shifts, as if he's a little surprised. "That's kind of amazing."

"Is it?" I ask. "Or just naïve?"

"It's rare," he says. "And no, not naïve."

I give him a look. "I bet you can't count your one-night stands on two hands."

"Ouch." He presses a hand to his chest, mock-wounded.

I narrow my eyes at him. "Are you going to tell me you've never had one?"

He raises both hands. "Totally serious. I've dated everyone I've slept with. For at least a few weeks. Sometimes a few tragic months."

I take another bite, letting the sweetness give me courage.

"Is Olivia the first person you've been in love with?"

He doesn't answer right away. Then, softer, "There was someone I was hung up on for a very long time. She wasn't available."

"Did she know how you felt?"

"Definitely not. It was complicated, and I couldn't tell her. Kind of made it impossible to even think of anyone else for years."

There's a current between us now. It's invisible, but electric, and unacknowledged.

I'm not sure I can take hearing more of his heartbreak. Instead, I lighten the mood. "You know, crème brûlée is technically healthy. Eggs are protein."

He smiles, just barely. "Always with the facts."

"I'm a wealth of semi-useless knowledge," I reply. "You should see me at parties."

"I'd like to," he says.

We eat a few more spoonfuls of crème brûlée before I break the silence again.

"How does it feel to be living the fairytale?" I ask.

"Fairytale?"

"You know, falling in love and living happily ever after."

He takes a moment before responding. "I used to love fairytales when I was a kid. They teach us to take risks, put ourselves out there."

"You don't think we're all really just driven by the biological urge to perpetuate the species?" I ask.

"No, Darwin, I don't."

"Come on, you can't tell me you haven't noticed that people who look like Olivia have an easier time at love than the rest of us?"

"You believe finding love is easier for people who look like Olivia? If you could trade places with Olivia, would you?" he asks.

I pause. "Well, that would mean I'd be dating you."

He says nothing.

"And we both know that would be impossible," I scoff.

"Do we?" he asks.

"Well, yeah. First of all, I'm not nearly perfect enough for you."

"You think I need perfect?"

"You've got perfect."

In the flickering dark, his hand shifts on the table and our fingers touch. Neither of us breathes. He flinches almost imperceptibly, then looks down at his spoon. One of the candles gutters, casting a jagged shadow across his jaw.

The moment hangs between us, tender and terrifying.

I want to rewind the last three seconds. Instead, I focus on my dessert and pretend like my cheeks aren't on fire. I don't know what I meant. I don't even know if I believe it.

Before I can say anything else, his phone buzzes. He glances at the screen.

"I should take this," he says, and heads out to the terrace.

I watch him through the glass as he lifts the phone to his ear. His back is straight, shoulders squared, voice quiet.

The dessert tastes different now. Richer. Sharper. And, I think, Gavin is a lot like crème brûlée. Once cracked, his hard exterior reveals a comforting, sweet, but complex inside.

And I am dangerously close to craving more.

CHAPTER 18

Plan Platonic

I AM NOT falling for Gavin Jones.

Nope. Absolutely not.

Not just because he's engaged to a woman *People* magazine once named one of America's Most Beautiful Humans.

Of course, I am not falling for Gavin because that would be monumentally stupid.

Even if he may have looked at me yesterday, for the briefest of seconds, like I was dessert.

Nope. I am not going to pine like an Emily Henry heroine. Just because a man moans over custard doesn't mean he's your soulmate.

Even if I'm still thinking about the moment his fingers brushed mine when he handed back the pastry torch, and I felt that ridiculous zing that no amount of logic has managed to kill.

It's not even about Gavin. It's residual Jared. It's just … emotional phantom limb syndrome. My heart reaching for something that's no longer there, like it forgot it's been cut off. Of course, I'd be drawn to someone who looks like Jared, sounds like him, has that same stubborn jaw and careful way with words. It's just my brain, scrambling for comfort. Familiarity. Not lust. Definitely not lust.

I make a plan anyway. The plan is to stay in the platonic zone for the next three months, then leave by enacting the following:

1. Avoid alone time with Gavin.

2. Channel all rogue attraction into garden work. Sweat out the feelings. Compost the longing.

3. Remind myself: this is temporary. He is temporary. I am here to heal, not detonate.

When I spot him on the patio through the kitchen window, lying on a chaise, barefoot, shirtless, hair still damp from a shower, a book resting against his stomach, my breath catches. He looks relaxed. Unguarded. A version of him I would fall for, if things were different.

I grab my gloves and flee on the bike to my safe zone.

I'M ELBOWS-DEEP IN garden soil, tearing at weeds with the kind of energy usually reserved for Black Friday sales and betrayal. Dirt cakes under my nails. I find a worm and scream only a little. Nature is healing, apparently.

I'm muttering "He's not yours, not yours, not yours..." when my phone buzzes.

It's a text from Kiki.

> KIKI
>
> Is it insane that I'm checking hotel availability on the island?

I call her, and she answers before the first ring ends.

"Okay, hear me out. I need air. Space. A place where no one is using 'synergy' unironically. And guess what? The Outlook Inn has a room available for the whole week. Can I come?" she asks.

My brain scrambles. "Wait—you want to come *here*?"

"To the *island*. You're just a bonus. A messy, emotionally fragile, crème-brûlée-hoarding bonus."

I laugh, the first real laugh of the day. "Come."

I can practically hear her grin. "Great. I already booked a ticket. My flight arrives in Bellingham tomorrow."

I let out a long breath. If anyone can distract me from Gavin and keep me from making an absolute mess of things, it's Kiki.

CHAPTER 19

Side Quests

THERE'S SOMETHING HOLY about the moment a ferry uncouples from the mainland. Like a quiet promise that says you won't be the same when you return.

The wake unfurls in widening rings behind us as we lean against the boat's railing, the wind pushing at our jackets and hair. Before us, the Salish Sea glimmers, blue-green and impossibly beautiful. We pass little uninhabited islands that rise from the water like the backs of sleeping creatures.

Kiki is cradling a lavender matcha latte like it's a therapy dog. She hasn't said much since I picked her up from Bellingham airport, which is how I know something's wrong. Kiki talks like she breathes—continuously, effortlessly. Silence is not her default setting.

"You came to check on me, didn't you?" I ask, gently.

"Of course I did," she says, but she's watching the water, not me.

"You moved to a remote island, you're trying to build a new life, and sending me photos of suspiciously adorable produce. It was time for me to check you weren't in a cult."

"And?"

"You might be. But your skin looks amazing, so I'm reserving judgment."

She smiles, but it doesn't quite reach her eyes. Not the way it used to.

"I'm glad you're here," I tell her.

She nods, pulls her jacket tighter, as the breeze kicks up, bringing with it the faint scent of cedar and salt.

"So…" I say, just to open a door. "This trip wasn't just about my glow-up and questionable life choices, was it?"

"You always did see through me like I'm a Hallmark protagonist pretending I don't still love my ex at Christmas."

"Which movie?"

"Pick one."

I wait. She doesn't make me wait long.

"Mel dumped me." She sips her latte. "This time it's permanent," she adds. "It had to be. I couldn't keep pretending."

I turn toward her, heart open, but quiet.

Kiki exhales, hard. "You know how in high school, all the other girls would whisper about who they wanted to kiss? Which boys they made out with under the bleachers, who had the best butt in jeans, who they wanted to lose it to at prom?"

"Sure."

"I felt… nothing. I thought I was a late bloomer. Or just picky. And I wanted to want it. I watched *Titanic* fifteen times, trying to get turned on by Leo in a waistcoat. All I got was frustration that Rose couldn't be bothered to lift a finger—and a weird fixation on lifeboats."

I laugh, gently. She lets out a breath.

"Now that I'm an adult, I like kissing," she says. "I love kissing, actually. I like the warm stuff, the kind of cuddling where your ribs hurt from how hard you're hugging. I love slow dancing in kitchens and napping with someone tangled around me. I love *love*."

She pauses. Looks at me.

"I just don't want to have intercourse. I never have. And for a long time, I thought that meant I was broken. Or traumatized. Or missing something fundamental. But I went to this conference last month for Asexual Awareness Week, and for the first time, I didn't feel weird. I felt named."

"You're a romantic asexual?" I ask, softly.

She nods, eyes brimming. "I didn't even know that was a thing. But it is. And I am."

"What are you feeling now?"

"Relieved. Terrified. Free."

"I'm proud of you." I give her a sideways hug.

Her shoulders drop like she's been holding them up for weeks. "Thank you."

"Do you want me to ask questions or shut up and sit with it?"

She gives me a real smile now. "Ask."

"Okay. Does it change what you want from relationships?"

"Maybe. I mean, it's not like I was killing it on the dating apps before. But now I get to be honest. Up front. The already small pool of possible partners just turned into a kiddie pool with a slow leak, but at least I won't be in it pretending I like the dirty water."

That gets a genuine laugh from both of us.

"What about love?" I ask.

"Oh, I still want it. I want a Nora Ephron movie ending, minus the sex montage. I want someone to curl up with and eat popcorn straight from the bag and fall asleep on the couch watching *Notting Hill* with. I just don't want the part where it ends with sweaty naked acrobatics."

"Fair."

"I kept trying to be the version of myself someone would want, and I kept leaving pieces of me behind to do it."

"Not anymore," I say, fierce.

"Not anymore," she echoes. "You know, the weirdest thing is that I feel more like myself than I ever have. But lonelier than I expected. Which is why I needed this trip. Not because I need to disappear. Because I needed to be seen. By someone who knows me."

I take her hand. "I see you. Always have."

She wipes her eyes, then immediately pivots. "Also," she adds with a sniff, "I want to help you get laid."

I snort. "Excuse me?"

"What? You've been heartbreak cooking and mooning around farmers markets like a Brontë heroine with a secret sourdough starter fetish. It's time."

"You really came here to help me rebound?"

"I came here to help you *thrive*," she says grandly. "But I am open to side quests."

"You've put thought into this."

"Oh, I have spreadsheets. And a moodboard. Think *Under the Tuscan Sun*. The woman gets dumped, then traipses off to France."

"Italy. Tuscan sun," I remind her.

"But don't you think France would've been nicer?"

I raise an eyebrow.

"Anyway," she continues, "Think *You've Got Mail* with the perky blonde in all her cute hats walking through Central Park, faking orgasms along the way."

I snort. "You mean *When Harry Met Sally*."

"God, the heartache that woman went through. The boxes and boxes of tissues, the confusion, the torture. And the guy she fell in love with was her friend."

"Okay, I think we went off track—"

"As modern women, we have to ask ourselves: Do we really think we'll find a Lloyd Dobler who's going to stand under our window holding a boom box and play a kickass song to prove his love for us?"

She pauses. "Why are you looking at me like that? What did I mix up this time?"

"Actually, you got the movie right. Threw me for a loop."

"Seriously, Ava. Is it even possible to find a Lloyd Dobler without going through a Costco supply of tissues?"

"First, I don't know the answer to that. Second, you do know they've made romantic comedies since 1990, right?"

"Have they? Because the ones I've seen don't deserve to be in the genre."

"And today's Lloyd Dobler would just text you a Spotify link."

"So bleak."

She doesn't say anything after that, and she doesn't need to.

Below, a shout rises from the deck. We both turn—and then we see them.

A pod of orcas, surfacing in unison. Five or six, maybe more, their slick black backs slicing through the water. One breaches—a full, dramatic arc—and the ferry passengers gasp.

"Oh my god," Kiki breathes. "Is that even real?"

She doesn't blink. Doesn't breathe. Just stares, like she's trying to memorize it.

"They're resident pods," I explain. "Gavin says they stay together forever. Matriarchal, too. The grandmothers lead."

We watch the pod in silence as it disappears in the waters beyond us. We both exhale, long and quiet, as the island comes into view, with its towering evergreens, sharp coastline, and a kind of beauty that asks nothing of you.

As we drive off the ferry, Kiki says something about the trees—how tall they are, how the air smells pure, scented with possibility.

I smile, but my stomach pulls a little.

Because now I know why she's here.

And I'm not sure what terrifies me more.

That she might succeed.

Or that I might want her to.

CHAPTER 20

I Want You to Want Me

REUNITING WITH KIKI feels like the universe finally sent in backup. I've never had a sitcom-style girl gang to get me through a breakup—just me and my slightly alarming coping strategies.

So I'm thrilled she's here.

Even if her main goal seems to be facilitating my sexual reawakening. Or, in her words: "Some deeply transformative pelvic alignment with a stranger."

It's both touching and mildly horrifying.

Life on the island has been breezy and low-stakes. Gavin and I slipped into a rhythm I didn't see coming, and I'm not sure I want to disrupt it by succumbing to some human chakra tune-up.

When she asked if I found Gavin attractive, I dodged. Said I couldn't picture myself with someone who didn't love music as much as I do. The man listens to nothing but classical. And I always said I loved how good Jared was with kids. The visual of Gavin stiff-arming a toddler like it's a grenade doesn't exactly scream "dad material."

It wasn't a lie. But it wasn't the truth, either. Just a half-cooked, self-preserving smokescreen.

Because the truth is, I can't stop thinking about Gavin.

The tires crunch over the gravel as the house comes into view.

"We're here," I say, but it comes out like a question.

Kiki leans forward in her seat, eyes scanning the property. "This certainly isn't a drawback," she murmurs, already looking suspicious. Like she smells romance in the air and plans to follow the scent to its source.

We climb out of the car. The ground stills beneath our feet, but the air hums—music, unmistakable, loud enough to rattle the windows.

Inside, sunlight slants across the foyer floorboards as we pause just beyond the threshold. In the living room, a man stands with his back to us, guitar slung high, fingers moving with easy precision as he plays.

Maybe Gavin's friend Quinn arrived early.

Kiki clutches my arm. "Who is that?" she stage-whispers.

"Hello!" I shout at the top of my lungs, hoping the stranger will turn around.

Kiki may not need or want sex, but she looks thrilled as she stares at the man's absurdly appealing backside. He has on a pair of old Levis and a tight-fitting plain black tee, and his hair is flopping all over the place as he lets loose and strums on his guitar while simultaneously belting out *I Want You to Want Me* by Cheap Trick like he has a personal, emotional stake in the outcome.

Kiki leans over. "I want him to want me."

Next to him is a gangly boy who looks to be about twelve, pure concentration as he, too, jams on a guitar. I look around for Gavin, but he's nowhere in sight.

The man drops to his knees, riding a guitar riff, selling the song's emotional thesis—wanting, needing, loving—with reckless conviction.

Okay, yes, we love you, but who are you? Where is Gavin?

The guy pulls the plug on the amp, and the music cuts off.

A beat.

He turns around, and it's—*oh, shit*—it's ... *could it be*?

It's Gavin.

This is not the man I told myself I wasn't attracted to.

Unspooled. Sweaty. Electric. And unrecognizable in the best possible way.

He wipes his forehead with the bottom of his tee, exposing a relief map of taut muscle and toned, forbidden territory.

Jesus. Abs. He has abs.

Kiki turns to me, her eyebrow raised so high it's practically on vacation. Because apparently my life is a romantic comedy now, and no one told me.

As Gavin sets his guitar down, she whispers. "Right. Totally not into music."

I try to speak, but all that comes out is an undignified squeak. "I swear, I had no idea."

"Hey, Ava. I didn't expect you back so early." Gavin gestures to the boy. "This is Micah. He lives next door."

Micah waves with a sheepish smile. "Hey," he says, practically blushing. He then turns to Gavin. There's clearly adoration and respect emanating from him.

Gavin puts his arm around Micah. "Great on that first guitar solo. Practice is paying off."

"Yeah, guess you were right about that." Micah beams. Like Gavin just handed him the keys to a secret club.

Kiki leans into me again. "Sucks with kids, too. Tragic."

I ignore her. Mostly.

"Micah, I'm gonna make my favorite not-so-fried-chicken sandwiches. Want in?"

He glances at Gavin, who nods. "Awesome. I'm starving."

Gavin claps him on the back. "Go wash up, then call Ana to let her know you're staying."

He walks toward us, and it's frankly criminal that a man can look like that. He's glowing, grinning, the very embodiment of undone, while I try to remember how to keep my knees from buckling.

"Hi, Kiki. It's nice to see you again." Gavin extends his hand out to her.

"Trust me, the pleasure is all mine," Kiki purrs.

"So," I say, trying not to sound like I've forgotten the English language, "when you said you used to be the lead singer in a rock band, you weren't kidding?"

"Why would I be kidding?"

"Right. Good question. Why'd you give it up?"

"Long, boring story. Besides, I don't think I was cut out for life on the road. As I'm sure you've noticed, I'm a homebody."

It comes back to me. The time Jared told me Gavin turned down a dream opportunity to travel the world with friends because Patricia had cancer, and someone needed to stay behind to help with Jared and Cari, who were still in school.

The more I learn about Gavin, the harder The Plan gets.

Kiki doesn't say a word. Just arches an eyebrow again like she knows exactly what my brain is doing. And she's not wrong.

In the kitchen, Gavin moves to the sink and starts rinsing out the coffee pot like it's nothing, like we're all just people here, not witnesses to his musical seduction of the universe.

I head to the counter and start prepping sandwiches. Or, at least, I try.

I grab some ciabatta and somehow forget how to slice. I turn the knife the wrong way, fumble it, recover with fake confidence, and pretend I'm not unraveling like a woman who just watched her maybe-crush shred a Cheap Trick solo in faded denim.

Kiki hops onto a stool at the island, watching me while she sips an espresso like it's tea in a Jane Austen adaptation.

She doesn't speak. She smirks. Which is worse.

When Micah returns, we devour our sandwiches, and the kitchen becomes a comedy club. He's got Kiki and me doubled over with a story about school cafeteria sabotage and an ill-fated pudding cup.

I'm laughing so hard I almost miss Gavin clearing our dishes. He's washing them in the sink. Rolled sleeves. Quiet competence.

When Micah is done telling his story, Gavin dries his hands on a towel and nudges him out of his chair. "Okay, scoot. They're too old for you."

"Thanks for lunch, Ava. It was nice meeting both of you." He shakes Kiki's hand. He starts to shake mine, but I pull him in for a hug. "Give us a call any time you're hungry."

He nods his head vigorously, and as Gavin escorts him to the door, I hear him whisper: "Ava is really nice. And, pretty."

"How come you've never commented on how nice or pretty Olivia is," Gavin responds.

"She's pretty, too, but I never get to visit when Olivia is in town."

It's absurd, but I glow anyway—because apparently even tween praise is lethal when Gavin is standing nearby to hear it.

I clear my throat and start wiping down the counter, like that's a normal thing people do after getting soft compliments from adorable kids and watching hot men do the dishes.

"Micah seems nice," I say.

Gavin leans against the counter. "He's a great kid from not-so-great parents. When they aren't home fighting, they're off traveling or having affairs, and leave him to pretty much fend for himself. I've known him since he was five. Anyway, he ensures I don't get rusty on the guitar."

He says it so offhandedly, as if mentoring a neglected kid is just something he does between conference calls and climate strategy meetings.

I don't know what to do with this version of Gavin—the generous one, the casual rock god, the man who's steadily wrecking my very careful emotional blueprint.

"Let's take these outside," he says, grabbing a pitcher of lemonade from the counter and tucking a couple of linen napkins under his arm like it's second nature.

Kiki and I each pick up a glass and follow him through the wide back doors, out onto a wooden deck overlooking the bay.

"This is Mom's favorite spot when she's here," he says, setting the pitcher down on a low table.

We settle into the chairs, the late afternoon sun lighting the twisting trunks of the Madrona trees. Sailboats drift in the distance, and for a moment, no one talks. We just take in the horizon, relaxing into our surroundings.

"Kiki, you used to work at *Pulse*, right?" Gavin asks, finally breaking the silence.

"Yep, until Ava rescued me." She clinks her glass with mine.

"She means got her fired," I add.

"Best thing that's ever happened to me." Kiki grins.

"What do you do now?" Gavin asks.

"I'm doing pop-up events for an underwear brand. While I look for something more permanent. Something creative." She pauses. "Actually, I haven't told anyone, but I have a side project."

She looks a little nervous—for Kiki—but excited, too.

"I'm contemplating a personal crowdsourcing project," she says, more cautious now.

"To manufacture the underwear?" Gavin asks, his business side intrigued.

"Not exactly," Kiki responds.

She hands Gavin her phone. I lean in to see the screen and try not to notice how ridiculously good he smells. It's a GoFundMe titled: **Freeze My Eggs, Not My Dreams.** The photo is of Kiki in a lab coat holding a tray of egg cartons labeled **HANDLE WITH CARE** and a bouquet of birthday balloons.

"Kiki," I whisper with realization.

"I want kids. I don't want a partner right now, maybe not ever, but I want a family. And this way, I buy myself time. I'm asking friends to buy me this instead of dinner or coffee or birthday gifts. Also, my video ends with me whispering, 'Ova and out.' So I kind of have to commit."

I burst out laughing.

"You're unbelievable," I declare as I embrace her.

"So, let me get this right. Instead of waiting around for Mr. Right while your ovaries age, you're going to freeze them so that when you want to have kids at, let's say, 40, your eggs are still 32, and you don't need a Mr. Right. How much does it take to freeze one's eggs?" Gavin asks.

"Ten thousand dollars," Kiki confesses.

"It's a lot of money, but people spend $40k on cars all the time. Having a child is way more important than having a car, isn't it?" Gavin asks.

"Way," Kiki says, grinning a mile wide.

I pretend his empathy for Kiki doesn't affect me. But my chest reacts anyway to his gentle encouragement. That way he has of making you feel like maybe your wildest plan is not so wild after all.

"It's a clever way to solve a problem," Gavin adds.

And, with that, he has won Kiki's heart. She stares up at him like he's singlehandedly restoring her faith in men.

"You know what, Gavin Jones, I like you."

"Same, Kiki. Now, if you'll excuse me, I'm going to take a shower and make myself presentable."

As soon as Gavin clears the room, she turns to me.

"If *that's* not presentable, I'm genuinely concerned for your safety."

CHAPTER 21

Girl on Fire

OLIVIA ARRIVED THIS morning with matching designer luggage and a breezy plan to hit the farmers market with Gavin before picking up Quinn, Gavin's business-partner-slash-best friend, who will be staying for two days.

Kiki is enjoying her Water's Edge room at the Outlook Inn, so I do the only reasonable thing a woman does when handed an unexpected pocket of freedom: I take a bath. A long, glorious soak in the hand-hammered copper tub that Patricia absolutely did not buy for its resale value.

My sore, post-gardening muscles practically sob as I lower myself into lavender-scented water. I stay until my thoughts start to blur at the edges, until I almost—*almost*—believe that Gavin's too-long stares and crooked smiles don't mean anything at all.

Afterward, towel-wrapped and still warm, I tug on the lacy red panties Kiki gifted me with a note that read, *For the next great mistake.* She may not be having sex anymore, but she's determined I will.

They're barely on when it starts: a high-pitched shriek.

Not human.

Mechanical.

Smoke alarm.

"Gavin?" I call.

He's probably still strolling the farmer's market with Olivia, bonding over fresh zucchini and emotional unavailability.

The alarm keeps shrieking. The house could be burning down.

Still damp, with only the towel over my underwear, I sprint to the kitchen, already thick with smoke. Through the haze, I make out bacon charred on the stovetop, a small flame shooting up from the pan.

I move on instinct. Flour. *That's a thing. Right?* I snatch the bag from the cabinet and toss a handful toward the flame in a reckless whoosh. The fire fizzles, but the smoke alarm keeps howling like it's personally offended.

I grab a dishtowel and jump, fanning at the alarm, trying to swat it into silence.

Then my towel slips.

As it hits the floor, I lunge to grab it—

—and freeze.

The alarm cuts out, but a man I've never seen before is standing in the doorway.

He's watching me, one eyebrow raised, one hand in his pocket, mouth tilted in a smirk like he's just stumbled into an off-Broadway performance of *Portrait of a Partially Nude Lady in Kitchen Fire.*

He's tall, lean, blonde, all sunlit edges and golden stubble. And those eyes: clear, sea-glass blue and very, very focused.

I don't move. I don't breathe. My heart thumps so loudly I half expect the alarm to start again in sympathy.

Then Gavin steps in behind him, suitcase in hand, and stops short.

His gaze flicks to me, takes in the smoke, the flour, the near-nakedness. He blinks once. Twice.

His jaw tightens.

I scramble to rewrap the towel around me. "The smoke alarm—"

"You must be Ava," the man says, with the kind of accent that sets off my fight-or-flirt reflex. Australian. Definitely Australian. "You make one helluva first impression."

His grin should be illegal in three states and supervised in the rest.

It's not flirtatious, exactly. It's amused. Intrigued. Like I'm a puzzle he's not sure he can solve but wouldn't mind trying.

Before I can demand who the hell he is—or where he gets those cheekbones—Olivia sweeps through the back door, earbuds in, sunglasses on, completely oblivious to the chaos in her kitchen.

Then she sees him.

"Quinn!" She throws her arms around him, but when she follows Quinn's gaze to me, her expression falters.

"Ava, why are you wearing a towel and covered in flour?"

It's not the question so much as the tone: one part concern, two parts judgment.

I open my mouth, but no words come, just heat and static and the low hum of humiliation.

Gavin elbows past Quinn and shoots him a look.

"Wipe that smile off your face, Romeo."

He turns to me, hand landing at the small of my back. "Can we talk? Now. Privately."

Even furious, he's focused. Controlled. And something about that—his restraint—makes me feel reckless.

He doesn't wait for my answer. Just steers me down the hallway, past the pantry and closed doors, until we stop outside the laundry room.

The door clicks shut behind us.

For a second, there's only silence. And him.

He's close. Closer than he should be. His arm brushes mine as he turns. He paces once, then faces me like I've personally offended his moral code.

"You're half-naked," he says, low and sharp.

"I was putting out a fire," I say. "Sorry if I didn't have time to don my ball gown."

His jaw flexes. "You didn't need to handle it."

"Well, I did. Because your fiancée tried to flambé bacon."

"Still." He rubs the back of his neck.

I narrow my eyes. "Still what? Should I have let your house burn down? Or maybe I should've waited for you and Olivia to come back with artisanal honey and put out the fire *together* as a bonding activity?"

His mouth tightens. "You don't have to be like this."

"Like what?"

"Combative. I—" He exhales sharply, dragging a hand through his hair. "It's like you want me to lose it."

"Oh, poor you," I snap. "Sorry my towel wasn't securely fastened enough for your delicate sensibilities."

His eyes drop to the towel now knotted at my chest. And then lower. And then back up.

His voice is rough when he says, "It wasn't about the towel."

Something electric sparks in the air between us. I can feel it tighten, coil around my lungs.

I should back away. I don't.

He takes a step closer.

My breath catches. "If you're going to lecture me, maybe don't do it while standing that close."

"Maybe don't run around the house half-naked when there are guests arriving," he growls, but his voice is husky now, all friction and contradiction.

"I didn't *run* around," I murmur. "I was in the kitchen. And I had a towel."

"You had red *panties* and a towel."

My mouth drops open. "How do you even—"

"Red lace," he says, eyes flicking downward again. "Hard to miss."

Oh.

Oh *no*.

I hate how my skin flushes. I hate how my pulse spikes.

He leans in, voice a velvet scrape. "You don't think I notice these things, but I do."

My back hits the wall before I realize I've even stepped away.

"And what, exactly," I say, trying to keep my voice steady, "are you noticing?"

His gaze drops to my mouth.

Everything slows.

He takes a breath, then straightens like he's just remembered where he is. Who he is. That he's engaged to a woman who can't operate a stove but knows how to apply lipstick with sniper precision.

"We should go back," he says. But his voice is rougher than before. Regretful, maybe.

"Good idea." *Let's go back to pretending none of this is happening.*

He opens the door without looking at me.

I follow anyway, heart pounding, towel still damp, and more confused than I've ever been in my life.

CHAPTER 22

Hunger & Heartbreak

After scorching the first batch of rice and a brief crisis of confidence, the paella is perfect.

Golden crust on the bottom, lobster tails curled on top, fresh Dungeness crab legs nestled among blistered cherry tomatoes and sweet peas. I've been chopping, stirring, and whispering spells into this pan all afternoon. Cooking has always been how I process heartbreak. And tonight, I'm doing it for Kiki to help her take back a dish that once symbolized the night she fell for Mel in Madrid.

"I want to let go of my love for Mel but not my love for paella," she confessed.

The garden glows like a scene from the movie *Amélie,* if Amélie had grown up watching Queer Eye and subscribed to *Magnolia* magazine. Kiki fell in love with it the moment I showed it to her. She admired the blooming peonies I coaxed into existence, the bright orange nasturtiums spilling over the raised beds, and the citrus trees in the l'orangerie finally bouncing back with fragrant blossoms. She has twisted lemon balm into the napkin rings for our dinner tonight and arranged dogwood branches in a piece of driftwood for a centerpiece.

She's healing the only way she knows how, by making beauty out of whatever hurts.

I know the feeling.

Except tonight, something is different.

Maybe it's the way my hands shook a little while I sliced the chorizo at the thought of being near Gavin again. Or how I couldn't stop remembering Gavin's breath on my neck in that tiny closet, or the joy on his face when he was playing guitar.

I try to distract myself by thinking about microgreens and plating style, about anything but him, which works until he arrives.

Hair damp from a swim in the Sound, shirtsleeves rolled up to expose his forearms, carrying flowers and a warm loaf of hearth bread from Brown Bear Baking around the corner because he knows it's my favorite.

Gavin moves through the garden like he belongs to it—like he belongs to this moment—and I hate the way my heart reacts before my head does. The way my pulse stumbles like it forgot its rhythm.

"This is really becoming a habit with you," he says, glancing at the table as I slide the paella pan onto a trivet.

"What's that?"

"Making dinners that look like something out of the pages of Bon Appétit for people experiencing heartache."

"I'll take that as a compliment," I say.

"Good. Because it was one."

Kiki slides in beside him, with a kiss on his cheek. "Hey, stranger. I've been hearing things."

He grins at her. "And yet you came anyway."

"Curiosity," she says, then gestures to the paella. "And crustaceans."

Olivia arrives overdressed in wide-legged linen trousers and a cream silk blouse that gleams under the string lights. Her gold earrings catch the last rays of the sun. She pauses just long enough to clock Kiki's outfit: patterned culottes, rhinestone collar, satin bomber with ABSOLUTELY NOT embroidered across the back. Her face stays neutral, but the judgment might as well be a full monologue.

"Well," she says, taking in the garden. "Someone's been busy. This is... quaint."

Kiki extends a hand. "You must be Olivia. I'd call it 'intentional minimalism with vintage undertones,' but sure, quaint works."

I clear my throat. "Just a little paella."

Then the gate creaks and we all turn.

Quinn enters like he's dressed for date night on the French Riviera. Tousled hair, Chopard vintage shades, white linen shirt sleeves rolled to reveal corded forearms, tan and tattooed, and carrying a bottle of $500 Barolo like it's a liter of Dr. Pepper.

He surveys the scene as he approaches, pausing on Kiki as she lights a candle, the rhinestones on her collar reflecting every bit of light.

He turns to Gavin: "Who's the genderfluid disco ball?"

Kiki straightens. "The disco ball has ears. And a name. I'm Kiki."

"She's tonight's guest of honor," Gavin says.

Quinn's expression shifts, less amused, more attentive. "Do you always dress like that?"

"Only on days that end in 'why not,'" Kiki replies.

Gavin's lips turn up, amused, as Kiki walks up to them.

"Chalk, meet Cheese," Gavin says. "Kiki, this is Quinn."

"You look like a walking art installation," Quinn says.

Kiki stares at him. I can't tell if she's about to kiss him or kick him.

"Thank you. And you look like you could convince people to buy coastal real estate in the South of France or jump off a yacht naked."

Olivia bristles, but Quinn laughs, genuinely, then turns to me as I lay grilled asparagus on the table. "And Ava, you're just as beautiful with clothes on."

My cheeks redden, and Gavin tenses next to me.

THE SCENT OF saffron, grilled lemon, and woodsmoke hangs in the air. Wine flows, candles flicker, and everything feels suspended in that golden hour between beginnings and endings.

Quinn takes one bite and makes a sound that borders on indecent. "I had a paella in Barcelona once that was so good it made me cry," he says. "But this beats it. And I was sleeping with the chef of that one."

Gavin nods. "This is the kind of food people think about when they're old. Like—'remember that paella we had on Orcas Island?'"

They're all looking at me like I've conjured something. Like I've turned grief into gold.

I turn to Kiki, the guest of honor, for her reaction.

"Mel who?" Kiki says it like a joke, but I hear the truth in it—she wanted to keep the paella, not the pain. Mission accomplished.

Even Olivia is smiling. "Seriously, Ava. You've outdone yourself. At this rate, you'll have proposals before dessert."

Kiki leans in, syrupy sweet. "Isn't that the saying? The way to a man's heart is through his stomach. Or maybe it's through his ego. Depends on the cutlery."

Quinn nearly chokes on his wine. Gavin laughs out loud.

Olivia's laugh carries across the garden—light, unselfconscious.

I watch her with something like envy, but not the bitter kind. I am seeing what Gavin sees in her.

Quinn is a natural storyteller. He recalls a summer spent pressing olive oil as a teenager, before realizing he was working for the Italian Mafia and being adopted by a Sicilian vineyard family whose daughter he fell in love with. I can sense Kiki resisting the urge to roll her eyes until she's halfway through her second glass of wine.

Then she leans toward me and murmurs, "Oh man. If I hadn't given up sex."

Quinn sputters. "Sorry—what?"

Kiki shrugs, serene. "I did."

He looks vaguely panicked. "You gave up *sex*?"

Kiki points her fork at him. "I know. Hard to understand for someone whose pheromones arrive anywhere five minutes before he does."

The table bursts into laughter.

Everyone but Olivia ladles seconds onto their plates, and when we're done with the paella, I serve the nasturtium-topped panacotta I made with rose syrup and pistachios.

As the plates empty, Gavin leans back full and satisfied, "I know people who would pay a lot of money for this."

"This definitely feels like it could be the start of something amazing," Kiki adds.

"Healing people's heartbreak through food. You did it for Isabel. You did it for Kiki tonight," adds Gavin.

"Pop-up dinners by Ava," Kiki says with excitement.

I feel the possibility unfurling in me like a bloom. A pop-up dinner garden.

"I event plan, you cook," she adds. "We get Patricia to do florals."

"The woman does have opinions about peonies the way most people have opinions about politics," I laugh.

Gavin nods. "Isabel mentioned she's ready to give up her lease."

Olivia turns to Gavin, her smile strained. "What would Ava do with a café on Orcas Island?"

"Cook," Gavin says. "Cure heartache."

"Yeah, and apparently it's easy to find a place to rent here, so long as you're cool with living in someone's converted tool shed for three grand a month," I say.

"There's a soon-to-be vacant apartment above Isabel's café," he replies. "You could live upstairs and cook downstairs."

Kiki clasps her hands like she's found religion. "Twenty-four-hour espresso access."

"It sounds too perfect."

"Then let's make it real," Kiki says.

Quinn holds his glass up. "To Ava not leaving us."

Something flickers in Gavin's jaw, a small shift, but enough that I notice.

And then I realize: Olivia hasn't spoken in almost a full minute. Her glass is half-raised, her gaze steady on the rim, like she's trying not to drop it.

The realization comes over me slowly, like surf dragging over sand: she doesn't like this. Not the flirting. Not me glowing under the attention of two men she's known longer, better.

Kiki sees it too and gives me the faintest warning glance.

As we finish the last of the wine and the dessert, the garden becomes quiet, until Olivia says, "Ava, that was amazing. I'd stay longer, but I have to pack for an early flight tomorrow. Would you like some help cleaning up before I head back to the house?"

"No worries, O, Gavin and I are on dish duty," Quinn responds.

Kiki and Quinn grab plates and walk them back toward the café kitchen as I extinguish the candles. Gavin gives Olivia a peck on the cheek, then watches her go.

"She's... really likable," I mutter, surprised.

"She is," Gavin says softly.

I don't look at him, but I feel it—the gravity between us. The kind you pretend isn't real because admitting it would make it impossible to ignore.

"You okay?" he asks, voice low, unreadable.

"Totally," I say, too quickly. "This is peak normal. Just me, on a remote island, talking to my ex's brother who is engaged to a literal swan."

He almost smiles. Almost.

He disappears into the café kitchen with the wineglasses, and I trail after him with the bottles, suddenly very aware of the sound of my own footsteps on the gravel path.

As Quinn passes, he murmurs, "I think Dad may be sore with me," like it's gossip we'll circle back to but never do.

Inside, the kitchen is warm from the oven's residual heat. Gavin's already at the sink, sleeves rolled, methodically rinsing glasses.

I take the towel from the hook, step beside him, and we fall into a rhythm that feels rehearsed, even though we've never done this before. When he passes me a glass, our fingers graze. It's the softest touch—barely there—but it sets off a flutter behind my ribs, like something winged trying to escape. He goes still. Not dramatically. Just enough for me to know it wasn't nothing.

THE HOUSE IS hushed, thick with the kind of quiet that only settles when everyone's gone to bed or is pretending to. I pad into the kitchen for water but pause when I catch voices drifting from the living room. Gavin. And Quinn.

"She's getting over a relationship with my brother. She's off-limits," I hear Gavin say.

"C'mon, mate. You can't have all the beautiful women to yourself," Quinn replies.

And then Gavin's quiet response: "To be fair, Quinn, you had Olivia first."

CHAPTER 23

Agaricus Bisporus & Magic Mike

DUE TO SLIGHT pressure from Kiki, I am wearing one of her very tight, very short red dresses, bright red lipstick, and heels higher than I've ever worn before. I glance in the mirror and barely recognize myself. I look like a version of me who says yes to trouble and maybe even starts it.

We find Gavin in the kitchen, reading *The Wall Street Journal*, his sleeves rolled, collar undone. He doesn't look up when I start explaining his food options.

"Okay, dinner is all set. I left directions on how to microwave everything. There's apple mint lemonade in the fridge."

"Okay, thank you," he says, still buried in his paper.

I should head for the door r—Kiki's already angled toward it—but I freeze. God, I hate this. Part of me wants him to notice. Not *us*. Me.

There's some ancient, forbidden part of my brain that feels powerful, dangerous even, armed with nothing but red lipstick and bare skin. Another, bigger part of me feels stupid for even caring.

Gavin is engaged. He's my employer. He's Jared's brother. He's—

Kiki coughs. Once. Then again. It's fake. A nudge.

"Hey, Gavin. Ava..." Her voice wraps around my name like a dare. "... and I are heading out."

His eyes flick to me. There's surprise, then something heavier, darker. The air has shifted slightly. He looks me up and down, and my skin prickles. My dress feels too tight; my neckline suddenly feels like a confession. My pulse stutters.

"What are you two doing tonight?" he asks, his voice pitched carefully neutral.

"We're getting Ava laid," announces Kiki.

I whip my head toward her, horrified. "Kiki!"

"What? That's the plan, right? Your first one-night stand?" Kiki turns to Gavin as if he's an impartial audience. "I didn't spend two hours getting this one into my dress and Spanx for some innocent girl-dinner-and-Netflix situation. Ava needs a one-night stand, stat. Right, Ava?"

Yes, the plan is to get laid so that I can forget Jared—*and Gavin*—once and for all.

Gavin's jaw tightens, but his expression doesn't change.

"Okay. Time to go." My voice cracks slightly as I dig in my purse, pretending to search for something. Anything to avoid his gaze.

"And dessert is gluten-free peach cobbler. Just nuke it for one minute and add the fresh whipped cream I made in the canister in the fridge. I repeat: the fresh whipped cream, not that fake fat-free rice milk canister of Olivia's."

Kiki elbows me. "Let's go, goddess."

Finally, I get up the courage to look him in the eye, taking a nerve-calming breath as I do. The mention of Olivia's name has erased the look of lust on his face. Or, it was never there and only imagined by me, which might make far more sense.

FOUR HOURS LATER, not having sex tonight feels less like failure and more like mercy. Right now, slipping off my heels and climbing into cozy pajamas sounds like the truest kind of pleasure.

Through the car window, I can see Gavin is up past his usual bedtime, pacing like a dad waiting for his teenager to come home from prom. As Kiki pulls the car to a stop to drop me off, I watch as he grabs something off the bookshelf and drops onto the sofa.

The door sticks as I push it open, and I stumble slightly, trying to enter quietly, but the wine still fizzes in my bloodstream.

Gavin looks up as I shut the door. His eyes flick to my impossibly high heels, to my dress, and then snap quickly back to my face.

"Hey." My voice comes out too chipper, too loose. I wince inwardly as I drop my purse on a chair.

"*The National Audubon Field Guide to North American Mushrooms*?" I read from the book in his lap, squinting.

"What? Who can know enough about the soil attrition rate"—he flips to a random page—"created by the over-farming of fleshy, spore-bearing *Agaricus bisporus*?"

"*Agaricus bisporus*. Uh-huh."

I take a step toward the sofa, and my ankle wobbles in my too-high heels. Before I can catch myself, Gavin's hand is there—steady, warm, curling around my elbow.

"Careful," he murmurs.

The feel of his fingers burns through my skin, sending a sharp jolt of heat to my stomach. He doesn't let go right away.

"You're tipsy."

"Am not."

"You're arguing like a tipsy person."

"Fine. Slightly tipsy."

"More than slightly."

The room spins a little, so I plop down on the far end of the sofa to stop it. He pulls his legs in, sitting cross-legged to give me room.

"If I had a time machine, I'd go back and murder the person who invented high heels," I grumble, as I loosen the strap on one of my heels to rub at angry red marks on my foot.

"You wouldn't use it to take out Hitler? Stalin? Whoever invented TikTok challenges?"

"Nope. High heels. Obviously, a man. Definitely a sadist. Who would you take out?"

"Does it have to be murder? I can't just go back in time and watch Queen at Wembley?"

"Sorry, this is what being back on the single scene does."

"Makes you homicidal?"

"And desperate for an accomplice."

He huffs a soft laugh, the corner of his mouth curving.

"You don't know how lucky you are to be engaged to Olivia."

Something flickers across his face. It's not quite a smile.

"No one-night stand?" he asks softly.

"Do you really want to hear about my, in retrospect, premature foray back into singledom?"

"I have a strong hunch it might be more entertaining than North American mushrooms." He snaps his book shut and gives me his full attention.

"Well." I lean back. "Turns out I'm not my type's type. The guy I was being set up with decided he doesn't date women who 'look their age.' He's five years older than me, by the way."

"Sounds like a moron."

"Oh, it gets better. The first guy who asked me to dance moved like he was auditioning for *Magic Mike: The Musical.*"

"Is that... bad?"

"I tried to keep up, but he was so wrapped up in his imaginary spotlight he didn't notice when I slipped away."

"I think I need a visual of this choreographed disaster."

"Not happening. Guy number three hadn't heard of Nick Cave or Mitski, but said he had heard of Bob Dylan, but couldn't remember any of the titles to his songs, except for, wait for it... *Born in The USA.*"

"Not everyone has great taste in music."

"Yeah, he said he liked 'real music,' the tortured meaningful kind. His examples? Nickelback. And... a Korean boy band he called 'art for the soul.'"

Gavin presses a hand to his mouth, trying to hide his laugh. "Nickelback and K-pop? That's... eclectic."

"Eclectic? Or criminal?"

Gavin's shoulders shake with laughter. It's deep and unguarded, and I want more of it.

"Maybe the dress was the problem," he says, his gaze flicking down for a split second before meeting mine again.

Ah. So, he noticed.

I grab a throw pillow and swat him lightly, but the air between us has shifted. His eyes have darkened. The heat in them makes my chest tighten.

"You're staring," I whisper.

"So are you."

The words hang in the space between us, crackling like a live wire. If I were sober, I would have probably reasoned it away, but I'm not sober, and I can *feel* it.

I push myself off the sofa, breaking the moment. *He's Olivia's. He's off-limits. You don't do this.* But I wobble in my heels. This time, I'm not quick enough to recover, and he's on his feet in an instant, one arm steadying me, the other at my back.

"You shouldn't be walking in those."

"I'm fine," I murmur, but the room tilts alarmingly.

"You're not."

Before I can protest, he sweeps me into his arms, bridal-style. My breath catches in my throat.

"Gavin, you don't have to—"

His chest is warm and solid under my cheek. He smells like vanilla and cedar and something uniquely him, and I have to fight the sudden, dangerous thought of pressing my lips to the skin of his neck.

"You're too good at this," I mumble, my voice thick with exhaustion and wine.

"At what?"

"Being… good. It's irritating."

"Go to sleep, Ava."

But I don't. Not yet.

As he lays me gently on the bed, I stir. My fingers curl into the fabric of his shirt. Our faces are inches apart, his breath warm against my lips.

"Do you always carry women to bed like this?" I whisper, a faint, tipsy smile tugging at my lips.

His eyes flicker, something unreadable flashing through them. His voice comes out low, controlled:

"Ava, you're asking dangerous questions."

And then he's gone.

I blink at the ceiling.

What did he mean by that?

I tell myself that it was nothing. But my heart is pounding like it disagrees.

CHAPTER 24

The First Time I Hear Him

I HAVEN'T SEEN Gavin since he carried me to bed last night. Not since he said my name like a warning. Not since I almost leaned in but didn't.

Today, I need distance. A distraction. Something that doesn't look like him or smell like him. So, when I find Nico's note (*Open mic tonight. Come watch me make a fool of myself?)* scrawled across the back of a compostable takeout lid, I take it as a sign. Not from the universe. I'm not that woo-woo. But maybe from the version of me who still wants to flirt, but without dire consequences.

The wind curls off the water, teasing the ends of my hair as I follow the path toward the cliffside lawn. The sky is that impossible Pacific Northwest blue, streaked with clouds. Fir trees line the bluff, their tips swaying, and below, the rocky shoreline dips into a narrow cove, the water calm and pale jade. Picnic benches are scattered throughout the grass like a scene from a summer folk festival, rustic cabins and a few tucked-away yurts dot the surrounding hillsides.

I spot Nico instantly.

He's perched on the edge of a picnic table, all easy limbs and unbothered confidence, his hair wind-tossed and his guitar balanced across one thigh. He's surrounded by three women—one lounging nonchalantly, one braiding the other's hair—but it's clear they're all orbiting him. He looks freshly tousled, like he just stepped out of a music video. He grins mid-story; something he's said makes all of them laugh, and for a second, I get it. The charm isn't just in how he looks. It's in the way the air shimmers when he talks.

Nico catches sight of me and lights up. As he heads toward me, the women glance over, clocking me with mild curiosity and maybe a touch of territorial suspicion.

"Ava. You made it!"

Nico embraces me like we're old friends instead of one-bag-of-gravel acquaintances. I don't mind. The island has that effect on people.

"You didn't tell me this place was straight out of a Bon Iver song," I say, taking in the sweeping view.

"Wait until the sun sets," he grins. "Full-on spiritual awakening."

Before I can respond, his hand lands lightly on the small of my back. Not possessive, just ... confident. Familiar. Or maybe I've forgotten what it feels like to be touched by someone who isn't breaking their own rules to do it. My skin prickles beneath it.

"Come on, I want to introduce you to someone," he says.

We weave through the picnic tables, his hand still gently guiding me, until we reach a tall man in a Patagonia jacket, his face friendly and open.

"Ava, meet Joe Brotherton, our fearless leader."

Joe grins and shakes my hand. "Welcome to our little corner of the world. Nico here is our star resident and—"

He turns to his right, and I glance over.

Gavin.

He approaches Joe's side, his expression unreadable.

Joe puts his arm around him. "And this is Gavin. The man who quietly helps support our songwriter residency, though he refuses to take any credit."

Gavin's gaze flicks briefly to Nico's hand still hovering near my waist. A flicker. A register. Then gone. But I swear his mouth tightens.

"Gavin and I know each other," I offer.

"Old family friend," Gavin adds smoothly. "And my summer chef."

His tone is light, but I catch the edge in it.

Joe claps his hands. "Well, you picked a good night. Nico's opening our open mic, but hopefully we'll get some other brave souls to follow."

The Doe Bay Café smells like cardamom. Inside, strings of mismatched lights zigzag over tables. Wildflowers fill mason jars. The walls are lined with photos of past performers—some famous, some not—but all caught mid-song, mid-feeling, mid-flight.

Through the windows, the cove shines in the last light. A couple of dozen locals fill the café with a reverent buzz, eager to witness something sacred.

Nico takes the stage with practiced ease. The first notes hush the room.

He plays three songs, lean and soulful. His voice is raw silk. By the end, the crowd is putty in his hands.

"Thanks for letting me warm up the stage," he says, tucking a loose strand of hair behind his ear. "Now, hopefully someone else is ready to take a swing."

A local singer, Stormy, in the back, boho dress, barefoot, takes the bait and walks to the mic with a fiddle. The crowd claps, easy and warm.

Nico slides back to our table and slouches into the seat beside me. His thigh presses against mine, casual and electric.

"What did you think?" he asks, voice low.

"Beautiful," I say, meaning it.

He grins. "I've got two more later tonight. But I'm more interested in your thoughts now."

He reaches for his drink, his fingers brushing mine, and I'm pleased to feel my pulse trip a little.

"Gavin, didn't you play guitar in college?" Joe asks.

"Only in private. And mostly poorly."

Nico laughs at Gavin's response. "Let me guess, a couple of sad chords and a Dylan impression?"

"More than a couple," Gavin replies coolly.

I laugh—too loud. "He won't get up there. No way." I reach for my drink.

Gavin's gaze drifts to where Nico's leg presses against mine. Then to my hand still on my glass.

Then he drains his drink like a dare. "Nico. Mind if I borrow your guitar?"

"Uh. Sure." He passes it over, curious.

I freeze. "Wait. Seriously?"

Gavin doesn't answer me. He just walks to the stage with an unhurried confidence.

He adjusts the microphone, then strums once. Then again. Then starts playing.

I recognize the chords to the Pete Molinari song: *I Don't Like the*

Man I Am. But Gavin slows it down. Gone is the bluesy bounce of the original. What's left is a haunting hymn-like confession.

His voice is gravel and velvet as he sings about restraint—about wanting someone he won't let himself have because he's not the man he needs to be. Every word lands heavy and raw.

His voice cracks at the edge, but it doesn't break. He sings like a man standing in a burning house, too lost in the music to notice the flames.

He sings like I'm the only person in the room.

Every line is a punch to the ribs. Not because he sings it to me, but because I believe he means it.

The trio of girls who were hanging on to Nico lean forward, rapt.

I can't breathe.

The song aches. It confesses. It apologizes. It pleads.

When the song ends, there's a beat of silence before the applause. I stand too fast.

"Excuse me," I murmur, pushing past someone's chair.

Out the back door, the night hits me in the face. Cool and salt-sweet. I step into the dark, heart pounding.

Gavin's voice echoes in my ears, haunting and hot.

My breath won't regulate. My chest won't unclench. Heat pools low in my belly and spreads, traitorous and terrifying.

I don't want this.

I want this too much.

I lean over the edge of the bluff and inhale sharply, trying to will the feelings down. Far down. I'm dizzy. Like I'm losing altitude without warning.

I picture his eyes as he sang. Unblinking. On me. The way he held every note like it cost him something.

Then I hear footsteps on the gravel path behind me.

A jacket lands gently across my shoulders. Gavin says nothing.

Neither do I.

We stand side by side, the only sounds the waves below, the wind threading through the trees, and the thunder of my pulse.

The jacket smells like cedar and something unmistakably him. I should shrug it off.

Instead, I pull it tighter. And let the feeling stay. Just for a minute.

CHAPTER 25

Garden & Table

Patricia could not have come at a better time. Officially, she's here to see her son. Unofficially, she's here for the island's acres of wildflowers, its salt-laced air, the way time slows enough to let you breathe, wander, and dwell.

The moment we embrace, I know she's also here for me. She smells like fig and fresh linen, and her arms feel warm, familiar.

There's something tucked behind her smile, something she's not saying yet, like she's savoring a secret she plans to enjoy telling.

Once we load her suitcase and she's buckled in, she turns to me. "We're going straight to the garden, right?"

Her enthusiasm catches me off guard, lifting me more than I expected.

We drive up Main Street toward the village, the afternoon sun flickering across the bay, the wind in our hair. I park in front of the garden, suddenly aware of how much I want her to love it. I value her eye—her instinct for beauty—and now that we're here, I realize: I'm nervous.

We step through the new wooden gate. Patricia pauses just inside, taking it all in slowly, as if she's giving each detail her full attention.

"This was a patch of nothing," she says. "Just dirt and dying trees and weeds."

The crushed granite paths catch the light in fragments. Raised beds spill over with kale and rainbow chard, their leaves bright and unruly. Mint patches crowd the corners where there's partial shade. Tiny-leafed thyme warms in the sun. Lavender hums under flitting bees, and nasturtiums ramble like they're trying to claim as much of the garden for themselves as they can. I trimmed back the lilac last week to show off the l'orangerie. Now it frames the glass as if it were part of the design. The rebuilt fence by Ezra, a local woodworker, is a piece of art made of weathered cedar. It creates a quiet border for everything we've coaxed into growing.

"You did all this?" Her voice is soft now.

"Isabel and Kiki and some new island friends helped."

I hesitate.

"And Gavin, in a way. He gave me free rein of the space and encouraged me to keep using it. Said the island needed something like this."

"That son of mine. Handsome and smart."

I don't reply. But my thoughts lead to an image of him: shirt sleeves rolled up, laughing in the garden at dusk, a quiet steadiness that's more comforting than I ever expected. I try not to smile thinking of him. I'm not supposed to think about him like that. Not with his fiancée somewhere in New York, planning a wedding. Their wedding. But the truth is, it's getting harder to pretend I don't notice the way he watches me when he thinks I'm not looking.

Patricia wanders toward the greenhouse and steps inside, hands clasped behind her back like she's in a gallery.

Sunlight streams through the glass panes. The trees have bloomed, their fruit just beginning to show: lemon, blood orange, more pomegranate—hints of what might be, if given time.

She claps her hands together in delight. "It's a real l'orangerie. Like the ones in Paris that grow the citrus trees in the winter. This," she says, "will be magic in the winter. Snow falling on the glass, candles on the table, velvet accents, the scent of apples in the air."

"I feel like I should be taking notes," I laugh.

"And the food is farm-to-table, right?"

"Tide to table, too," I say, with a grin.

"What a setting. Texture, fragrance by nature... edible petals from the garden to scatter on cakes and salads."

I nod, heart knocking.

"It started as a distraction. Then I needed it. Now I think I want it to be a kind of supper garden. Culinary pop-ups by reservation. For people who want to love better, or differently. After heartbreak. During it. Despite it."

She tilts her head. "For the heart-hungry."

I smile. "Yes. That."

I watch her, the way she moves through the space, seeing it, really seeing it. My mom would've done that, too. She had a quiet reverence for things people made with their hands: Gardens. Meals. She would've loved this place. She would have loved Patricia.

I swallow against the lump that always rises when I think of her. *Would she have believed I could do this? That I might build a life out of broken and dying things?*

"I was talking to Marisol," Patricia says, breaking the silence.

My stomach knots. I never called Marisol back after I left Pulse.

Not even when she left a kind, confused voicemail. I pulled an Irish exit and never looked back. I couldn't bear to explain how someone like Valerie had made me feel small in a job I once loved.

"She fired Valerie and left her husband. She wants to host her divorce party here. She saw Kiki's Instagram post—the dinner you made last week. She said it looked like hope on a plate."

"Seriously?"

"She wants to celebrate starting over. And this is the place. You are the person."

That undoes me. I press my hand to my chest. This little space that has helped me stay upright. *Could it be that for someone else, too?*

"I wish my mom could've met you," I say, the words out before I can stop them, then more quietly: "She would've wanted to be part of this."

"She's here," Patricia says. "In everything you're growing."

She puts her hand on my back to comfort me.

"Would you consider doing the flowers?" I ask.

She points toward the ceiling of the l'orangerie. "A chandelier made of fir boughs, fresh peony, and dahlia blooms would look amazing. Candles nestled in. Something wild but romantic."

"Is that a yes?"

"You didn't think I'd let you and Kiki have all the fun, did you?"

"We'll need more seating," I say. "And decor."

"Which is why we're going to Smörgåsbord," she says, triumphant. "You have to meet Melanie Trygg. She's a designer with the best eye for textiles and is completely ruthless about cushion quality. She'll have what we didn't know we needed. Then we'll swing by the pop-up for 45 Three Modern Vintage. Staci's bringing in furniture from her shop in LA. It's always crawling with celebrities. You'll want to be friends with her. Everyone does."

Smörgåsbord and the vintage pop-up are even better than I imagined. Melanie has us dreaming about linen and velvet, and Staci somehow manages to talk about mid-century Danish teak as if it were poetry. They are one more example of the island's strange gift for assembling the right people at precisely the right moment.

We find a dozen mismatched wooden chairs, sun-worn and quietly elegant. Two antique garden benches, and moss-colored velvet cushions so lush they pull us to their side of the shop. Patricia picks one up and holds it up to me.

I raise an eyebrow. "Velvet? On an island that gets nine months of drizzle?"

Patricia doesn't blink. "They're absurdly beautiful."

"They really are." I run my fingers along the fabric, and there's no going back. "Fine. We'll pretend we're impractical artists who believe in microclimates and miracles."

She grins. "We are."

Patricia runs her hand over a stack of soft ochre linen napkins. "This palette—ochre, lichen, mushroom—is beautiful. But we'll need height and some contrast. Maybe some purple delphinium. Something architectural."

We end up sketching the floral displays and layout on the back of a napkin, crouched beside a stack of brass candlesticks. The party begins to bloom in ink: chairs arcing under string lights, florals suspended from the greenhouse ceiling like a baroque painting.

My breath catches. It's more than one party starting to take shape, and I remind myself that everything about this island is like a summer love: lush, intoxicating, temporary.

We load the last cushion into the hatch, and Patricia pauses, gazing out toward the view of the Salish Sea. Sailboats and catamarans drift past as if they have nowhere in particular to be.

She says it almost offhandedly, like she's trying the idea on. "Liam and I have talked about retiring here."

I see it for them. Morning walks in the fog along the rugged coastline. A steaming Hot Stella at Darvill's Bookstore on snowy days. The endless summer flowers, the farm fresh fare, and the way the community folds around you like a quilt.

"I can see you here," I tell her confidently.

For me, there's the garden. The meals pulled from the land and the sea. The work that feels like tending, not just surviving. It's not just a distraction anymore. It's a rhythm. A kind of quiet belonging I didn't think I'd ever feel again.

And softly, finally, I let it surface: I can see myself here, too.

CHAPTER 26

Ninety-Six Words for Love

PATRICIA, GAVIN, AND I make dinner together like it's the most natural thing in the world. Grilled halibut with Peruvian aioli, mashed potatoes so creamy they deserve a sonnet written about them, and Apple & Olive Oil Cake from an Ottolenghi recipe that feels half spell, half dessert. Even before we take a bite, I know I'll remember this meal forever.

Golden light filters through the garden-facing windows, soft and slow. We clink glasses of mocktails made with Girl Meets Dirt shrubs and toast to Patricia's visit.

There's a tenderness to Gavin tonight. The way he ribs Patricia, eyes crinkling at the corners. He makes her laugh in a way that is not performative. Just honest. Familiar. Like muscle memory. She nudges him, calls him incorrigible, and he smiles like he's ten years old again.

And I'm undone.

Not by his hands or his voice or his irritatingly well-fitted shirt.

By this: the way he looks at his mother like she hung the moon.

The way his eyes flick to mine and linger a beat too long.

It's nothing. It's everything.

We talk about Marisol's party in the garden, about island sunsets and grazing tables, and the citrus trees beginning to bloom. Patricia tells a story about Gavin's childhood obsession with dinosaurs that has him groaning and me nearly snorting.

By dessert, I know the truth. Or at least, I start to.

That these are two of my favorite people. Not Patricia and Jared. Patricia and Gavin.

When did that happen?

I glance across the table. Gavin's smiling at something Patricia said, tipping back his glass, and I'm struck again. Not just by his face, but by the space he takes up in this room. In me.

Why did it take me so long to notice how dangerously attractive he is?

Because I wasn't looking. Now I am.

I reach for my water, my neck warm with the kind of heat that has nothing to do with temperature. I glance toward the window, pretending to admire the madronas glowing in the last light of day.

Patricia wipes a crumb from her lip, then turns to Gavin. "Honey, have you and Olivia set a date yet?"

The question lands like a glass shattering at the edge of the table.

Gavin's knee shifts under the table. Close enough to brush mine. He doesn't move it away. He may not even feel it, but I do.

"Olivia's been busy taking meetings with producers who want to steal her away from *Wake Up, America,*" he says. "And I've been out here."

"It's been almost a year," Patricia says.

Gavin grins at her, but it's the kind that hides things. "Let's be real, Mom. You're more excited about the floral arrangements than the wedding."

She gasps in mock offense. "You wound me."

He raises an eyebrow. "Admit it."

"Okay, fine. I've had your wedding florals planned since you were two." She leans toward me conspiratorially. "But I doubt Olivia and I will ever agree on style. And be warned: I've never seen a bride make it to the altar without at least three full meltdowns."

"Even you?" Gavin teases.

"Especially me," Patricia says, laughing. "Ask your father. I cried so much the week before our wedding, I'm surprised he still showed up."

"I can't imagine Olivia crying," I say before I think better of it.

Gavin's mouth twists into a smile that doesn't quite reach his eyes. "Come to think of it, I've only seen her cry once. And that was *before* we were dating."

He glances at me, this time with something unreadable.

"You two, though," he says, "You cry at the drop of a hat."

"We can't help it if happy things make us cry," Patricia says, her voice warm as she reaches for my hand. "Ava and I feel things deeply."

I squeeze her fingers, grateful.

"I have a theory about that," I say.

Gavin lifts a brow. "Is there anything you don't have a theory about?"

"Well, yes. Many things."

Like why I suddenly want to memorize the shape of your mouth.

Like why it hurts when you talk about your fiancée.

He tilts his head. "Let's hear it."

I tell them about my college roommate Asha's grandfather, a famous palm reader from Madurai. The year-long waitlist because people believed in him so much. How he looked at my hands and told me I was in my seventh and final life.

"He said it was an honor. That I'd learned everything I was meant to learn. That my soul would finally rest."

"Moksha," Patricia says quietly.

I nod. "No more reincarnation. No more heartbreak."

Gavin leans in. "So … you cry because …?"

"That's my theory. I cry at beautiful things because my soul knows it's the last time it gets to experience them. Last time I get to watch a mother kiss her newborn's head. Last time I get to hear children sing in a choir. Or—"

"A field of wildflowers as far as the eye can see," Patricia adds.

"Yes. That. It's joy and grief tangled together."

Patricia's eyes well up. Mine do too. She takes my hand again and holds it tight.

"See?" I laugh. "Happy crying."

But it isn't just that. It's the idea of losing this. This bond I have with them. And when I glance over at Gavin, he's watching me. His eyes dark with something I don't recognize—or maybe don't want to name.

I hold his gaze. I should look away. I should. But I don't.

Patricia is watching us now, too. Like she's trying to watch a movie she's seen before but can't quite remember how it ends.

And then, the strangest thing. Not a thought. Not even a realization. Just a knowing.

It rushes through me like a whisper and a wave.

This brother.

My heart—so quiet for so long—slams against my chest.

The voice is not gentle. It doesn't ask. It declares. Like my heart has been waiting for the most inconvenient moment in the world to raise its hand and shout.

I want to argue with it. To remind it that he's engaged. That Olivia exists. That this is ridiculous.

Instead, I keep looking.

"Gavin?" Patricia says. "What do you think of Ava's theory?"

He startles. Blinks. Looks down at his plate.

"Sorry, I drifted. Must be the wine."

He's lying.

And I can't stop wondering where his mind just went.

I STEAM MILK for cappuccinos, guiding the wand just beneath the surface until it stretches into light, airy foam. But my eyes are on Gavin and Patricia in the dining room, swing dancing. Chuck Berry's *You Never Can Tell* crackles through the speakers, its bright, brassy piano riffs ricocheting off the walls.

Patricia flicks her fingers beneath her chin and slides them out in front of her eyes—mock sultry, full Uma Thurman energy—and Gavin, God help me, mirrors her. Deadpan. Committed. He shimmy-shuffles backward, shoulders rolling, then pinches his nose and does an exaggerated water wiggle like he's cannonballing into an invisible pool.

They're pure joy—spinning, twisting, laughing.

Then he pulls her back in, smooth as silk, spins her once, twice, dips her low enough that she squeals.

This is the real Gavin, I think, as a lump forms in my throat. He's been rationing this version of himself. Keeping it carefully folded away. But up close, I see it—because Patricia knows how to unfold him.

And that Gavin pulls me in like a riptide.

The song ends in applause and breathless laughter. Gavin's phone buzzes. He checks the screen, expression shifting into something more contained.

"Olivia," he says, already stepping away.

Patricia lifts her cappuccino. "Come on," she says to me. "Let's give the groom some privacy."

We carry our drinks out to the back veranda.

"Since when does your son have hips?" I ask.

Patricia laughs. "Surprised he can dance?"

"I mean—" I wave vaguely toward the living room. "He was swing dancing like he's been rehearsing for a retro dance competition. I've seen him parallel park with less confidence."

She grins. "When I was sick, someone had to take Cari to and from her ballroom dance classes."

Patricia's voice softens. "He didn't want her to quit. So, he learned the steps. Waltz. Foxtrot. Even a little rumba. He'd practice with her in the living room after homework."

The image lands somewhere under my ribs.

We step fully into the night air. It's cooler, salted faintly by the ocean. Patricia settles onto one of the chaises, and I follow.

Above us, the sky opens wide and unapologetic, dotted with stars.

"So, I guess the brooding billionaire businessman routine is… performance art?"

Patricia's eyes sparkle. "My son contains multitudes."

She takes a sip of her cappuccino, then pauses before speaking.

"By the way," she says, like she's casually ordering coffee, "Gavin's the one who told Marisol about the dinner. Sent her pictures. Told her to call you."

I pause, hand gripping my mug.

"He did?"

She smiles. "He sees what you need. Even when you don't think he does."

We're quiet for a while, letting the stars do their job.

"Love that you can actually see the stars here. I never noticed them in New York City," I say.

Patricia sips, then nods slowly. "Stars remind us that sometimes you can't see light without some darkness."

I think about what she's saying. *Would I have seen the island's beauty—the garden, the friendship Gavin offers—if I hadn't first been lost?*

"How are you, really, Ava?"

"I still think about Jared. I miss him more than I should. Working for Gavin and building the garden has been a great distraction, but there's still something missing."

Tears come, but not the poetic kind from earlier. These clock in, do their job, and leave my chest lighter.

I haven't grieved Jared. Not really.

Now I do.

And underneath the ache is ... space.

Patricia gently places her hand on my shoulder, part comfort, part grounding.

I wipe my eyes. "An Inuit friend once told me there are a hundred words for snow in the Inuit language. First fall, dangerous crust, powder."

"I've heard that, too," Patricia replies.

"I wonder if they have different words for different kinds of tears?"

"I don't know the answer to that, honey, but I do know that in Sanskrit there are ninety-six words for *love*."

My mind drifts to the framed cards on Gavin's wall. "The art in the dining room?"

"I found them in India. Collected them over time on two trips there. I don't have all 96, but ..."

"They're beautiful."

"They're a good reminder that we're lucky to have any kind of love in our lives."

Could Jared be a different card?

Maybe our love was respect, creativity, and habit.

A bright card, but not *the* card.

"Thank you, Patricia."

"I haven't done anything."

"Actually, you have. I just figured out how I can keep Jared in my life."

"That's wonderful, Ava," she claps her hands together, delighted.

"You know, you've been taking care of me since I met you."

"Well, you've been taking care of my sons. First Jared. Now Gavin. He looks good, by the way," Patricia says.

"I've been feeding him well. Did you know he considered coffee a food group? I've also tricked him into eating more raw vegetables."

"That's not what I'm talking about," she replies.

"Oh?"

"He looks happier than I've ever seen him look. Content. Like a man in love for the first time."

"That's great, right? He and Olivia *are* about to get married and start a new life," I remind her.

"I don't think my son is in love with Olivia, Ava."

My pulse betrays me before my voice can, so I say nothing.

We watch the sky. And I wonder if love is what's been blooming all around me while I wasn't looking. A hundred kinds of snow. Ninety-six kinds of love.

And yes—Gavin.

CHAPTER 27

How the Light Gets In

I WAKE STILL carrying the sound of Gavin's voice.

Not the clipped tone he uses when he's exasperated or hiding behind sarcasm. This was something else: the low, steady ache when he sang at Doe Bay.

I dreamt about his hands, not on me, but on the guitar. The effect was the same.

I need air. I need clarity. Which is maybe why I text Jared. He's spending the summer working on his first solo photography exhibit—black and white portraits of people and their found families—for a show at Perry & Carlson gallery in nearby Mount Vernon.

We plan to meet at Orcas Island Winery, a barn and vineyard tucked against the base of Turtleback Mountain. He used to say the light was different, more honest, in the Pacific Northwest, and that's why he loved shooting here. Now, I know what he means.

He ferried from the mainland, ostensibly to deliver hard-to-find peonies for his mom, but really, I think, because he knew I needed this. Us. One last untangling.

Arthur, the tiny winery dog, greets me at the path and trots beside me like a loyal usher. Inside, Tera Andaya, the co-owner, waves from the tasting bar, her mesmerizing hazel-green eyes catching mine with their usual warmth.

The barn smells like grapes and cork and hay. Swallows flit in and out of the walls like they're part of the design, and the Orcas Project wine bottles are lined up along the shelves, whimsical animal labels winking at me like I'm in on the jokes. Tera pours two glasses that I carry out to one of the wooden picnic tables under the Hemlocks, just as the clouds begin to break.

Jared is already seated, sketching in his notebook with that look he gets when he's half in this world, half in his own.

He looks up and smiles, familiar, fond.

"Hey," I say.

"Hey. You look... islanded."

I glance down at my soft sweater, the streak of dirt still on my wrist. Probably from the lavender I transplanted this morning.

"That obvious?"

He shrugs. "Only in the best way."

We clink glasses. The wine is clean and quiet, like stone fruit and slow mornings, like it doesn't need to prove anything.

We sit in the stillness a moment too long. Then I ask, "Do you think we mistook being safe for being in love?"

He doesn't rush to fill the silence.

"I think we loved each other the best way we knew how," he says. "But maybe we confused comfort for a full yes."

He pauses, before asking, "Why didn't you ever push for more? For marriage?"

I stare out at the vineyard, its vines lush in the summer light.

"Because," I say quietly, "something in me never fully agreed. There was always a sliver of silence inside me when I pictured our future. Not dread. Just... absence."

Jared nods like he already knew the answer but needed to hear it out loud.

"I'll miss watching you cook," he says. "It was like watching someone sculpt a meal in the middle of a windstorm. Total chaos. But damn if it didn't always taste incredible."

I smile. "I'll miss calling you when I hear a song I love. Or watching you transform dumpster dives into gallery art."

He chuckles. "We really were magic."

I reach into my tote and slide out a small item wrapped in cardboard, opening it to reveal one of Patricia's Sanskrit cards bearing the word Maitri.

I lay it between us on the table.

"Have you heard there are ninety-six words in Sanskrit for love?"

He glances down, recognizing the ink. "The cards mom collected."

I nod. "Do you think it would be weird if we let go of one kind and chose another?"

"You mean like platonic love?"

"Exactly."

He's quiet. Thoughtful. Not uncomfortable, just measuring.

"Okay, it's weird," he says. Then shrugs. "But since when have we been afraid of weird? Maybe the spectrum of love is as wide as the spectrum of sexuality."

I exhale. I didn't know how much I needed him to say that. To say that choosing differently doesn't mean we failed. It just means we evolved.

"Absolutely. It's like the first law of thermodynamics."

He glances over. "Remind me—that's the energy one, right?"

"Yeah. Energy can't be created or destroyed. Only transformed."

I pause, watching the light bend over the hills.

"My mom used to say something similar in her very Buddhist, very poetic way. That nothing truly disappears. It just transforms. Becomes something else."

He nods slowly. "So we don't lose things. They just change form."

"Exactly." I look at him, and this time, I don't look away. "Even us."

I smile. And this time, it's clean. Untangled from grief. Grateful, even. For the version of us that could hold steady when everything else fell apart.

The wind lifts through the vineyards and brushes against my arm like a benediction.

"Can I still call you when I hear a great song?" I ask.

"Only if you promise to cook for me when you're in town."

We laugh, but there's a reverent kind of ache beneath it, the kind you feel only when you're brave enough to let go without bitterness.

As we rise to leave, Jared reaches into his coat pocket and pulls out a white envelope.

"One more thing," he says, handing it to me. "You and I were supposed to go, but you shouldn't miss it. Gavin agreed to take you."

I open it. Two tickets to see Leonard Cohen in Vancouver.

My heart tugs.

"Does Gavin even like Leonard Cohen?"

Jared shrugs. "He said yes. That's something."

A long silence stretches between us as I picture Gavin next to me in a dark concert hall. His shoulder near mine. His silence saying more than lyrics ever could. I think about the space I would need to keep. The boundaries I'm not sure I trust myself to uphold.

"Are you sure?" I ask.

Jared doesn't answer right away.

He just watches me. And smiles.

"Ava," he says, "Gavin has been showing up for you in ways I never could. Maybe he deserves this more than I do."

Jared stands and presses a quick kiss to the top of my head—like a brother, or the very best kind of friend.

"Text me photos," he says, already heading toward his car, Arthur padding along beside him, tail swishing in the golden grass.

I stay longer to watch the light shift across Turtleback Mountain, the last swirl of wine catching the sun in my glass.

I wasn't wrong to keep loving Jared.

Just wrong to stop at one kind of love.

CHAPTER 28

Love in the Backseat of a VW Beetle

I STARE AT my reflection and second-guess everything.

Black dress? Too pretty. Silk blouse? Too hopeful. Slouchy sweater from the night at Doe Bay? Too full of memory.

I settle on a camel-colored tee and black jeans. I throw on my favorite thrifted blazer and vintage lorgnettes, the ones Jared found in a dumpster dive behind MoMA, and I've since strung on a chain. The outfit says: I am composed. I am not unraveling. I am not thinking about a man I should not be thinking of.

This is not a date, I remind myself. Gavin agreed to the Leonard Cohen concert out of obligation, not desire. He's just the understudy. A placeholder. And whatever this is between us should stay in its place.

But when I walk into the garage, overnight bag in hand, and find

Gavin already standing there with his leather duffel, something in me catches.

He looks up. His expression is unreadable.

We both glance at the Defender. The back tire is completely flat.

"Should we put the spare on?" I ask.

"Long story, but there is no spare," he says, looking irked.

"Okay. What about the other car?" I nod at the covered one next to his.

He hesitates. Shifts on his feet.

"I... can't."

I narrow my eyes. "Can't, or *won't*?"

Another pause. A sheepish glance.

"Oh, my God." I gasp, dramatic. "*You* can't drive stick?"

"I'm from New York City," he says. "I can barely drive at all."

I start laughing. "This explains *so much.* And here I thought you were some kind of off-grid alpha man."

"Smoke and mirrors." His mouth twitches, almost a smile, and it feels like a reward.

I laugh. "Lucky for us, I can." I hold out my hand for the keys without thinking.

He drops them into my palm, and his fingers graze the inside of my wrist. Just skin catching skin for a half second too long. His gaze dips to the point of contact like it's a problem he can't solve. Then glances away.

He lifts the car's cover, and my heart stills.

The Beetle. The car that Patricia and Liam fell in love in during their first road trip. The one from the old photos in their foyer. Her in a mini dress with a daisy tucked behind her ear, Liam grinning at her like he couldn't believe his luck.

I've heard the stories. I've imagined them, both of them on their first of many adventures, windblown, young, and in love.

"Why is this here?" I ask softly.

"They had to sell it when Mom was sick," he says. "I tracked it down a few years after that."

He shrugs, like it's nothing. "I thought maybe someday I'd restore it and surprise them with it. Dad used to say only Mom could make sleeping in the backseat of that Beetle feel like the Ritz. First road trip they ever took, the engine died outside Reno. They didn't have money for a motel, so they folded the seats down and made a night of it."

A small huff of breath. "He always said it was the best night of his life."

His mouth lifts, almost against his will. "He asked Mom to marry him the next morning."

I smile despite myself. "He said once you've survived a breakdown in the desert together, you might as well make it official."

He glances at me. "You always liked that line."

"I did," I admit.

WE PULL OUT of the driveway and head toward the ferry landing. After a wait, the deckhands wave us forward, and the boat's ramp clanks beneath the tires like the car is being swallowed by a metal mouth.

On the mainland side, almost two hours later, we ghost through the tiny town of Bow—if we blinked, we'd miss it—and then Gavin has me take the turn that spits us onto the coastal highway, trees unfurling from rock like green silk caught in the breeze. The Beetle smells faintly of old leather and salt, like the ocean's been living in it, and, beneath that, something unmistakably him.

"What kind of companies does Venture Haus invest in?" I ask, casual on purpose.

"Quinn's reach is pretty broad," he says. "Fintech, infrastructure, anything venture-scale. If it has a shot at a billion-dollar outcome, he'll look at it."

"And you?"

"I only scout and invest in public benefit corporations," he says.

"That's... specific."

"It's a filter," he says. "The company's mission has to be baked in. Not just promised."

"And founders?" I ask. "Do you have a theme?"

"I tend to back women and LGBTQIA founders."

"Because they're more profitable?" I ask.

A corner of his mouth lifts. "The data *is* pretty consistent: they yield more revenue per dollar invested, and better returns. They also create more jobs and show more innovation."

"And yet," I say, "they're not the ones usually getting the checks."

"No," he says, and there's nothing soft about it. "And, when they do get backed by other companies, they get less."

I let that sit between us for a beat. The road hums. The trees flash by like a film reel.

"So," I say, "you're not just being principled. You're being strategic."

A quiet exhale, almost a laugh. "I believe you can be both."

Then, after a pause, his voice drops. "It's also because the founders I back build like no one's going to rescue them. Because most of the time, no one is."

Something tightens in my chest.

His phone lights up in the console. He glances at the name, and whatever expression he'd been wearing shutters.

"Sorry," he says, already reaching for a single earbud. He taps it in, and answers so softly I catch more rhythm than words. Low. Tense. Private.

He turns his face slightly toward the window, like he's trying to keep the conversation from spilling into the space between us.

"Vancouver," he says. A long pause. "I told you, no reporters yet ... If I hear from anyone, I'll call. Olivia. Let me just … Fine. I'll call you after the concert."

He hangs up, jaw tight. His stare locked out the window.

"Everything okay?"

He runs a hand through his hair. "Relationships are... complicated."

"You're talking to someone whose ex is now dating men. So, yeah, I get complicated."

I glance at him again, at the tension in his shoulders, and think about the Beetle. The way he couldn't let it go. Maybe he's like me. Good at holding on. Terrible at knowing when to let go.

He's quiet. Distant in a way that doesn't feel cold, just *unavailable.* And maybe that's what I want to understand. Not just what went wrong. But how it ever began. And before I can stop myself—

"So, how did you and Olivia get together?" It slips out more casually than I meant it to.

Gavin glances at me, weighing whether to answer. I brace for a vague deflection. Instead, he exhales.

"She was dating Quinn when I met her."

"Wait—*your* Quinn?"

He nods. "They were good together. Still are, in some ways. Both extroverted. Both are obsessed with being seen. I was the quiet third wheel who got dragged along to rooftop parties and told to flirt with trust fund girls."

"What changed?"

"One night, she showed up on my doorstep. She said she spotted Quinn at a party with an up-and-coming blond actress. When she confronted them, she learned that they had slept together. The blond was all too happy to reveal it. Olivia collapsed into my arms, and I sat her by my fireplace, and I let her talk. And cry. I didn't touch her that night, but I wanted to. She was..." He stops and corrects himself. "... *is* beautiful. Whereas before I thought there was a stand-offishness to her, seeing her so vulnerable deepened my crush into something more."

Something twists in my chest.

"I talked to Quinn the next day. He admitted he didn't want commitment and gave me his blessing."

"And then?"

"She came back the next night. We talked. For hours. At some point, she asked me to kiss her."

Smart woman.

"I knew she wasn't over Quinn, but I didn't care."

"And that was it?"

He shrugs. "She stayed the night. We've been together ever since."

A long beat.

"Bet you left a trail of broken hearts before her," I murmur.

"Just mine."

I look at him. That wasn't a throwaway line.

He adds quietly, "She never knew I was in love with her."

My voice is gentle. "You mean... someone else?"

He nods, eyes back on the road. "Her heart was with someone else. Always was."

He doesn't elaborate. I don't press.

But my mind is already turning.

Almost as if to change the subject, he plugs in his phone, and classical music floods the car. Shostakovich.

I groan.

He arches a brow. "Not a fan?"

"I like classical, but not every day. Definitely not on a road trip."

"It's the only common ground with Olivia. Otherwise, it's me and twelve Katy Perry remixes on loop."

He scrolls. Lands on something else.

Dylan's *Shelter from the Storm* starts to play. I exhale. The tension in the car softens.

Then *Magic in the Air* comes on. Then a punk cover of *Stand by Me.* Then The Ellis Court's *Let Your Song.*

I pull into a gas station.

I snatch his phone and scroll. "We do need fuel," I say, trying to sound breezy. "But first I need to know who made this playlist."

Dozens of songs. All of them from the mixed CDs Jared made for me. Every single one meaningful. These songs were the soundtrack to our relationship. Not just romantic background noise—these songs earned my love. My trust. My respect. We first fell for each other over five of them. Songs no one else even knew I loved.

All of it hits me at once.

Some women swoon over a man in a tuxedo. I swoon over a man who curates the perfect soundtrack.

I glance over at Gavin. He's watching me.

Just this quiet, curious look, like he's trying to solve an equation and realizing the answer might be more complicated than he thought.

"Did Jared make this playlist for you?"

He blinks. “What?”

“I mean... It’s full of my favorites. Jared and I once made a theoretical wedding playlist. This is oddly close.”

He gives me a slow, wicked smile. “Just how do you think baby brother got his taste in music?”

I sit there, stunned. *What if the things I loved most about Jared weren’t even his, but Gavin’s all along?*

And then I hear myself say it, too soft to be casual. “He used to make me mixes. Label them in his messy handwriting like it was a love language.”

I keep my eyes on his phone because looking at Gavin feels like staring into a solar eclipse. “I’d get them at my door, before we were really even dating. No note. Just… music. Like he was afraid of saying the wrong thing.”

I sit back in the seat, my fingers drifting to my mouth without thinking. I press them there. Gently.

His eyes flick from my mouth to my hand, then back again—and he doesn’t look away fast enough.

“He wasn’t afraid,” he says, quietly. “He was careful.”

The air between us turns thin. Like the car is holding its breath.

I swallow. “Where did he learn to do that?”

A beat. Gavin’s eyes stay forward, but his voice drops. “He’d sit in my room when he was fifteen. Steal my headphones. Ask me what mattered when it came to love and pretend he wasn’t taking notes.”

I finally look at him. “So, you—”

His hand reaches over, slow, like he’s giving me time to pull away.

“Let me,” he says.

His fingertips brush mine as he takes his phone back. It should be accidental. Except neither of us moves fast enough to make it purely an accident.

"Anyway," he says, and the word lands like a door closing gently.

Before he can cue the next song, his phone lights up again in the console between us.

The name flashes into view: Olivia.

His jaw tightens. He doesn't answer. Just watches it ring out.

Then a text alert slides across the screen, and I watch him read the message on his phone.

And whatever had softened in him seals back up.

His posture shifts beside me—not dramatic, just a retreat. He leans his head lightly against the window, his brow furrowed.

"Everything okay?" I ask.

"It's not," he says quietly. "But there's nothing I can do about it."

There's something final in the way he says it. Not angry. Not frantic. And suddenly the car feels much smaller.

So I do what I always do when things get emotionally claustrophobic.

I unplug his phone and plug in mine without ceremony.

"Okay," I announce, as if presenting a thesis. "Nobody gets to existentially brood on a coastal highway. It's against maritime law."

He makes a soft sound that might be disbelief.

I scroll, decisive.

"There is exactly one guaranteed serotonin override."

Then—

I'm Gonna Be (500 Miles) kicks in at a polite volume as I pull us back onto the road.

"You can't just deploy The Proclaimers like emotional Novocain," he says.

"Watch me."

"That song is a blunt instrument."

"It's a precision tool."

"It's musical populism."

"It's joy," I counter. "No one can stay in a bad mood during this song. It's physically impossible."

He turns his head slightly toward me, studying me like I'm a case study in reckless optimism.

"I could name ten bands that would do this with more nuance."

"Name three."

He opens his mouth, then closes it.

I crank the volume.

I sing. Loud. Off-key. Fully committed.

//And I would walk five thousand miles—//

He turns the volume down.

"That is not the lyric," he says.

"Yes, it is."

"It is not."

//And I would walk five thousand more—//

He presses his lips together like he's attempting containment.

"You are adding a zero," he says. "It's five *hundred* miles."

"Who only walks five hundred miles for someone they love? That's barely a gesture."

He finally looks at me, and I can feel the armor lowering.

"Five hundred is already absurd," he says. "That's the point."

"Have you ever walked five hundred miles for someone?" I ask.

His gaze lingers a second too long.

"Yes," he says quietly. "Metaphorically."

The air shifts.

I swallow.

"Well," I say, aiming for light and landing somewhere near honest, "I'd walk five thousand. For the right person."

The song barrels on. He doesn't sing. But when the chorus hits again, I sneak a glance at him.

He's trying—visibly trying—not to smile.

And for now, that feels like something.

CHAPTER 29

The Man with the Golden Voice

The Queen Elizabeth Theatre rises like a jewel box in the heart of downtown Vancouver. Inside, the air hums with low conversation and the rustle of coats being removed, purses placed between heels. The seats are plush and wine-colored, bathed in the soft gold of the chandeliers.

From the mezzanine, the stage is a study in precision, with velvet curtains drawn tight and lights glowing like halos above the empty microphones. There's an ache of anticipation in the room, reverent and electric, like everyone's holding a collective breath.

Somewhere nearby, someone is wearing sandalwood. The scent rises above the old theater scent, heady and grounding.

I brush against Gavin as we find our seats, and every sense seems turned up too loud. The velvet of the armrest. The cool air against the back of my neck. The accidental press of his knee against mine.

The crowd, a mix of all ages, is abuzz with anticipation. Leonard

Cohen hasn't toured in a decade—part of that time spent in a monastery—and this might be everyone's last chance to see him live. You can feel it in the way people lean forward slightly, clutching programs, whispering like they're in a church.

I am beside myself as we wait for the curtain to rise. I'm so excited that I grab Gavin's arm and squeeze it.

He puts his hand on mine, and I mean to pull away, but I don't. His hand is warm, still, heavy in the kind of way that says, "I've got you."

He's looking at me. Really looking. Like he's trying to match the version of me in his memory with the one in front of him.

Then, slowly, he pulls his hand back.

"I forgot something." He reaches into the interior pocket of his blazer and pulls out a little wrapped gift.

"What's this?" I ask, surprised.

I gently pull the ribbon off, placing it in my purse, then peel back the wrapping paper. It's a first-edition copy of *Book of Longing* by Leonard Cohen.

My breath catches. My eyes well.

Gavin's face shifts, uncertain. He pulls out a handkerchief and hands it to me.

"It's a happy cry," I whisper. "This book reminds me that we still love each other in some way."

Gavin stiffens. "Excuse me?"

"Jared. I've been wanting a first edition of this for years." I clutch the book to my chest. "It must've been hard for him to find."

"Yeah, about the book, Ava—"

The stage curtains pull back, and a nine-piece band and backup singers walk out to wild applause.

Whatever Gavin was about to say gets swallowed whole.

Then Cohen walks out in a sharp suit, bolo tie perfectly crooked, a sly grin on his face. He doffs his hat in a deep, almost reverent bow.

"We really began this tour four years ago, when I first dreamed about it," he says. "I was 74 then—just a kid with a crazy dream."

The crowd roars with laughter, completely under his spell.

As he sings *Hallelujah*, I feel like I'm falling into something I can't climb back out of.

Somehow, even at 78, Leonard Cohen is obscenely sexy.

I lean in and whisper, "Warning: I may throw my underwear on stage."

Gavin leans in close. Too close. His breath brushes my cheek.

"I may be throwing mine first," he murmurs.

I gasp a laugh, then swallow it. Because suddenly, there's not enough air in the room. His mouth is close enough to graze. My chest is buzzing.

I feel his knee bump mine. He doesn't move it. Neither do I. We're both staring forward, but every nerve in my body is tracking him.

I don't need him to look at me again. I can feel it anyway, that gravitational pull like we're already halfway to the thing we're not supposed to do. My skin remembers the weight of his hand. Everything inside me is leaning, inching, aching.

In between songs, Cohen shares seductive tales and wry observations. His voice is gravel and silk. It's the sound of someone who's known ruin and wanted it anyway.

After the third song, he pauses and confesses: "I hope this isn't the end. I want to start smoking again when I make it to eighty. But if that should not come to pass," he says, "and we do not meet again, I promise you tonight we'll give you everything we've got."

And suddenly I forget everything. Olivia, Jared, even the plan.

It's just me. And Gavin. And Cohen's golden voice.

It feels right.

More right than I've felt in years.

THREE AND A half hours later, the concert ends with a bittersweet standing ovation.

As we're swept outside in the press of the crowd, we get jostled hard. I lose my footing and Gavin pulls me to the side. But a new surge pushes me forward, right into his chest, his back hitting the wall.

He catches me. Holds me.

His chin rests on my head. My cheek against his chest.

And now, I am not okay.

I feel everything. The heat of him. The tension. The way his arms don't want to let go.

My body responds before my brain can catch up. It's an ache and a want I've never felt before.

I tell myself I'll step back the second the crowd thins.

But when the moment comes, and I try to pull away, he tugs me gently back.

I need to pull away *without* looking at him. Because if I look at him, I am doomed. A few moments later, I see another break in the crowd, and I do as I planned.

Do. Not. Look. Back.

"Let's go, Gavin," I say through gritted teeth, without looking at him.

"Ava, wait." He yanks me again.

I stop. I look around us and up at the sky, anywhere but at him. We are now under a grove of trees bursting with small purple flowers. The trees are creating a canopy over the walkway we are on, their limbs romantically lit with twinkling lights. All around us, people are laughing and smiling, dressed in their finest date clothes.

This is not the place to stop. This is a place where people fall in love and hearts get into trouble willingly.

"Ava."

I close my eyes, suck in a gulp of air, and brace myself as I turn to him like nothing is amiss.

"We should get going," I say, only half-looking at him, my eyes focused on his chest, the voice shouting at me again. Shouting Gavin's name. Seeing him a little makes me want to see him more, and my eyes disobey me, traveling up his body to his face. I stop when our eyes meet. And now I find that I cannot take my eyes off him.

There goes my stupid plan.

He is standing before me, his eyes alight with something I can't name, but I can feel. Joy and grief and hunger, all of it braided together. His eyes are riveted on my lips, and I can feel something in my core responding. There's more desire, I realize, in Gavin *not* kissing me than there ever was in Jared or anyone else actually kissing me. I exhale his name in a breathy, vulnerable gasp—and that's it.

The plan was never going to hold.

I let him pull me toward him, and for a second, I think he's going to kiss me.

But he doesn't.

He just *holds me*, forehead to forehead, his breath mingling with mine, his hands solid on my hips like I might float away.

And somehow, that's worse. Or better. I don't know.

What I *do* know is that I need to move.

"Let's go," I say, my voice rough and low.

"I completely agree," he says, gaze lingering on my mouth like it already belongs to him. His voice is wrecked. Like he's been trying not to want this and failed.

CHAPTER 30

What Happens at Leonard Cohen, Stays at Leonard Cohen

THE HOTEL ELEVATOR ride feels like an eternity. We don't speak. We don't look directly at each other.

But I see him watching me in the mirrored panel, and I stare right back, our reflections braver than we are.

Cheesy elevator music hums softly, breaking the spell just enough to make me ache for it again.

When we reach the room, he opens the door, and I barely have time to think as he pulls me into it, shedding our coats as we stumble in, breathless and unsure. Our mouths are so close I can feel the warmth of his breath, and suddenly my knees threaten betrayal.

But he steadies me. His hands stay right at my waist again—firm, like he's afraid that going any further will break us both.

And somehow, that restraint makes it worse.

My body is thrumming, every nerve wide awake, and still, it's the nearness that undoes me. The wanting.

I press my forehead to his.

Our breath tangles between us. Shared and shallow. His hands shift—slowly, carefully—one brushing just beneath the hem of my shirt.

His fingers graze the bare skin of my lower back. Nothing more. But it's everything.

"I've never felt like this," I whisper, the words small and raw between us.

He exhales like I've knocked the air from his lungs.

"I know," he says. "Me neither."

For a second, we just breathe each other in.

My hands curl in his shirt, desperate to hold on.

And then the truth finds me. Sharp and cold. Like a light flipping on in the middle of a dream.

The desire doesn't vanish. It just makes room for guilt.

"Gavin—"

He pauses, lips on the nape of my neck.

I press my hands to his chest.

"Olivia."

He stills.

I whisper it another way, softer this time.

"She doesn't deserve this."

What I don't say is: *But I do.*

I watch as something drains from him—the lust, the joy, the heat that held us together for a breathless moment.

He exhales.

I step back, slowly. One inch. Then another.

"Gavin," I say, my voice cracking. "We should stop."

He doesn't move for a beat. Then he nods.

"I know."

The space between us stretches. My skin feels cold.

"I'm sorry."

"Me too," he says, then turns and disappears through the door to the other half of the suite.

I sit on the bed, still clothed, shoes and all, staring at the wall like it might offer clarity.

The want is still there.

What hurts most is knowing this wasn't just reckless desire. It was a kind of love. One with a name I don't know, but one of the ninety-six, I'm sure.

The kind that aches.

The kind that knows it isn't our time, but wishes, stubbornly, illogically, that it could be.

CHAPTER 31

Tower of Wrong

When I awaken the next morning, I discover that Gavin has already left the hotel room. There's a text on my phone:

> GAVIN
>
> Something came up. Had to fly to NYC. —G

I stare at the message, rereading it three times, waiting for my heart to do something other than sink.

I figure it's a lie, or at least a half-truth. But I'm too wrung out to chase it. And, maybe a part of me is grateful that he's disappeared before I had to face him in the morning light.

We crossed a line. And then I stopped us.

But the stopping didn't make it any simpler.

THE HOUSE IS quiet and empty feeling, so I spend the day in the garden. The sun is out, but I can't feel it. My hands are in the soil, but it's not grounding me. I'm trying to plant something, but everything inside me feels uprooted.

I tell myself over and over that we stopped. Olivia didn't deserve it. No matter how much I dislike her—which, let's be honest, is a lot—she doesn't deserve betrayal. But that doesn't mean I don't feel it.

That hunger. That need. That unbearable clarity that something real was happening between us.

It's not just guilt that's following me. It's *wonder*, too. The kind that rearranges you. I let myself feel it. *Just for today*, I tell myself. Then tomorrow, I'll put it away and try to be his friend again. If I can be friends with my ex of eight years, surely I can be friends with a man I've only *almost* kissed.

But it was more than that, wasn't it?

Gavin arrives home late the next day and walks through the kitchen, his jaw tight, expression unreadable. He doesn't look at me.

"Hey," I say softly, turning from the stove. "Can we talk about it?"

He pauses. Doesn't meet my eyes. "There's nothing to talk about. It happened." He shrugs. "We stopped it. That's what matters."

I blink. "That's *all* it was?"

"We had a moment. You were missing my brother. That night was complicated."

He says it like a surgeon. No feeling. Just precision.

"Gavin, you don't look like you're fine."

"Ava, the world doesn't revolve around you."

The words hit harder than they should. He exhales, already regretting them, but not enough to take them back.

"I'm exhausted," he adds. "And I have some things going on that I'm not at liberty to discuss. So please. I'm going to my study."

He walks away, and I let him go. Because chasing him would hurt more than watching him leave.

Actually, I prefer the world not to revolve around me. But the truth is, we are all our own sun, no matter how much we don't want to be at times.

I call Quinn. Not because I want to see him. Because I need to feel like someone still wants to see me.

"Dinner?"

"Sure." I curl into the corner of the couch. "That sounds—"

The phone is snatched from my hand. Gavin presses **'End Call'** like he's swatting a fly.

"What the *hell*, Gavin?"

"You don't need to throw yourself at Quinn."

"Excuse me?"

He exhales. "You're doing something reckless to feel wanted. I get it. I've done it. But don't. Not him."

"Wow. Thanks for the slut-shaming. And also—why do you care?"

His voice lowers. Rough. Tired. "Because I know exactly what he wants."

"What do you want, Gavin? To protect me? Or to punish me for stopping something you were never brave enough to finish?"

That gets him. His eyes flash. But he doesn't respond.

"Forget it. I'm going to dinner," I say.

"I don't want him anywhere near you."

"News flash: I'm an adult, and *you* are not my father and definitely not my boyfriend."

I grab my coat and bag. But when I reach the front door, I realize my keys are in the kitchen.

Of course they are.

I take a breath and open the door anyway.

QUINN'S CAR PULLS up, headlights flashing across the drive.

Gavin follows me outside.

"You're not going," he says.

"You don't get to decide that."

"I do when it's Quinn."

"You've been weird about him since the beginning. What the hell is going on?"

He doesn't answer. Just steps forward, putting himself between me and the car.

"Gavin."

Quinn steps out of the car, his brow furrowing as he looks from me to Gavin. "Everything right, mate?"

"Turn around," Gavin says quietly.

"Excuse me?"

"I said leave."

Quinn laughs. "You're not my bloody boss."

Something dark flashes in Gavin's expression. It doesn't read as rage. It's something worse.

"I've seen the photos, Quinn." His voice is flat. Dangerous.

Quinn's jaw tightens. Not anger. Something closer to shame.

"Gav—"

"Don't," Gavin says.

Quinn looks at me then. And for a split second, I see it—regret. Not for getting caught. For something else.

"This isn't her fault," he says quietly, then gets back into his car and drives off.

I whirl on Gavin. "What. The hell. Was *that*?"

He opens his mouth. Closes it. Rubs his hands over his face.

"I can't," he says. "Not yet."

"Try."

"I'm trying to keep you from getting hurt."

"Funny, because right now, you're the one doing the hurting."

I HAVEN'T SPOKEN to Gavin for three days.

I think about texting Kiki.

But what would I even say? *Hey, I almost kissed my ex's brother and then stopped myself. Thoughts?*

Kiki would come running if I asked. But right now, I don't want to talk.

I want to un-feel. To undo. To forget.

I leave food out for him, but I don't check whether he eats it. I move through the house like a ghost. The only place that still feels safe is the garden.

I'm halfway through texting Jared—half a tattle, half a cry for help—when there's a knock on my door.

"Ava," Gavin says quietly. "Can I talk to you?"

I don't respond. I'm too angry, too afraid of what I might say.

"Dinner's in the fridge," I muster. "That's all I have for you tonight."

Minutes later, I hear the microwave beep. The soft scrape of a fork against ceramic.

I made him a dinner like I always do. And he ate it like nothing's changed.

But everything has.

And we both know it.

CHAPTER 32

Love and Other Perishables

It's been days since the Quinn mess, and Gavin and I have barely exchanged syllables, let alone made eye contact. This morning, he looked like a ghost of himself: dark under eye circles, shirt wrinkled, tie missing, not even pretending to read *The Wall Street Journal.* Before he left for a two-day work trip, he set his phone on the counter while he hunted for his keys. The screen lit up with a stack of missed calls, all from Olivia.

Whatever's happening, he won't tell me. But it's eating him alive.

And I'm still mad. Or confused. Or both.

The house is too quiet, and I am having way too many arguments with myself. I need to get out. Breathe some different air.

I drive into town for eggs and yogurt and maybe—let's be honest—just to feel a little less like I'm pacing in my own brain.

Island Market has been family-owned since 1897, and it still feels like it. There's a community corkboard covered in handwritten notes about lost keys and found kayaks, shelves stocked with handmade sourdough hearth loaves from Orcas Island Bakery, too many kinds of kombucha, and air scented with island-grown pears.

The magazine rack by the register is small: *Bon Appétit*, *Food & Wine*, *Magnolia*. Because Orcas Island does elderberry syrup and hand milled soap by Island Thyme, but it doesn't do gossip rags.

Or so I thought.

I spot a woman in pristine white hiking boots and a fur-trimmed Arc'teryx jacket that's never seen a trail and makes zero sense in September—she's clearly not from here—holding a copy of *National Enquirer*. The tabloid looks like it stowed away in her tote from Sea-Tac, its crinkled pages as loud and misplaced as her outerwear. It's like a flamingo appeared in the Arctic.

On the cover: a photo of a couple leaving The Plaza Hotel. Even from five feet away, I recognize the curve of Olivia's cheek. And Quinn's jawline.

Headline: *Sweetheart Host Olivia Wood in Tryst with Ex.*

Subheading: *Spotted Leaving Plaza Hotel the Morning After.*

My stomach drops.

I step closer, heart pounding. "Excuse me. Could I borrow that for a sec?" I ask the woman. She hands it to me, amused.

I stare at the page. It's definitely them. Olivia and Quinn. She's tucked under his arm, her hand pressed to his chest, his lips inches from her ear. The Plaza's gold revolving door glints behind them like a spotlight.

Suddenly, everything makes sense.

Gavin isn't moody. He's devastated.

And I've been too busy being mad to see it.

I rush outside and call Patricia. My fingers are trembling as I type her name.

"Is it true?" I ask, before she can even say hello.

She sighs. "You saw the photos."

"Yes."

"It's true. Gavin just got confirmation yesterday. His PR team was trying to get ahead of it, but it's already out."

"What can I do?"

There's a pause. Then:

"Chocolate croissant bread pudding," she says.

CHAPTER 33

Some Assembly Required

Gavin won't be back until tomorrow night, his assistant, Yumi, tells me when I call his local Venture Haus office. He's in NYC for meetings. PR triage. Probably doing that thing where he pretends he's fine when he's falling apart inside.

That gives me thirty-six hours.

Just enough time to give him something he'd never ask for—but Patricia and I agree he clearly needs.

The recording studio sits at the far edge of Gavin's property, wrapped in warm cedar, softened by ferns and moss, and perched above a bluff where madrona trees twist out of rock in a constant reach for the sun. Through the tall windows, you can see all the way to a scattered chain of uninhabited islands, like a trail of secrets leading toward the horizon.

I walk the path past the olive grove and the half-split woodpile. I carefully slide open the studio's door. It smells like sawdust and plastic. Like something unfinished.

Because it is.

The inside is frozen in time. Not abandoned. Not even neglected. Just paused.

A Steinway grand sits under a tarp in the corner. When I lift the cover, a soft plume of dust rises. The instrument is timeless and elegant, its keys a little cold, but when I press one, it sings. Just one clear note, resonating against bare plywood walls.

The mixing board inside the sound booth is still in its box. Cables and converters lie in a pile like a puzzle he never gave himself time to solve. No drywall, no lights. Only a single suspended mic, swinging a little in the breeze.

Gavin never finished the space. Of course, he didn't.

He was too busy helping everyone else.

I call Duke first, because Sara says Duke can fix literally anything and owns enough tools to justify their own storage shed, which Sara calls "The Museum of Questionable Purchases." Also, he works fast, especially when bribed with homemade ramen.

I text Duke's friends, Jake and Kevin, local sound-engineering legends. There are whispered stories on the island about how they once rewired a haunted theater in Prague and engineered an album in a cave.

They reply immediately: "For Gavin? We're in."

Within hours, we have an army. Islanders show up without being asked. A baby-faced electrician named Colton arrives barefoot, carrying a coiled snake of wires and a thermos of coffee the size of a keg.

A woman named Libi, who once got a loan from Gavin to save her shop in town, sets up a table of pears and Lum Farm cheese like she's catering a farm wedding. Theresa, a memoir writer from Doe Bay who is allegedly on deadline, ends up alphabetizing Gavin's vinyl collection with the manic energy of someone avoiding their manuscript at all costs.

Micah from next door spends the afternoon chasing off the angora goats before they can headbutt the Steinway or harass the crew. He takes the job very seriously. The goats do not.

A famous music composer named Jim Bredouw volunteers to tune the piano because this island, apparently, does nothing of consequence casually.

We sweep. We sand. Jake runs cables. Duke installs light fixtures. Someone finds a salvaged rug and unfurls it. It smells faintly of cedar and lemon oil.

I ferry espresso, figs, brownies, and gratitude. I don't know if I've ever been part of a community like this. Not one that shows up simply because someone good needs something.

By nightfall, the space is transformed.

The walls are up. The floor gleams. The mixing board is installed and live, glowing as if it's waking from a dream. The sound booth is finished. The overhead mic hovers above a newly placed stool. I hang soft Edison bulbs in a line, casting a warm glow over the piano.

I run back to the main house and find his guitar, the one with the tiny chip on the neck. He once told me he got it in Galveston, Texas, on a road trip before everything got serious in his life. He didn't say so, but now I know it was before he gave up his dream to help his family through Patricia's illness. I wipe it down and place it beside the stool. The final touch.

I pause, look around.

This isn't just a studio anymore.

It's a space that says: *Your dreams matter, too.*

CHAPTER 34

If Pigs Could Fly

I DID IT. I committed the most reckless act of love I could think of: I made brisket. On three hours of sleep, with sore arms and sawdust in my hair, I pulled off a twelve-hour gamble involving smoke, meat, and my last shred of pride. If nothing else, it'll sedate Gavin into a food coma so deep, he won't have to think about Olivia for the next ten hours.

But when six rolls around and he's not home, my stomach knots.

I call Yumi at Venture Haus. She tells me Gavin is holed up in his office, the door shut, showing no sign of leaving.

"Tell him there's an emergency," I say.

"An emergency?" she asks, skeptical.

"Yep. At the house."

Fifteen minutes later, I hear a car door slam, the crunch of gravel, the sound of someone running toward something they care about.

Then the front door swings open.

"Ava?" he calls, already halfway down the hall. "What's going on? You didn't answer your phone."

He's breathless. His hair mussed. Chest rising fast beneath a soft, black tee. His eyes scan the house, sharp and worried.

And suddenly I feel the weight of what I've done—not just the trick, but the gesture.

Not just the food, but the invitation.

I take his hand. He's warm and real and here, but he hesitates, still not sure there isn't a crisis or a trap.

"Come with me," I say.

Outside, I let go of his hand and step aside.

The madrona trees catch the last light of day, all copper and flame. The sea below murmurs against the rocks. Somewhere in the distance, one of the goats bleats, offended, maybe, that they weren't invited.

I've dragged the patio table into the middle of the backyard, lit it with floating candles and strings of flickering votives overhead. The good china is out. Bottles of his favorite beer gleam with condensation. The outdoor fireplace glows beside us, throwing golden light across the seagrass.

The air smells like smoke and brisket, and something sweeter and tangier underneath—a secret barbecue sauce I didn't even know I had the wherewithal to make.

He stops. Takes it all in. For a moment, he says nothing, then, "Who is all of this for?"

"You."

"You did this for me?" he asks, softer now.

I nod. My heart is a cannonball rolling down a hill. My throat is full of words I haven't figured out how to say.

He stares at me, quiet.

"I'm so sorry, Gavin. I heard about Olivia and Quinn. And I've been… awful. I was so busy being angry, I couldn't see you were trying to protect me. You've been trying to protect me all along. You're always looking out for everyone. Patricia. Jared. Isabel. Micah. Me."

My voice catches. I didn't plan this part. I didn't expect to feel so much.

"I just wanted to do something for you," I whisper. "Even if it's small. Even if it's just dinner."

He exhales. A breath that sounds like it's been stuck in his chest for days.

"There was no way you could've known," he says. "When we drove to Vancouver, I'd heard the news, but Olivia wouldn't confirm it. The next morning, I had messages from reporters—well, vultures—asking for confirmation. Some even offered me money."

I wince. His voice is steady, but it hurts him.

"That's why I've been distant," he adds. "I didn't know how to tell anyone. I almost told you on the road trip. But I didn't even have all the pieces yet."

I remember that call. The way he looked out the window, like the truth was too dangerous to touch.

"It's humiliating," he says. "But now that it's out, I'm relieved."

He glances away, and for a second, he looks younger, lighter.

"Maybe this will help," I say, stepping aside.

Slow-smoked barbecue brisket glistening under the lights, okra fried to a perfect crisp, jalapeño purple potato salad with crème fraîche and vinegar.

It's not fancy. But it's mine. And it's his. And it's ours, somehow.

He steps forward. A grin curves slowly across his face.

"It's all my favorites. How'd you know?"

"A little birdie told me."

"Mom," he says, knowingly. "I haven't eaten in three days, so I'm making up for that tonight."

"Good. I made enough to feed you and the goats."

We take our seats, Gavin at the head of the table, me at his right. We fall into a rhythm, passing plates and pouring drinks, like we've done this every night for years.

And maybe, in some quiet universe, in another lifetime, we have.

He tries the brisket first, then the potato salad. Washes it down with cold beer. Turns to me. His eyes are soft, open, and clear.

"Like?" I ask.

"Love," he says. His voice is low. Sure. The way you sound when you mean it.

He takes another bite. Chews. Swallows. Then glances over at me. "This sauce is incredible. Where'd you learn to make it?"

The question opens a door in me I didn't know was closed.

"My dad," I say quietly. "He made it every summer. Said it came from *his* dad, a butcher in Texas, who traded two full briskets for the recipe from a guy named Papa Dee, whose barbecue was legendary. But Papa Dee never gave my grandfather the amounts, just the ingredients. Dad used to joke that the sauce was part science, part séance. You had to feel it to make it."

I look down at my plate, then back at Gavin. "I think that's what this is, tonight. It's me trying to take care of someone the way he took care of me."

Gavin doesn't speak right away. Just reaches across the table and touches my hand. It's the gentlest thing. The kindest.

Watching him eat, seeing joy return to his face like sunlight spilling through a window, I feel it hit me:

He deserves this. The care. A night without armor. And not just because he's generous, because he's good. Deeply, impossibly good.

This is what I know how to do. Feed the ache. Turn heartbreak into hunger, and hunger into something warm and shared. Kiki said it. Gavin did, too. And maybe now I believe them.

We eat like we haven't in weeks. We talk about everything: music, dreams, the story of his escaped goats. Everything except Olivia and Quinn.

It's the best time I've ever had with Gavin.

Maybe the best time I've ever had with anyone.

And I realize, with a sharp tug in my chest, that I don't want it to end.

When we finally stop laughing long enough to breathe, I stand.

"I have one more surprise."

He arches a brow. "There's more?"

"Come on."

I take his hand and lead him past the trees to the studio.

WARM LIGHT SPILLS through the studio windows, soft and golden, like it's beckoning us.

Gavin stops short. His breath catches. "I don't even know what to say."

Inside, the transformation is complete. Thanks to Duke and half the island. The smell of citrus oil and fresh-cut cedar still lingers.

The grand piano is uncovered, shining under the lights. The custom mixing board is connected and glowing in the sound booth.

But what stops him is the guitar. His guitar. Resting beside the stool under the suspended mic.

He steps forward, awestruck. "You did all this?"

"With a lot of work from all the islanders you've helped. They were happy to return the favor."

When he picks up the guitar and strums it, I can tell he's remembering the night at Doe Bay, when he sang *I'm Not the Man I Want to Be.*

"You give so much to everyone else," I say.

He crosses the room slowly, running his hand along the polished edge of the mixing board, then across the keys of the piano. He presses a single note: a clean, resonant C.

I want to say something comforting, or profound, or maybe even flirtatious, but what tumbles out instead is this:

"I thought maybe after losing the love of your life, you could use a space that gives something back."

He doesn't move. His hand hovers just above the piano.

Then, he says, quietly, "Olivia was never the love of my life."

"Oh," I say, and it's all I can manage, because the air between us suddenly feels dense with meaning. My heart pounds so hard I'm sure he can hear it.

The silence stretches between us, thick as honey. I swear, if he touched me right now, I'd combust.

"Okay, great, *so*… dessert?"

He turns, his mouth twitching at the corner like he knows exactly what I'm doing.

"Dessert," he echoes, his voice lower now, a shade rougher.

Outside, I glance over my shoulder. He's still behind me, and his eyes haven't left me—not once.

We walk the short path, our footsteps crunching softly over the gravel, between the studio and the main house in silence, but it's not empty. It's charged; every step pulsing with the words we haven't said.

At the porch, I push open the screen door. I don't have to look to know he's close. I can feel him, steady and electric.

"Dessert needs to be served warm," I say, stepping inside with a slight wobble that's part wine, but mostly the way he's been watching me all night.

"You do have room for dessert, right?"

"Who needs six-pack abs," he says, his voice low, amused.

"That's the right attitude," I laugh.

I open the oven and pull out the pièce de résistance: chocolate croissant bread pudding, golden at the edges, the custard set and gleaming. The scent alone could break hearts. I dust it with powdered sugar as Gavin watches, quiet now, brow furrowed like he's trying to solve something.

"Is that—?" he asks.

"Your great-grandmother's *If Pigs Could Fly* Chocolate Croissant Bread Pudding," I say, grinning.

"That's impossible," he replies.

"Clearly it's not."

"Mom always said it's a secret recipe and she would never give it to anyone but family ..." He trails off, a smile building on his face.

I am smiling, too. The Jones family is my family. And, taking care of Gavin in his time of heartbreak feels like what family would do.

"I really want us to be friends," I practically whisper.

"What if I don't want to be friends?"

He reaches up, brushes powdered sugar from my chin with his thumb, slow and deliberate. My breath catches. I try to answer him, but one needs air to speak, and I can't seem to find any. I glance up at him. I can't tell whether he's thinking about kissing me or asking for a fork, so I change the subject as I cut into the dessert.

"Gavin, why didn't you invite me to your engagement party?"

His hand lowers, but his eyes stay on mine. "Because I thought you'd be a distraction."

"It's not like I knock over chocolate fountains or light things on fire in public."

"It wasn't that."

"Then what?"

He exhales. "It was Olivia's day."

"It was your day, too."

"Yes, but Olivia was the one who'd always dreamed about her engagement party."

"I still don't understand. If you were embarrassed by me, you can tell me. I know I'm not as polished as Olivia. I know Patricia probably forced you to give me a job, and you pitied me, but I'm a lot more resilient than you might think."

His jaw tightens. "Do we have to do this right now?"

"Your mom trusted me with the family's secret recipe," I say quietly. "You can trust me, too."

He steps forward, close enough that I can feel the warmth of him. Then, slowly, he reaches out and tucks a lock of hair behind my ear, his knuckles grazing my cheek in a touch so gentle it steals my breath.

"It wasn't pity. It wasn't embarrassment."

"Then *what*?"

He leans in, voice low. "It was you. You were the distraction. I didn't want Olivia to see the way I looked at you."

My heart stops. I blink at him, stunned. And then—

He kisses me. Softly. Like he's afraid I might vanish.

It's not a kiss that demands anything. It's a kiss that says, I see you. I've seen you for years. And I kiss him back like I finally believe it.

I break away, a little lightheaded, my heart pounding, my eyes still closed.

"*Mmmm*... did I say dessert's ready?"

"Surely it can wait?" he laughs.

"Patricia was adamant that it be served warm."

"That's why microwaves were invented."

"So that people can make out while their dessert gets cold?"

"Now you're catching on."

His fingers toy with the buttons of my blouse—slow, teasing—as if unwrapping a secret. I let out a shaky breath.

The kitchen smells like sugar and heat and something wild. My skirt brushes higher as he steps between my legs, his hands sliding along my thighs like he's memorizing the landscape. His mouth finds the soft space just below my collarbone, then his breath is hot through the lace of my bra. My nipples tighten beneath the damp fabric.

He pins me gently against the wall, his kisses growing hungrier, his hands still careful, still coaxing. Mine curl into his shirt, not tugging him closer but anchoring. Letting go and holding on at once.

"Gavin ..." I murmur, voice hoarse.

He stills. His forehead rests against mine.

"I think you were trying to explain that you don't hate me," I say.

He exhales, warm against my cheek, and his fingers find another button on my blouse. It slips free with a soft pop.

"It was the opposite," he says.

Then another button.

"I think I was struck by you, the first time I met you."

His knuckles brush the skin of my chest, and I swear I feel it all the way through me.

"I couldn't get you out of my head. Ordinarily that would mean I'd ask you out, except ..."

Another button.

He's not even looking at what he's doing. Just me.

"You were dating my baby brother."

I swallow hard. "Right."

The last button slips free. His gaze drops to my chest. Just for a second. When he looks back up, something's shifted. His eyes are darker now. I can sense him struggling to hold onto the thread of his thoughts.

"I thought Olivia deserved to have an engagement party with a fiancé who wasn't infatuated with another woman in the room. I couldn't risk having you there, for her sake."

My heart aches. Because I'm not sure if I'm more shocked by the word *infatuated* or the way he's looking at me right now, or the realization that I am the woman who broke his heart. That Gavin has loved me all these years.

My blouse hangs open between us, but he doesn't touch me. Not yet. It's like he's waiting to see what I'll do now that I know.

I should say something. Anything. But the words are stuck in my throat, tangled with all the years I didn't know how to see him this way.

"I am sorry about Olivia," I manage.

"Don't be. It's not the first time."

That stops me. "What?"

"Why do you look so shocked?" he asks.

He slides my top off of me, kissing the space between my breasts, slow and reverent.

"I can't fathom why any woman would cheat on you. At least now that I know you're not a jerk."

He laughs, throwing his head back. The sound is warm and gorgeous, and it sparks heat low in my stomach.

"You're attractive, intelligent, kind," I go on, my voice thinner now, barely trusting itself.

"You think I'm attractive?"

"Let's just say that if you kissed me again, I wouldn't stop you."

"And if I wanted more than a kiss?"

My pulse stutters.

"You'll have to find out," I whisper.

Then, without warning, he lifts me in his arms.

"Gavin!"

"We're not stopping now," he says, carrying me down the hallway.

The bedroom is dim, moonlight filtering through gauzy curtains.

He lays me down gently on the bed, then slides my skirt down my legs.

I'm in nothing but a bra and panties. Thank God I went with black lace. Matching, even. The nicest set I own, which feels—suddenly—like a life choice I should be proud of.

His eyes sweep me—lingering without rushing—like he's trying to take me in and not overwhelm me at the same time. His voice comes out wrecked and reverent.

"You're fucking beautiful."

The moonlight catches the tension in his jaw, the way his chest rises like he's wrestling something physical. He strips off his shirt, and for a second, I forget how to breathe. His body is all quiet strength: broad shoulders, a lean waist, and along his ribs, the ink isn't decoration, it's a small private litany: the Sanskrit words for love, split into its truest forms—familial, platonic devotion, romantic—as if he's sharing his life philosophy in plain sight.

He comes back to me, hands framing my face like he needs to be sure I'm real. And when he looks at me, my stomach flips. It's not just desire, but the weight of all the years I didn't see what he was carrying.

His voice drops, rougher. "I've wanted you for so long."

No flourish. No bravado. Just truth.

His words do exactly what I'm afraid they will do: they crack something open.

Because the wanting is big enough to scare me.

"What if I'm not..." My voice catches, and I hate that it does. I force it steady. "What if I'm not all you imagined I'd be?"

He doesn't answer right away. He just holds my gaze.

"Do you trust me?" he asks.

"Yes," I whisper.

He reaches for a lavender silk tie hanging on his bedpost, gathers my wrists above my head, and loops the tie around them, slow, gentle, knotting it loose enough that the silk slides instead of bites. A suggestion of restraint, not a trap.

"Just for the record," he murmurs, mouth brushing ear, "I've never tied anyone else up in my life."

Heat floods low and fast. Of course, he hasn't. Of course, this is him. Thoughtful even when he's losing control.

His mouth finds mine again. Then my neck. My stomach.

His hands explore with a devotion that borders on worship. He moves like he knows exactly where to touch and how long to linger. My body hums, arches, reacts before I can think.

His fingers graze under my bra, then trace the straps to the back.

"Front snap," I murmur when he fumbles.

His mouth never leaves my body as he undoes the clasp of my bra, one-handed.

"You're scarily good at that."

I feel the smile on his lips as he cups my breast, thumb rubbing over the peak, then lowers his mouth. When his lips close around my nipple, I make a sound I can't take back. My back bows. My wrists pull against the tie as he sucks, slow and indulgent. It's not just desire. It's reverence again. Like he's thanking me for existing.

"I've dreamt about this," he says, voice low, certain. "About you under me."

Something unspools deep inside me at the way he says it, like the wanting isn't just sexual. It's emotional. Physical. Total.

He shifts lower, kissing down my stomach, then the softest parts of me, until his hands slide beneath the waistband of my panties. He peels them away like he's unveiling something sacred. The air hits me and I shiver hard.

And then—his mouth. Hot. Devoted. Every movement deliberate, every stroke of his tongue a confession. I gasp, buck against him, not even trying to hide how badly I need it, need him.

My wrists strain again, the knot loosens with the motion, the silk sliding, giving. The restraint turns into friction, turns into hunger.

"Gavin—" I gasp. It's not a plea. It's surrender.

He doesn't stop. He goes deeper into it like he's determined to take me apart with his mouth before he asks anything of me at all. Like the first time is his to give.

I'm shaking when one wrist finally slips free. The instant it does, I reach down and thread my fingers into his hair, holding him there. Anchoring. Because I can't bear the distance even for a breath.

My hips lift, chasing him. He meets me—steady, relentless—until the pressure builds too fast, too high.

I come with a gasp that borders on a sob, my body breaking open around his mouth, my hand tightening in his hair like it's the only thing keeping me on the planet.

When the tremors start to ease, I pull, gentle but urgent, drawing him back up my body because I want him. All of him.

He climbs over me, mouth wet, eyes wrecked, and the sight of him like that hits harder than the orgasm. My other wrist is loose now, the tie forgotten, hanging from my skin like an afterthought.

I lift my hips, desperate. "Please," I whisper. "I need you."

His breath stutters. He kisses me. One quick kiss, like he's barely holding on, then another, deeper.

He reaches into the nightstand drawer without looking. A soft scrape. The rip of foil.

The sound alone makes me clench.

He rolls the condom on fast—no hesitation, no fumbling—then he's back over me, braced on his forearms, eyes locked on my face like he won't let this happen without seeing me.

And then he's inside me.

A stretch. A fit. A breathless, perfect fullness.

He goes still for a beat, forehead dropping to mine, eyes searching my face like he's checking for pain, like he'd rather take himself apart than hurt me.

I clutch him closer, nails in his shoulders. "Don't stop," I breathe.

That does it.

He starts to move, slow at first, controlled, as if he's trying to make it last and also trying not to lose it. My body meets him, chasing the friction, the fullness, the way he fills every hollow place like he belongs there.

His mouth finds mine again, swallowing every broken sound. My legs wrap around him. He groans my name like it hurts, like it's relief.

The rhythm builds. The room narrows to skin and breath and the wet heat between us.

I feel it coming again, sharp and fast, and he must feel it too because his eyes go darker, his grip tightening, his mouth at my ear.

"Look at me," he breathes—not gentle now. Not polite. A need.

I do.

And when we shatter, we do it together—eyes open, mouths parted, tangled, breathless, and undone.

CHAPTER 35

If You Love Somebody but Nobody Knows, is it Still Love?

My body knows where I am before my brain does, because the sunlight lands differently in this room. The bed is warm, and I'm bare, tangled in sheets that smell like salt, cedar, and him. I shift, and Gavin shifts with me. His leg slides between mine, his hand resting on the curve of my hip like it forgot how to let go.

"This isn't my room," I murmur, voice still sleep-rough.

"It is after last night." His mouth is just beneath my ear, his breath warm against my skin, his hand gliding from my hip to my breast.

"You always wake up like this?" I ask, voice rougher now for an entirely different reason.

"Like what?" he murmurs, kissing the spot just below my jaw.

"Like you've got nowhere else to be."

He lifts his head just enough to meet my eyes. "I don't."

There's something devastating in how he looks at me. Like I'm the secret he's finally allowed to share, and this morning, this bed, this mess of limbs and affection, is everything he's ever wanted.

I curl closer, tracing the Sanskrit tattoos twisting around his rib cage with my fingers.

"You've been holding out on me, Gavin Jones."

He hums, kissing my temple. "I've been holding back for *years*."

I let my hand rest over his heart, and for a moment, we just stay like that—quiet, close, breath syncing.

Then his lips find mine again, slow and unhurried. Just his mouth on mine, his body pressed against me, the faint scratch of stubble against my cheek, and the ache in my thighs reminding me of every spontaneous, perfect decision we made last night.

When he finally pulls back, he groans, resting his forehead against mine. "We should probably get going."

I grin, eyes still closed. "Didn't we already do it twice?"

He laughs, the sound low and delicious. "I'm not talking about sex." A beat as his mouth finds mine again. "Though I could be persuaded into a round three."

Eventually, he slips out of bed and pads across the room. I miss the weight of him immediately. He's standing by the window in nothing but boxers, sunlight kissing the curve of his back, catching in the mess of his hair. The sight of him—barefoot, golden, unguarded—does something dangerous to me.

There's a wild, undone beauty about him in the morning, as if the night didn't quite finish with him. And I feel him everywhere, the memory of him, still humming beneath my skin. His gaze finds me in the reflection of the glass. He doesn't blink. Doesn't move. It's as if he's still trying to memorize me, even now.

"What time is it?" I ask, stretching on instinct. His gaze traces the path of my arm, then drops to just above where the sheet dips, barely covering me.

I watch his throat move like he's just swallowed a thought.

Two identical dings break the spell. My phone, his phone, both lighting up on the table behind me.

I ignore it. He doesn't.

"It's Jared," he murmurs. "He says he can't wait to share his *big news*."

I groan. "The only big news I want right now is whether you're coming back to bed."

"Trust me. If we didn't have to get going," he says, as if it pains him to say it.

I sit up, clutching the sheet to my chest like it might help me think. "Get going where?"

"Jared and John. Brunch."

"Oh. Crap."

Gavin crosses the room and presses a kiss to my bare shoulder, like it's habit. Like we've always done this. "We could save time if we shower together," he says, brushing my hair off my neck.

I glance at him sideways. "And water. Think of the planet."

He grins. "Exactly. Responsible and efficient."

"I like a man who's practical," I murmur, already reaching for him again.

Half an hour later, we have been anything but practical. As I step out of the shower, I somehow feel both clean and dirty.

THE SUN IS high by the time we're on the road, windows down, our fingers laced on the console between us. Gavin drives like the world isn't going anywhere without him, slow and unbothered, while I sneak glances at his profile. He looks content, as if he's exactly where he's meant to be.

"You know those giant road signs with the numbers on them?" I ask.

"Yes?"

"They suggest a driving speed, Grandpa. You can actually get a ticket for going too slow."

"What's the hurry?" he says, grinning. "The slower I drive, the longer I get to be alone with you."

I bite my lip to keep from smiling too hard.

He's right. If I could bottle this exact feeling and sip it through fall, I would. We ride the rest of the way grinning, our fingers still laced.

Maybe seeing Jared and John is a blessing in disguise. Otherwise, my mind might fixate on post-coital questions about commitment and the meaning of what we did and when we can do it again.

Soon, I hope.

THE ORCAS HOTEL perches on a hill as if it knows it's the prettiest thing around—classic white clapboard siding, red gables, wraparound porch, and just enough faded paint to feel historic instead of haunted. It's been overlooking the ferry landing since 1904, watching strangers come and go with the tide.

We pull into the gravel lot just as the latest ferry unloads, a stream of cars rolling off while foot passengers blink into the bright morning like they can't quite believe how lucky they are to be here.

Inside, the café is all creaky wood floors, lace-curtained windows, and that cozy hush you only get in places with that much history—or really good muffins.

We see Jared sitting at a table for four, standing to greet us, a huge smile on his face. He looks good. Not Gavin good, but good.

He pulls me into a big bear hug, and I'm pleased that it doesn't make me miss what we had. It just makes me happy to see him.

I glance sideways and see Gavin watching. Not with jealousy, but maybe curiosity. After a few seconds, he clears his throat, and Jared releases me to hug his brother.

"Good to see you, too, Gavin. John's just parking the car. He'll be here in a sec."

We sit, order coffees, and turn to each other.

"You look great, Jared. It's really good to see you," I tell him.

"I'm so glad you guys could make it. I have something I really want to tell you." He can barely contain his excitement.

"The last time I heard those words, my world turned upside down," I tease, sipping water.

"I'm getting married," he says.

I spit my water, spraying the table.

Gavin wipes it up with a napkin as I choke out, "Very funny."

"Seriously. I'm getting married."

"To John?" I ask.

"Yes. Of course, to John."

"That's ridiculous."

"What do you mean, 'that's ridiculous'?" His voice rises.

"Jared, you just came out. He's the first guy you've even dated. You're probably just afraid to date anyone else."

"Don't reduce it to that."

"I'm not reducing it," I say. "I'm saying maybe you don't have to make the biggest decision of your life in the same year you blew up ours."

"Okay, kids, let's take it down a notch." Gavin puts his hand on my arm to calm me as some of the diners glance our way.

Jared eyes Gavin's hand on my arm, waiting to see if I pull away. He looks from me to Gavin and practically winces.

"Are you kidding?" He turns to me. "You and Gavin? You hate him."

"You hate me?" Gavin says, mock-wounded.

"I don't hate you."

"But he said you hated me."

"Gavin. This isn't about you. It's about Jared."

"Exactly," adds Jared. "I thought my best friend and my brother might be supportive or even happy for me."

Gavin raises an eyebrow. "I haven't even said anything yet."

"Exactly. Not saying anything is just as bad. Just answer me. Are you two sleeping together?"

"Well," Gavin says, leaning back with a slow smile, "I wouldn't say we're getting a *lot* of sleep."

I slap Gavin on the shoulder.

Jared grits his teeth. "Great. You're judging me for falling in love, while you're hooking up with someone you didn't even like three months ago."

"Hey!" Gavin protests. "Still here."

Then, turning to me, "You really hated me?"

"Gavin, we can talk about it later. Of course, I never actually hated you."

I turn back to Jared, but he stands abruptly, bumping into a good-looking guy with wavy blonde hair approaching the table.

"Hi!" he says, smiling, then glances around at our strained faces. "Bad time?"

"Yes," Jared says. "We're leaving."

BACK HOME, I throw open cabinets, yank ingredients out, and bang pots with theatrical fury.

"What are you doing?" Gavin asks.

"I'm baking."

"Want help?"

"No, but you can watch." I pour a pile of pecans on a chopping board and grab a cleaver. Gavin looks like he's worried this could be dangerous.

"Do you want to talk about it?" he asks.

"No," I say, letting the cleaver drop with a CHOP!

"Are you sure?"

"No. Yes! Ugh!" *CHOP!* "How could Jared find someone so quickly?" *CHOP!*

"I... it's... just..." I start crying and set the knife down.

"Thank God," Gavin mutters, sliding the knife away.

He looks helpless, and it hits me—maybe he's never done this. Olivia probably didn't sob while baking.

"What did Olivia do when she got upset?"

"She got distant. Cold. You're... not that."

I sniffle. "So, I'm irrational and emotional?"

"You're passionate. Real."

His kindness breaks something open.

"We were supposed to be the ones planning a future. I don't want him that way anymore, but I still worry about him. What if John isn't good enough for him?"

I reach for the cleaver again.

"Are you sure you should be around sharp objects?" Gavin asks. "What are you even making?"

"The most addictive chocolate, pecan, coconut bar on the planet. With Gavin cracker crust."

"That's not a real ingredient," he says.

"Is now."

I melt chocolate. Dip a finger. Suck it clean.

Peace.

"Did you know chocolate triggers the same chemicals in the brain as falling in love?" I dip again and extend it to him.

"Want to taste?"

"I want to do more than that."

He pulls me close and sucks the chocolate off my finger while holding my gaze.

A jolt of heat sparks low in my belly. "Do you really have to leave tonight?"

"Yes, I do. Sorry, but this trip has been planned for months. It's only for three days." He lifts me up, and I wrap my legs around his hips. "But we've got four whole hours before I leave."

Everything else fades away as he kisses me. We're only hands, breath, heat. It takes a moment before I realize the doorbell has rung. Not once. Twice.

He kisses me again, more passionately. The doorbell rings again.

"You know we have to get that," I say.

"I beg to differ."

He pulls my hair back to blow on my neck.

"Oh, god … maybe you're right," I gasp.

My cell phone rings. I look at the caller ID as Gavin nibbles at my earlobe. "It's your brother."

"The petulant one who just ditched us at the café? Not interested."

There is banging on the door. "Ava, I know you're in there," Jared yells from outside.

"It's a bluff," Gavin says. "We could go back to bed."

"Tempting. But not the right thing to do."

"Doing the right thing is overrated."

My phone dings with a text from Jared.

"He says he knows where your hideaway key is."

"Damn that key."

"Gavin. He's coming in."

Gavin laughs as I fix my hair.

"How do I look?"

"Ravishing."

"Seriously."

"Lipstick's a little smeared."

Before I can reach for my mouth, Gavin swipes his thumb across my lower lip, slow like he's got all the time in the world.

His eyes flick to mine. Dark. Amused. Possessive.

"There," he murmurs. "I prefer it smeared. But I'll be civilized."

The doorknob turns. We hear Jared letting himself in.

Gavin snatches a pen and a Post-it and writes on it.

"What are you doing?" I ask.

He holds up the Post-it so that I can see what he has scribbled: **Note to self: Change the locks.**

He sticks it to the wall, front and center, and impossible to miss.

I plant a quick kiss on his lips. "Thank you for being patient."

"Just make sure he's out in less than an hour."

I'm relieved to see Jared and a little bit satisfied that he looks embarrassed. Not that I was an angel, but still.

Jared opens with, "Can we talk?" The question is directed at me more than Gavin.

I nod. We've never stewed over anything when we were in a relationship, and I'd love to keep that up in our friendship.

We sit down in the living room, each of us on one side of Gavin's

L-shaped sofa. I pull a pillow onto my lap for comfort. Gavin, I notice, is keeping his distance, sitting in an armchair off to the side.

"You tell me everything, Ava. How could you keep this from me?"

"You kept things from me, too. The fact is, the rules have changed fast. Maybe faster than we were ready for—because we both know this is not about John."

Jared nods, softening.

"When I told you about John, I felt judged. And part of me—the selfish part—was jealous that your bond with Gavin might be stronger than ours was. I hadn't fully let you go."

"It doesn't mean anything that I didn't tell you about Gavin. We've only been together for a day. And, it's all your fault anyway. I thought he was a stuck-up jerk."

"Hey! Still here." We both laugh, but Gavin doesn't.

"Don't worry," I assure him. "I don't think that anymore."

"Thanks, I guess."

I turn back to Jared. "You know what Leonard Cohen does to me."

He laughs. Then, together, we both say, "I'm sorry."

"I don't know what came over me," Jared adds. "I was defensive, and I was judgmental."

"No, I was those things, and—"

Jared puts his hand up to stop me. "Wait. You don't have to apologize. I know you were looking out for me. Both of you have always been the most important people in my world. The two people I could count on when times were tough. Gavin, you showed me how to ride a bike and be a man. Ava, you showed me how to be a friend and a romantic partner. It would be a stroke of good fortune if you two found each other.

Have Gavin and I "found each other"?

"But I didn't come out just to be out," Jared says. "It's always been about love. You were the only woman I could love. John's the only man. Why waste time looking for someone else when I already know I've found the person I want to be with for the rest of my life? I want both of you to be at our sides when we marry. Ava, will you be my maid of honor? Gavin, my best man? It would mean everything."

I DROP GAVIN at the ferry terminal for the night's last boat to the mainland, both of us still buzzed on good wine and the relief of having made peace with Jared.

"Dinner was great, wasn't it?" I ask, knowing he was as relieved as I was to mend things with Jared.

"Yes, dinner was good, but it was missing a much-needed side of sex."

Gavin tucks a strand of hair behind my ear, then tilts my chin up for one last kiss—slow, greedy, like he's memorizing the shape of my mouth.

When he pulls back, he's still close enough to whisper: "Until further notice, you're my only one-night stand."

I smile. "And I fully intend to ruin that stat."

As he boards the ferry, I stay behind, pulse thrumming, lips tingling, heart cracked open in the best possible way.

CHAPTER 36

Hungry Love

THE GARDEN LOOKS even more cinematic than before, with pots of rosemary now flanking the walkway and stakes of soft landscape lights winding their way along the path and through the citrus trees like fireflies in formation. Next to the l'orangerie door, more herbs, a pile of much-needed gravel, and bags of bark have been delivered since I was last here.

Kiki stands in the middle of the l'orangerie, hands on her hips, assessing the light, the layout, the vaguely magical scent in the air. "Okay, I know this isn't technically our place," she says, "but we're absolutely claiming credit for the vibe."

I set a crate of mismatched dishes on the table—vintage plates, chipped mugs, someone's old porcelain swan—all rescued from the Exchange, a place built by islanders to leave what they don't need and take only what they love. It's part thrift store, part magic trick. The only rule is: pay what you can.

"And here I thought the vibe came from Isabel and Batu adding these lights, and hauling in a literal ton of gravel, rosemary, and bark."

Kiki lifts a brow. "Isabel and Batu didn't do any of that."

I pause mid-unpack. "What?"

"They left town two days ago. They're in Port Townsend visiting Batu's sister."

I blink at her. Slowly. Like an idiot. Because of course.

It was Gavin.

Kiki watches my face for all of three seconds before smirking. "You didn't know it was him."

"I—no."

She crosses the room, opens the tall windows until the breeze lifts the hem of her dress and sends the lilac swaying. "You're so doomed."

"Oh, am I?"

"Yeah. You've got post-sex soul haze."

I look up from my stack of plates. "The *what* now?"

"You're looking at everything like you're in a romance directed by Sofia Coppola. Smeary light. Long silences. Existential yearning. Full-blown moodboard vibes."

"Am not."

Kiki gives me a long, appraising look as we both take a seat. "Did you do it in here?"

I nearly drop a plate. "What? No!"

"His living room?"

"No!"

"The porch swing?"

"Jesus, Kiki."

"Come on, give me *one* room to cross off my fantasy list."

I bite my lip to hide the smile. "Fine. The kitchen. Well, we started there at least."

Kiki throws her hands in the air. "*Yes.* That tracks. Messy. Close to snacks. A room you know your way around."

I shake my head, laughing as I pull out linen napkins. "We are not talking about this."

"We are absolutely talking about this. You had kitchen sex with Gavin Jones. Your boss and former nemesis. The man with the midnight blue suit that makes him look like Mr. Darcy if Mr. Darcy had a turntable, a wine cellar, and opinions about first pressings."

"It was a great suit."

"It was. But apparently not as great as what's *under* the suit."

I toss a napkin at her. She catches it one-handed.

"Anyway," I say. "We're here to talk about *Marisol's party.* Not my sudden descent into cliché."

"Right," Kiki says, sobering as she pulls out her tablet. "Is the menu confirmed?"

I nod. "She wants Coastal Mediterranean–inspired. Seasonal, something elegant but rustic."

"So basically: she wants to feel like Anne Hathaway fell in love with a local while making tapas on a TikTok-viral island. White Lotus vibes minus the dead body."

"Exactly," I laugh. "We've got the figs. We've got the saffron. Isabel's on the bread. I have the Ladies Hunting Club on speed dial if the meat doesn't get delivered. The only possible wrench in our plan is that she's requested we add a short set of live music."

"What about Nico's local musician friends—Pedro or Madison West? Maybe they can play a set together. And for dessert—"

"I was thinking a galette with plums from West Beach Farm."

We fall into the rhythm of the planning. It's easy, collaborative, full of our usual shorthand and spiraling daydreams. But somewhere between the handwritten menus and floral mockups forwarded by Patricia, Kiki goes quiet.

She's fidgeting with her bracelet.

"You okay?" I ask.

She looks up at me, then exhales. "I haven't told you the big news yet."

"Oh no. You're moving to Hawaii with the goat wrangler."

"No," she says, laughing. Then: "My GoFundMe got fully funded."

"*What?*"

"An anonymous donor gave half the ask in one donation. Just like that. I'm freezing my ovaries, Ava."

I launch myself at her, squealing and hugging, nearly knocking over a bottle of wine. She laughs into my shoulder, her body shaking.

But when we pull apart, I'm frowning.

"What?" she asks.

"Do you know who the donor was?"

"Nope. But I have a guess."

I stare at her.

"I think it was Gavin."

I go still. "Why would he—?"

"Because he *listens.* Because he gives a damn. Because that man looks at you like he wants to build a world around you and then make room in it for your best friend."

"Well, shit."

My phone buzzes on the table between us.

Kiki's eyes flick down, then back up to mine.

I don't even have to look. I already know.

GAVIN

> New York's louder and faster after a summer on the island. And not the same without you. Let me know if you need anything else for the event.

Something warm and unsteady spreads through my chest.

Kiki grins. "And there it is."

"Don't," I say weakly.

"I didn't say anything."

"You didn't have to. Your face wrote a whole press release."

Later, we sip rhubarb spritzes under the ginkgo tree.

"You know," Kiki says, "people are starting to talk."

"About what?"

"About us. About the dinners. A woman named Liberté asked if we'd consider catering a dinner next spring for KIXP radio. Katie from the Outlook Inn asked if we'd be open to doing all the pre-wedding events for their couples."

My heart stutters. "Seriously?"

"Seriously. Which is why," she says carefully, "I think we should name this thing."

"Oh god."

"Two words."

"I don't know. That feels *not* temporary."

"Hungry Love."

I open my mouth to argue—and then don't.

"Okay," I say. "I kinda love it."

Kiki beams. "I knew you would."

We head to the café kitchen, glasses in hand, the rosemary brushing our legs on the path Gavin lit without telling anyone.

My phone buzzes again.

GAVIN

Also ... last night? Yeah. Still thinking about it.

I smile despite myself.

Kiki doesn't miss it.

"Oh," she says. "You are so gone."

I laugh, watching the sea breeze move through the garden, catching on the ginkgo's leaves, making them look iridescent.

"Do you think you could stay here?" she asks. "Build a life?"

I watch overhead lights flicker on one by one, feel the garden holding its breath.

"I don't know," I say honestly. "But I don't think I could do it without you."

She bumps my shoulder. "Good. Because I could definitely get used to living on a beautiful remote island with produce so sexy it deserves its own OnlyFans."

CHAPTER 37

Soft Launch

THE FIRST HUNGRY Love video goes viral while I'm waiting on the dock at Rosario Marina.

It's a ten-second reel Kiki filmed of me spooning whipped chèvre onto a wood-fired flatbread, then topping it with halved figs, charred at their edges and sweet in the middle. She added an original guitar riff by Mandy Troxel and stitched it with a clip of the ginkgo leaves fluttering above the l'orangerie.

I didn't even know she'd posted it.

The clip of the figs—bursting and caramelized against the charred flatbread—fades into sunlight streaming through a hops vine, and the internet collectively loses its mind.

Now it has 140K likes and a comment section full of: *Where is this?! Taking my honeymoon here. This is what my heart wants. Looks like a cure for Divorce Blues! What happens when you put a female chef on a remote island, with a camera, and aesthetic autonomy.*

The second video Kiki posts doesn't even feature me; just a slow pan across the garden, then Eastsound Bay, then a crate of sun-warmed Shiro plums from Susol Orchard. By lunch, people are DMing us asking if we host retreats and weddings.

The third is of me again. Specifically, me with flour on my cheek, plating practice plum galettes, laughing at something Kiki said off camera. I didn't know I could look like that. Like someone whose happiness is tethered to a place where she can finally stay.

They say the island knows who to keep and who to spit back.

A few months ago, I stepped off a seaplane here at Rosario with a rolling suitcase and a grudge. I didn't know a single person. Not even Gavin really.

Now I'm leaning against his car, wind tugging at the hem of my dress, waiting for him to come home.

The seaplane skims in low over the water, floats hissing against the surface. The same sound that startled me on that first day. Now it's the sound of belonging.

Brett—the crab guy from the dock—hoists a trap up beside me. We graduated to first names last month, but today he calls me "Chef," and I don't correct him.

The pilot, Derek, steps out first. He spots me walking down the dock and grins.

"Still here, huh?"

I shrug. "Still temporary."

His grin widens. "That's what they all say."

When Gavin steps off the plane, his eyes find me instantly.

His leather weekender is slung over one shoulder. His boots are salt-smudged. His hair is mussed from wind and travel.

He slows when he sees me. Not surprised. Just certain.

"Miss me?" he asks, his hands going to my waist the second he's close enough.

"Only in a completely normal, emotionally well-regulated wa—"

He kisses me before I can finish the sentence. Deep and hungry, right there on the dock, like he's making up for every minute he was away.

In the car, he drives with one hand on the wheel and the other over mine.

I glance down at our joined hands, his thumb brushing slowly across mine.

"Weird. Same car," I murmur, thinking back to when he picked me up all those months ago.

"Same girl?" he asks, not quite teasing.

I smile out the window. "Not exactly."

He grins as the road curves beneath us. "That first day, you looked like you were already planning your escape."

"I was."

"And now?"

I roll the window down. The scent of kelp and cedar spills in—sharp, green, unmistakably island.

"Now it's hard to imagine leaving."

He pulls onto the road, sunlight striping across the windshield.

"Then don't."

WE MAKE IT to the garden just before golden hour.

"I wanted to show you something," I say, pulling him through the gate.

The lilac is in full bloom now, lush with perfume, vines curling like ribbon around the archway to the l'orangerie.

As we push open the doors, the scent rises around us, warm, sweet, intoxicating. Inside, the light is soft and low, filtered through citrus leaves and glass. The gravel has been raked. A new antique velvet table runner runs the length of the table.

The rosemary is blooming at the edges, tiny pale blue flowers curling open at the tips, like even it is drunk on the heat.

I glance around the l'orangerie, and all the magic a group of women can make when no one tells them no.

"It's kind of unbelievable that this all came together," I say.

Gavin smiles, slow and easy. "It came together because you did."

I shake my head. "I know you helped more than I realized. I couldn't do this alone."

He steps closer, voice low.

"You didn't have to. People rearrange around you, Ava. That's what you do. You walk in, and somehow everyone wants to make room for you."

His words land somewhere between my ribs. I don't say anything. Instead, I press my hand to his chest and walk him backward until he hits the edge of the table. His hands are already on me, pulling me in.

I let him kiss me like he's been waiting since takeoff. His hands slip beneath my dress, dragging it up with a reverence that makes my pulse stutter. I reach for his belt as the garden hums outside, heat curling low in my stomach. We crash onto the table, mismatched plates rattling like they're applauding. It's desperate, breathless, and so stupidly good I could cry.

Later, we lie tangled on the cool tile floor, warm skin against stone, the scent of lilac drifting through the open window.

I think about what it would mean to let this be real. To stop preparing for disappointment as if it were the forecast.

Gavin traces a line along my shoulder. "You ever think about what this could be?"

I keep my eyes on the ceiling. "You mean like a business?"

He's quiet a beat. Then: "Sure. That too."

It's the closest he's come to saying it, to revealing he wants more.

And I don't answer. Because I know what I'd want to say: *I want this. You. The garden in bloom. The dirt under my nails. The insane ferry schedule. The slow mornings, the sea planes and the way you look at me like we've already made it and you're just waiting for me to believe it.*

But I've trained myself to expect the fall.

So instead, I kiss him, softly at first, then deeper, and pretend I didn't hear the question.

Because when things are this good, the fall feels inevitable.

CHAPTER 38

Partly Cloudy with a Chance of Something Beautiful

THE RAIN STARTS before breakfast, soft and spiteful, the kind that doesn't soak so much as seep, like it's trying to convince you to give up.

Gavin's on a last-minute trip to Vancouver, which means I've been able to focus on wrangling Marisol's party. And by "party," I mean "potentially rained-out disaster with a grazing table."

"It's fine," Kiki says, arms crossed, as we stare out at the half-assembled stage. "Maybe the rain is the vibe."

"We don't have a tent," I remind her.

"Yet."

Patricia materializes beside us in patterned rain boots, holding two steaming mugs like a woodland apothecary who moonlights as a floral stylist. She hands one to me with a serene smile.

I take a sip and immediately regret it. "What is this?"

"Rose hip and nettle," she says. "Immunity in a cup. We can't have anyone getting sick."

"Tastes like boiled socks."

"That's the nettle." She grins, then flips open her clipboard. "Slight update. Marisol texted. Jamila Robinson, editor of *Bon Appétit*, is coming, and Padma Lakshmi's team has confirmed. Padma's bringing a producer from HBO Max, possibly scouting.

"Scouting... what?"

"Something about a show featuring female chefs in remote locations. And—" she glances up— "Kris Tompkins might boat over."

"The *actual* Kris Tompkins?" I ask. "Conservationist, founding CEO of Patagonia, saver of rain forests?"

Patricia nods. "Apparently, she loves it when chefs use native ingredients. Just don't say 'foraged' too many times."

Kiki groans. "Our dinner party just turned into a tasting menu for the planet's coolest women."

"And about seventy-five guests total," Patricia adds. "Half of them booked a float plane."

Kiki groans. "Which means we need more shuttles."

I take a long breath. *Okay.*

The prep list is already a novel. I still have to finalize the new courses due to ingredient availability, harvest the last of the squash blossoms, preserve the rose petals for the dessert, and somehow transform the garden into an outdoor dining room with enough seating and shelter to look as if we planned it that way.

"Let's add 'sourcing tarps' to the list," I say. "And ask Veronica at Orcas Rentals if she's got dance floor ideas that won't become Slip 'N Slides if it rains."

"Done," Kiki replies, already texting.

I walk back to the garden with Patricia, who's humming under her breath. The herbs are soaked, the greens drooping like they know something we don't. We pick around the edges, gathering nasturtiums, mint, and baby arugula.

"What if I screw this up?" I ask her quietly.

"You won't."

"But what if I do?"

She stops beside the rain-slicked path. "It'll still be beautiful. Because your heart is in it."

I stare at her, momentarily undone.

Then I do what I always do when emotions creep up where they don't belong: I get back to work.

I tug my hood over my head and start harvesting. At least the mint is still perky, even in the rain. The butter lettuce may be too tender. Thank God the Garden Club advised me to plant hearty Kale. There's sorrel, calendula, and baby beets. If I can coax enough flavor out of this garden in 48 hours, we might just pull it off.

Inside the kitchen, other helpers—people I barely knew a month ago—are peeling carrots, chopping onions, and debating whether the vegan appetizer should be a mini tart or a canapé.

This is happening. It's real.

I glance at my phone to check the time just as it pings and a text from Gavin arrives.

> GAVIN
>
> You sure you don't want me to fly back early to help?

I hover over the keyboard.

Then I lock my phone and slide it into my pocket.

I want him to see it when it's done. When it's glowing, and messy, and mine.

For now, I'm not the girl waiting for the guy.

I'm the one setting the table.

CHAPTER 39

Into Her Arms

I NEVER EXPECTED my life to take another 180—this time in a garden full of strangers on a remote island in the Pacific Northwest—but here we are.

Marisol's friends are a wild, wonderful bunch. One minute, I'm deep in conversation with Miranda Otto, Nicholas Galitzine, and Bradley James—all somehow even cooler in person than on screen. Five minutes later, I'm wedged between Ali Hazelwood and Abby Jimenez, holding my own in a hilarious debate about fictional boyfriends. Next, Marisol is introducing me to Samuel W. Gailey, whose feminist backlist once launched me into a full-blown BookTok spiral.

If I hadn't just fallen head over heels for Gavin (a fact I still can't say out loud without wanting to both cry and twirl), I'd be sorely tempted. Samuel is disarmingly handsome in a literary, brooding-but-kind-of-knows-it way. Think rumpled vintage blazer, black jeans, combat boots, and the kind of glasses that say *I read French philosophy but also appreciate a good IPA*.

I fangirl a little over his latest book, *Come Away from Her*, and he hands me his card and says I should call him for lunch so he can tell me, "all the real secrets."

The party hums around me. Flowers hang artfully from the string of lights, and I catch a glimpse of the food table. Nasturtium-infused pidés topped with smoked eggplant, figs, and prosciutto are a full-blown hit. The editor from *Bon Appétit* is licking her fingers without a shred of shame, and Padma and her crew are going back in for thirds. I take that as permission to breathe.

The Dungeness crab salad is my favorite thing on the menu, not because it's the prettiest—though it is, all pale microgreens, paper-thin daikon, and avocado fanned just so—but because it belongs to this place. Tide to table in the truest sense. I caught the crab myself, out on a boat with Brett at sunrise, hauling cages up from eighty feet of cold Pacific water. My arms were shaking. My shirt was soaked. But the payoff was this: sweet, clean meat, barely dressed, with just a drizzle of orange-miso-sesame aioli to let it shine. The effect was unexpected umami.

There's something heady about feeding people this way, about knowing exactly where your food came from. The land. The sea. Me.

Marisol floats by in sapphire satin, every inch the woman who just scorched the earth of her past and made it look effortless. She pauses beside me, eyes sweeping the table.

"This," she says, "is proof you'd make an amazing editor at *Pulse* if you ever want to come back."

Her words land lightly—like an invitation—but I feel the weight of them. A few months ago, I would have reached for that offer like a lifeline.

Now?

I smile. "Thank you."

It's not a no.

But it's not a yes either.

Across the garden, I spot Liam under the ginkgo tree, alone with a drink, and wander over.

"Ava, it's been too long."

"I was just thinking the same thing."

"What's going on with you, besides throwing this spectacular party with my beautiful wife?"

I'm about to go with small talk when I see him. Gavin.

The air leaves my lungs. His tie is loosened, jacket slung over his shoulder, sleeves rolled. He looks like he walked out of a movie where he saved the world at the exact right moment. I didn't think he'd make it tonight. Not with two delayed flights.

He's scanning the crowd, and then he finds me. That grin, the one that makes my knees unsteady, spreads across his face.

"I'm in love with your son, Liam."

"Oh, sweetheart. I know it's been rough, but you've got to get over Jared."

"Not that son, Liam."

Liam looks to me, then to Gavin, whose gaze is riveted on me.

"I suppose that's why I had *two* sons." He puts his arm around my shoulder and squeezes me affectionately. "To make sure you got into this family one way or another."

Patricia approaches. "It's a great turnout, isn't it?" she says. "I think we'll get more work from this than we can handle." She turns to Liam. "Maybe we can move out here earlier than we planned."

"Sweetheart, Ava just informed me she's in love with our Gavin."

"Yes, I know she is dear."

"You mean I'm the last to know?"

"I never told Patricia," I say. "I haven't even told Gavin. I only just figured it out."

Patricia cups my face and kisses my forehead.

"So, do you two think I should tell him?" I ask.

They answer in stereo: "Definitely."

Gavin walks up just then. "Mom. Dad. Why do you look like the cat that swallowed the canary?"

Liam pats his back. "Good to see you, son."

"Hello, honey. Gotta go check on Isabel."

They both make their exit far too casually. As if this isn't the moment everything may tilt. Like I'm not standing on the edge of something irreversible.

Gavin turns to me. And everything else—conversation, music, ambient hum—fades. I want to touch him, but I restrain myself. He hates PDA; he used to roll his eyes when Jared kissed me in public. *But now?* He doesn't hesitate. One second, I'm standing there, stunned stupid by the sight of him, and the next his hands are in my hair, and his mouth is on mine. It's not a chaste, hey-good-to-see-you kiss. It's a remember-this, rewrite-everything kiss. The kind that short-circuits thought and rewires memory. I forget the garden, the guest list, my own name. When he pulls back, just slightly, I forget to breathe until he presses his forehead to mine.

"Okay," he says, voice low, a little hoarse. "Parents were being a little weird."

I laugh. "You made it."

Before I can assemble words, Kiki storms over, headset askew, eyes wide. "Please tell me the singer showed."

"No singer," I say, keeping my voice even.

"Marisol wanted *live* vibes. At least a five-song set, thirty minutes.

This is bad," Kiki says. "This is her redemption party, Ava. Her 'I divorced the sockless fraud and now I'm thriving' comeback."

"Remote island thing. No plan B," I shrug.

Kiki blinks, then actually sags, as if the air goes out of her. "But the editors of *Goop* and *Poosh* are here, judging us."

Gavin doesn't say a word. He absorbs it. His gaze skims the garden: the small stage we rigged for ambiance, the mic, the guitar case. Then he leaves us.

Kiki frowns. "Wait. Why is Gavin walking onto the stage?"

I do my best innocent shrug. "Maybe he's trying to help?"

She narrows her eyes. "You're smiling."

"I always smile in a crisis," I reply.

"No, you look like you're about to get away with something."

I flash her a grin. A grin that once got me out of calculus and into an advanced French pastry class.

Onstage, Gavin pulls the guitar out, recognition flashing across his face, then a tilt at the corner of his mouth, the kind of private expression a person has when they open a drawer and find a memory inside.

He looks for me. Finds me. The look he gives is not a smile so much as a secret—warm, complicit, a soft *I see you* from across the garden.

He strums one note. Then another. The hush comes slowly. First, the people closest to him, then a ripple across the crowd. By the time he starts to play, every head is turned toward him.

He sings *Poison Cup* by M. Ward. Slower, stripped. Tender. The audience bends toward him like flowers to the sun.

By the second song, *True Love Will Find You in the End,* people are swaying. Servers stop mid-step. Someone near the firepit whispers, "Is this guy famous?"

Tara says, "He should do this professionally."

I don't say anything. But I think: He did. Once.

He doesn't say anything between songs. He just plays. Two originals, raw and gorgeous. Then *Into My Arms* by Nick Cave.

He sings about leaving someone untouched. About loving her as-is. About only asking the universe for one selfish thing: to direct her into his arms.

It's the kind of song—and he's the kind of performer—that grips your ribs from the inside.

This is where he belongs.

Not because the crowd is rapt, but because his whole body settles into the shape of music—shoulders loose, hands sure, breath steady. He gave this up once. For Patricia. For the family. For certainty. And here he is again, coming back to himself in front of almost a hundred people and me.

More reactions bloom around me.

Kiki has one hand on her headset and the other over her mouth, eyes glossy and disbelieving. She doesn't even pretend to manage anymore; she just listens.

"This," Marisol whispers, "is what a second act sounds like."

Patricia presses her fingertips to her lips, not bothering to hide the happy tears. Liam stands tall beside her, pride so evident in the set of his shoulders you could hang a coat on it.

And me? My chest is a fuse. I feel the rightness of it like heat. I'm not just in love with him; I'm in love with this new version of him. The one who didn't vanish when life got complicated. The one who could still be recovered.

Olivia arrives on the last verse.

She slips in at the far edge of the lawn, all smooth silk and sharpened cheekbones, and stops dead. Her eyes track the line from

Gavin on stage to me and back again, reading the air like a lawyer reviewing evidence.

She would be a fool not to feel it—the current running between us. It's not a look you can dismiss. It's a frequency.

Gavin holds the song's final note. Silence lands. Then the applause rises fast, full-bodied, and I can see he's a little stunned.

He sets the guitar—*his* guitar—back in its case, and for a beat, he doesn't move, letting the sound wash over him. Then he finds me in the crowd again, and things new and old pass between us: recognition, gratitude, want.

Under the soft spin of a Miel song, he meets me on the dance floor. He doesn't make a show of it. He just offers his hand, and I take it, and we sway in our small circle.

His chest brushes mine, familiar and electrifying. He smells like cedar and some cologne I now associate exclusively with orgasms. I notice his tie—the lavender one. It's knotted casually at his throat now, but I can feel it like a phantom touch. A reminder of everything his hands have done to me.

His mouth is near my temple as he whispers: "There never was another singer, was there?"

I tip my head up at him, a sheepish smile giving me away. "I didn't lie," I say. "Technically."

A quiet laugh, close enough that I feel it. His thumb sketches a half-moon across my wrist.

"Mad?" I ask, barely above the music.

"Not even close." He breathes out. "That's the best I've felt in a long time."

He doesn't explain the rest, but he doesn't have to.

"I have something I have to tell you," I say.

He stops dancing. I don't need to look behind me to know that Olivia has approached.

"Gavin, I need to talk," she says.

"Now isn't the time."

"You haven't answered my calls. We are still officially engaged." Her words do not seem to be moving him in the slightest. She tries a different tactic. "If we're going to end things, I should at least get a chance to explain my side."

"We were supposed to be on the *same* side."

"If you'd let me finish… I want to say that *I'm sorry*. It was a stupid mistake. We've been together for three years, Gavin. Don't I at least get to say goodbye?"

Gavin turns to me. "Ava, do you mind if I speak to Olivia alone for a minute?"

I absolutely mind. A lot of things can happen in a minute. Every minute, there are 250 babies born. In one minute, lightning strikes the Earth 6,000 times. Oprah makes $523 in one minute. But I smile. "Of course not. I'll check on the staff."

I stand in a place where they cannot see me. They are in *my* garden in a dark corner, away from the throngs of people, heads huddled in intimate discussion. Olivia seems to be humbling herself. Gavin has his arms crossed, keeping his distance. Olivia's head drops on her chest. *She's pulling out the crying card. Of course, she's nowhere near me on the crying spectrum. No shoulder-shrugging-snot-dripping-swollen-eye-crying* for her. No, of course, she looks ethereal when she cries. Like a sad angel sent from Heaven to grace us mere mortals with her presence. Gavin uncrosses his arms and puts his hands on Olivia's shoulders. *No.* She looks up at him through those insanely thick eyelashes of hers. *No!* He says something, then she nods and leaves. And now Gavin is looking for me. *Me. Not Olivia. Me.*

He finds me beneath the tree again, hands in his pockets like they might keep him grounded.

"Hey." His voice is low. Worn. "Olivia wants to try again. One more chance."

A pause. Then: "I told her I love her. But—"

The word hits me like cold water. Love. Not loved. Not used to love. Love. Present tense.

Of course he loves her. Three years together. Engagement rings. Families. History.

"Let's forget about Olivia. This is your night. What did you want to tell me when we were dancing?"

He says it too easily. Like the word *love* didn't just happen. Like it's something we can step around.

My throat tightens. "Gavin, what are we doing?"

"Ava—"

"What we had ..." I shake my head, and force a shrug. "It was a moment. A good one. But that's all."

His brow furrows. "That's not what it felt like."

The last thing I want is to fall madly in love with another guy who isn't sure what he wants. We may not be talking about something as insurmountable as being on opposite sides of the spectrum of sexual attraction here. Still, we are talking about the spectrum of Olivia; naturally gorgeous, voted "woman men most want to go to bed with," perfectly-mannered, Hampton-bred vs. me, Ava, girl who lacks the accessorizing gene, homeless, soon-to-be unemployed, obsessed with food, cries at the drop of a hat, and has to have guys tie her up the first time they have sex with her just so that she can relax. Of course, he's confused. I wouldn't want to leap into my arms either. I decide I will make this easier on myself. Easier on Gavin.

"Gavin, you said you love her. What you and Olivia had is real.

You sent save-the-date cards for god's sake. What you and I had… well, chalk that up to Leonard Cohen, and rebound sex."

"Is this what you were trying to tell me on the dance floor?"

"Yes," I lie. "The sex didn't mean anything." *It meant everything.* "You were the closest thing I could have to Jared if I couldn't have him."

The words are knives. I know exactly how deep they'll cut.

Part of me wants him to fight for me. If he really loved me, wouldn't he?

"Ava." His voice is ragged now. "What are you doing?"

"Giving you an out. If you and Olivia make sense, don't throw that away for a two-night stand."

"You're not."

"We'll see Gavin. We'll see."

And that's it.

I walk away.

Not because I want to.

But because I don't believe I'm someone worth staying for.

PART THREE

WHEREVER

CHAPTER 40

I've Lost Him but I'm Not Lost

THE MORNING AFTER the party, the sky is already slipping toward grey. Western light—soft, seaworn, a little apologetic—seeps through Gavin's kitchen window and lands on a note, folded over with just an 'A' on the front. I stare at it, afraid to read it and longing to read it at the same time.

When I open it, I'm crushed a little bit more, which should make it easier to let him go, but it doesn't. A single piece of paper. The handwriting is his, but the tone is not.

Gavin: Ava—Take your time moving out. I won't be back for three months—NYC stuff. Make yourself at home until then. —G

It's the kind of message that reads like permission, not goodbye, and that hurts in a new way. It feels like I'm a subletter he barely knows instead of the woman who kissed him like her lungs depended on it, then walked away because she thought it was the right thing to do. There's nothing sentimental here. No clue what he's feeling, except I'm easy enough to let go that it only takes a two-line text.

By late morning, I'm back at the garden.

The air still smells like night-blooming jasmine and burnt sugar. There are champagne corks in the flower beds. Candle stubs leaning sideways in the dirt. The aftermath of Marisol's party is everywhere—but Gavin isn't. I walk the path we danced on. Stand under the same tree where I told him a lie dressed up as logic.

What we had... it was a moment.

I scrub until my knuckles sting and my eyes blur, the ache in my body a welcome distraction from the one in my chest. When Kiki arrives, I tell her everything. She gives me a good hug, then understands that I need to work, to move, to distract. We stack glasses. Re-line the prep tables. Rewire the market lights. Re-pot fallen rosemary bushes. The soil is still thick under my nails, but I feel hollow. Like I packed my heart into one of the catering crates and sent it off to be sterilized.

We've accepted dinner reservations for locals through the next month, which feels like both a tether and a dare. I throw myself into prep. I map out menus. Rotate seasonal ingredients. Start a spreadsheet Kiki will mock for being neurotic and then secretly copy.

It helps. Until it doesn't.

Because when I stop moving, the questions flood back in.

Should I have told him the truth?

Did he believe me when I said he didn't matter?

If I convinced him to walk away in one conversation, how much did he really care?

After the garden has been restored, Kiki and I drink a bottle of Syrah and talk about future options. We could go back to Brooklyn. Marisol made it clear that we are both welcome to return, with promotions and raises. Kiki could keep up with her freelance event jobs. I could scrounge up some remote editing work. We say it like we mean it. Like we're not both looking at the sky here, as if it holds secrets we haven't finished uncovering.

Three days after the party, the press requests start coming in.

A food editor from Portland—*one I've been quietly stalking for years*— calls.

A podcast on relationships wants to talk to us.

Padma wants to feature us on her show.

A woman from New York—the kind of cookbook editor whose authors win James Beard awards and casually thank her in their acknowledgments—emails to ask if I've ever considered writing one.

She mentions the way I plate. The way my menus read like a story. And, most of all, how I seem to understand heartbreak well enough to cook someone out of it.

I reread her email three times.

It would be easier to say yes if I knew where I'd be in three months.

Out of what we say is just curiosity, Kiki and I tour a cottage for rent with a questionable smell. Then, a tiny house with a composting toilet that makes Kiki say she'd rather die. We look at a space above a bait shop that shakes whenever someone closes the cooler. I start to wonder if this whole experience was a beautiful, painful summer fantasy. A fever dream with heirloom fruit.

One morning, I walk the long loop around Mountain Lake. The wind slices through the cedars, cold enough to make my breath visible. Fallen leaves skitter across the path in wet clumps, and the lake looks dark and endless. I walk until my fingers go numb and my thoughts don't. Until I've circled the entire thing and I still don't know what I'm doing here without him.

Then I step back into the garden for a pro bono reception for

HALO—the Hub for Arts & Literature on Orcas, one of those essential island nonprofits that everyone supports in one way or another. This is the kind of community where people sit on boards, bake for fundraisers, and volunteer at beach clean-ups. When they asked if I'd cook for their winter artist showcase, I said yes before thinking too hard. I use the profit from Marisol's event to cover the costs. No budget, no staff. Just me, feeding the island in the way I know how.

They asked for simple comfort food. There are about ten sit-down restaurants on the island, but none that serve Italian, so I go with that. I make the pasta myself—hands floured, dough elastic and golden in the cold morning light. A shredded kale Caesar with lemony white anchovy dressing and buttered sourdough croutons. Pappardelle in a simple cream sauce made with garlic, sun-dried tomatoes, and scallions, dotted with local spot prawns, the color of late-October sunsets. And a centuries-old recipe for the dessert zeppole—tiny, golden, warm—served on a platter with a pot of blackberries I preserved back when everything still felt possible.

A musician named Lilo Sánchez plays an acoustic set in Spanish and English, and a guest named Mary asks if she can sell my flavored olive oil blend at her Orcas Village Store at the ferry landing.

Kiki stops by for the end of it. Through her eyes, I can see how heartbreakingly sweet the reception is. Twenty people, ages 28 to 88, gathered warmly in the l'orangerie.

"If we leave, I'm going to have to grieve aggressively," she says.

I laugh, but something sticks in my throat.

I still don't know if I should stay. But I know I want to.

On a Wednesday, Patricia offers to make me lunch.

"Nothing urgent," she says lightly. "Just a winter morale boost."

We sit in Gavin's dining room with the *96 Words for Love* on the wall next to us. I'm two bites into my croissant abricot from Brown Bear when she slides something across the table. A key. And an envelope.

"I know we agreed to not talk about Gavin, but I think this is a worthy exception," she says, voice soft but steady. "He asked me to give you this."

Inside the envelope is one of the Sanskrit cards. There's also a note.

Ava—Isabel's café and the apartment over it are yours. So is the garden. You made them yours anyway. I just caught up. —G

I look up at Patricia, who meets my gaze calmly.

"He wanted to make sure you had a place," she says. "Not because you needed him. Because you didn't."

"I don't know what he would have said," I say. "I don't know if he left because I asked him to or because he wanted to."

Patricia smiles, a little sadly. "He left because he thought you didn't love him back."

My throat closes. I want to say something—anything—but nothing fits in the space between what he gave me and what I never gave back.

I close my eyes.

There it is.

The fault line. The break I made. The thing I never said.

I should have told him the truth. That when I pushed him away, it wasn't because he didn't matter. It was because he mattered *too* much. That I loved him so much it scared me. That I was lying when I said we didn't matter. That I was only trying to give him an out because I didn't believe I was someone anyone would choose twice.

But I didn't.

Now he's three thousand miles away. And I am sitting here with a key to something that feels like both an ending and a beginning.

Patricia reaches for my hand. "He may not come back the same. But he left something true. That matters too."

I walk back through town alone with the key in my pocket. The village is quiet this time of year; a third of its small shops, with hand-painted signs, are shuttered for the season. Still, a few windows glow warmly behind glass, and I nod to the familiar faces inside. I didn't plan to make a life here. But somehow, piece by piece, I did.

The garden is no longer lush, but it's not entirely dead either.

Most of it has gone to seed or sleep. But there's a kind of beauty in that, too—the way something can be pared back to almost nothing and still insist on being alive.

The wind has teeth now. The winter sky is pearl-grey and swollen with rain, but it hasn't broken. Not yet.

He never said he loved me, but I know I loved him. And I know I'm not sorry. And in the hush before the downpour, maybe, for now, that has to be enough.

CHAPTER 41

This is Where You'll Find Me

THERE'S A KNOCK, then Gavin's front door opens without waiting.

Kiki walks in first, already in full command, hair up, sleeves rolled, jaw set. She's carrying packing tape and a latte the size of a vase. "Okay," she says. "You don't have to say anything. We're doing this."

Behind her is Melissa, with moving blankets and the severe competence of someone who has never once in her life dropped a box labeled FRAGILE. Right behind her is Sara, arms full of Tupperware, produce bags, and moral support. We are apparently doing this as a unit.

"Is this a rescue or an intervention?" I ask.

"Yes," Sara says, and pulls me into a hug that lasts just slightly longer than I would have let it if I wasn't this tired. "We're mad on your behalf, but we'll save that for when you're not still in yesterday's sweatsuit."

"We brought labels," Melissa says, like this is triage. "And snacks. And ibuprofen. Also, Tara's already at the new place."

"She is?"

"She closed the Barnacle for an hour," Kiki says. "She said, and I quote, 'no one relocates after a romantic crisis without a cocktail.' She's breaking in your kitchen."

"My kitchen," I echo, like I'm trying on the shape of the words.

I've decided on six more months. Of the island. The garden. Hungry Love. Which means, for now, I'm saying yes to the apartment from Gavin—for me and Kiki.

We kick into motion, falling into roles without saying a word. Kiki starts boxing up my cookbooks, muttering that I'm not allowed to buy another unless I get rid of two. Melissa breaks down my bar cart like she's deactivating a bomb. Sara wraps the Ayame Bullock bowls I've been collecting in dish towels, sighing over each one like it's a rescued duckling. I go through the pantry, then my room.

I'm weirdly stunned by how much there is to box—my shoes by the door, my spices in his cabinet, my sweater on the chair in his bedroom—like somewhere along the way I stopped "staying here" and actually moved in without noticing.

On the third trip out, we line the cars along the driveway: Gavin's Defender on loan, Melissa's Wagoneer, Sara's sprinter van with the back full of plants. We pull out one after the other, a slow little caravan that looks suspiciously like a funeral procession—if funerals involved bubble wrap and an irresponsible number of throw pillows.

It's only two miles to the apartment, but the drive feels longer, like I've crossed some quiet border between the version of my life where Gavin and I were inevitable and the one where we very much aren't.

The key turns easily in the lock, and I swing open the door. I haven't had the time or the heart to see the apartment before this.

This isn't some so-so extra space. It's beautiful. Way too beautiful.

High ceilings. Light everywhere, most of it natural. Wide-plank floors refinished to the color of honey.

The living space is big, open, and soft. There's a deep, brand-new sofa. A reading chair. Actual rugs. The master bedroom is off to the left with a queen bed, linen duvet, and the window angled so you can see both the water and the garden from where your head would rest on the pillow. The bathroom has a clawfoot copper tub like the one I just left at Gavin's.

It's more than a place to crash. It feels like he built me a landing.

My jaw drops when I see the kitchen. A long window over the sink that frames the ocean like it's art. There are granite countertops, a butcher block island, and open shelving. And he's stocked it. Of course, he got the kitchen linens I was coveting from Material Wit. He always notices the details I don't say out loud. My favorite cookbook—the one that got destroyed in the bacon fire—is already on the counter. And, my mother's pan. I thought I left it in the café kitchen, but he must have moved it here when I wasn't looking. The thought is a fist and a balm at the same time.

"Oh," Sara says softly.

"Yeah," Melissa agrees.

Tara is already in the kitchen, sleeves rolled, shaking something in a steel shaker. The air smells like citrus and gin.

"You're late," she says without turning. "I started without you."

"What are we drinking?" Kiki asks, instantly revived.

"French 75s," Tara says. "Modified. Day appropriate. And I used Girl Meets Dirt pear shrub instead of simple syrup, because we're soothing and fortifying at the same time." She pours pale gold into little coupe glasses she must have brought.

"They're not too sweet," she adds, pouring. "You do not need sweet right now."

Sara sips and groans. "God, I love you."

"And," Tara adds, "Martha brought art."

Martha is there, stepping down from a small ladder in the dining room, to finish the last adjustment on an oil painting that's centered on the main wall. She wipes her hands on her jeans and looks at me. "It brings out the light in this room," she says simply.

It's one of hers. Sea layered into rock, then sky, with softer streaks of pale light underneath like something is surfacing.

My throat does an awful, grateful thing.

She gestures to the big corner window. "It's a reflection, and an abstraction of the view out your window."

I walk to the window.

From up here, I can see Eastsound Bay, restless with whitecaps, a dusting of fresh snow blurring the edges of the tiny island just offshore. A Great Blue Heron stands in the shallows, still and solitary, like he's waiting out the cold because leaving wasn't an option. To my left, the garden. The beds we carved out. The trellises we built. The lavender Kiki and I tucked in after dark with phone flashlights. The irrigation Duke and Batu wrestled into working. The little corner where Isabel swore nothing would grow, and then thyme exploded out of pure spite. My garden. And I am somewhere between the two, unsettled, but staying.

Sara sets another box down on the island and exhales. "This is gorgeous."

"I told you," Kiki says. "Our girl is not moving into some sad interim crash pad. She is ascending."

Kiki walks down the short hall, peeks into the bedroom that will be hers, then turns toward the window. She stares for a moment, like she's surprised to see the garden right there, impossibly close. "I've always dreamed of a commute I could count in footsteps," she says. "Bonus points for edible landscaping."

Melissa rearranges my spices by cuisine. Kiki plugs her charger in her room and leaves a toothbrush in the bathroom like a cat marking territory. Tara writes HYDRATE on a Post-it and slaps it on the fridge. Sara puts lemons in a bowl like a magazine spread. Martha moves the living room rug two inches to the left and says, "There."

Tara hands me a cup. "To first nights," she says.

Sara clinks. "To gorgeous rent-free situations."

Melissa clinks. "To that novelist who was undressing you with his eyes, because we need bench depth."

Kiki clinks. "To my new commute, Hungry Love, and whatever the hell comes next."

By early afternoon, Martha's painting catches golden-hour light, and it looks like someone lives here. It looks like *I* live here.

"Call if you need us," Melissa says as they head out.

"I will," I say, and mean it.

When everyone finally leaves, it's just Kiki and me, for a moment, before she heads to the monthly Ukulele Jam on the interisland ferry.

"Emoji me a raccoon and a wine glass if you need me," she says.

"Deal."

She hugs me and goes.

The apartment goes quiet. Not empty. Quiet.

For a second, I can't breathe. Because it hits me all at once: I've built this. With help. With love. With mine-ness. I'm not just the girl who followed a man here and then lost him. I've taken root.

CHAPTER 42

Ramen Remembrances

WHEN YOU LIVE on a rural island in the Pacific Northwest, winter teaches you how to be still. More than half the restaurants shutter for the season, the ferries run late or not at all, and the dark comes early, slinking in by four o'clock. There are no malls, no chain stores, and nothing stays open very late.

I've had to cancel three Hungry Love dinners due to ferry crew shortages. The weather's been brutal, and sourcing ingredients on the island this time of year is like playing Iron Chef with one arm tied behind your back and a three-item mystery basket you didn't choose.

Kiki is off island for a week, which means the apartment is quieter than usual. Without her soundtrack of movement and color, I do everything I can to distract myself from the silence. From the space he left behind.

I joined the local Romance Book Club because I want to believe in love again.

I joined the Somber Sisters Book Club because I suspect it might be hopeless.

And when I finish our club picks, I cross the street to the bookstore, craving espresso and something less tangible. Maybe distraction. Maybe company. Maybe a room where my chest doesn't echo back everything I'm trying not to think about.

OUTSIDE, THE WORLD is fog and rain; in here, it's paper and warmth. Darvill's is the only shop open seven days a week, even in the off-season, because as Sara says, "Everyone deserves somewhere warm to duck into when the rain won't stop."

The staff has become like family over the last few months.

Ashley, tall and wry with a resting-bookworm face, lights up when I talk romance books with her. She figured out my weak spot for Mhairi McFarlane. Becky's my go-to when I'm chasing literary fiction that bruises. Kelly, with her legendary cackle, knows which cookbook to hand me when I'm spiraling.

And Gray—gentle, soft-spoken, razor-sharp—always finds the most surprising titles. She's mixed Asian-Latino-Scottish like me, and though we haven't talked much about that, there's something grounding in just seeing her. She's studying publishing at Emerson and comes back to the island during breaks to work at the bookstore. Her taste is precise and expansive—Ocean Vuong, Kazuo Ishiguro, Sally Rooney—and she never recommends something that won't make me feel deeply.

Elaine's got me covered for soul-nourishing nonfiction—the kind that makes you believe people can change, even when you can't.

Ocean, her four-year-old daughter—quiet, wide-eyed, always in mismatched socks—lives in the kids' section. She curls up in the window nook like a little forest nymph, reading under a string of paper lanterns as seals and seabirds and the occasional orca drift by in the Salish Sea just beyond the shoreline.

Today, Sara seems to read something in my expression, like an aura she knows how to translate. She hands me *Meet Me Tonight in Atlantic City* by Jane Wong. I devour it in a night. I laugh into my sleeve, cry into my pillow, and wince at the chapter where a white boyfriend infantilizes and fetishizes her.

The next morning, I return to Darvill's Bookstore, wrecked, mascara-smudged, and starving for more.

Elaine slides *Crying in H Mart* by Michelle Zauner across the counter, like she's setting down a bell I've been avoiding ringing, but maybe that's the point.

Gray recommends *Feeding Ghosts: A Graphic Memoir* by Tessa Hulls, about Chinese mothers, inherited silence, and the things families pass down without meaning to. It just won a Pulitzer, and the editor, Daphne, lives on Orcas, which everyone treats like proof that the island holds literary magic.

I leave with my arms full and something knotted tight in my chest.

Back at the apartment, I light the fireplace and curl up with a blanket and start to read. But my brain won't stay still.

I bought the books for distraction. What I got was a reckoning and the realization that no one ever let me mourn.

When Mom and Dad died, there was no memorial. Instead, there were social services, foster interviews, and bouncing from one school to another. We had been new to town, and Mom and Dad hadn't made friends yet. We were a self-contained universe, just the three of us who didn't need much more. And when that universe broke apart, there was no one left to remember them with me.

Now, the grief is loud. It has edges. It's not just the persistent ache of absence I've known all these years, but the sudden need for a mother I can't call. A mother who could hold me through this kind of loss—two heartbreaks in less than a year.

Not the loss of men who mistreated me or ignored me. No, they were the kind of men who treated me like a queen. Who gave everything they had. Until they didn't.

It's not lost on me that all the books I've clung to lately are by Asian authors, with food and their mothers prominently featured. I didn't have a fraught relationship with my mom like Michelle Zauner, but the question she asks—"Am I even Korean if my mother doesn't exist?"—lands like a sucker punch.

I'm half Japanese. *But now that Mom's gone, what does that make me?*

I don't have an answer. Grief and identity are braided so tightly that I can't untangle one from the other. So, I head to the kitchen.

I cook like I'm trying to conjure her.

Not the easy weeknight ramen I've made on autopilot for years.

The real ramen.

The kind of ramen my mom used to make, every winter, with religious dedication. The two-day, bone-boiling, noodle-making, soul-excavating kind.

I start by buying pork bones from Lum Farm. Boil them down into a cloudy, rich broth over twelve hours, skimming and stirring until the whole apartment smells like salt and marrow. I make noodles from scratch, adding baking soda to give them bounce, running the dough through the pasta machine in rhythmic turns until my shoulders ache and my mind finally shuts up.

At hour six, I Google "is it normal to feel emotionally manipulated by a stockpot" and the internet is unhelpful, because the internet has never met me or my mother.

I soak wakame. Stir in miso. I make jammy eggs, medium-boiled and marinated in sake, mirin, and soy.

I braise pork belly that I marinated overnight in garlic, sugar, and sake to make chashu, and add it to the broth in strips. Three hours later, the meat melts in my mouth.

The ramen is salty and rich and gloriously umami-deep. A portal and an offering.

And it's mine.

And it's the perfect dish to cry over—because you can blame the steam.

Later, sleep folds around me like silk, and for once, I wake the next day like something has been lifted.

I make garlic somen noodles with homemade chili crisp. Then curry over rice. Tatsuta-age. Soboro-don. Anything that keeps my hands busy.

I don't stop until I collapse.

I don't make any of it to feed anyone else's hunger or heartbreak. Just my own.

And maybe that's what this week was for.

The dinners I had to cancel. The books I wasn't ready for. The food I didn't need to serve. The silence I kept trying to outrun.

It wasn't distraction. It was remembering.

And the remembering—whether I wanted it or not—was a kind of letting go.

CHAPTER 43

Blind Spots

HUNGRY LOVE BEGAN as a way to keep my hands busy so my heart couldn't be. Somewhere along the way, it became real. The calendar is booked solid for months, which feels less like luck and more like a kind of momentum I didn't realize I could build. The nights that sell out fastest aren't the fancy ones. They're the heartbreak dinners—quiet, candlelit, carefully crafted, where every course is designed to carry someone from one version of their life to the next. People don't always say what they're coming for. They don't have to. I can tell by the way they hold their menus—like they're waiting to be told what happens next.

Kiki keeps insisting this means something, that I should let it. But part of me feels like the island is Gavin's, and I'm still learning how to belong to it without him.

Tonight is different, though.

Not because the garden is fuller, or the food more ambitious, but because—for once—no one is here to be healed. No one booked the garden because they were left, or lied to, or loved someone who didn't love them back. Tonight, the story belongs to someone else.

It's Samuel Gailey's book launch party. His publisher wanted New York City; Samuel insisted on here, on the island, in the garden, tucked into the l'orangerie.

He's lived on Orcas for years, long enough that no one calls him 'the writer from LA' anymore, and the baristas at Dragonfly start making his coffee the second he walks through the door. He likes the solitude. Not loneliness—solitude. (I heard him explain the difference once, like it was an argument he'd already won.)

He likes that it takes him exactly thirteen minutes and forty-four seconds to get from his place to town, and that if he leaves at the same time every day, he will inevitably run into Bella walking Risha, or Eava pushing Mona in her wheelchair, or old man O'Connell with his basket of mussels on Crescent Beach like he's been sent out by the ocean on an errand.

Samuel likes being able to count on things. It's one of the many reasons he is dangerously appealing to someone whose life currently feels like a dropped plate—noise, sharp shards, no way to pretend it didn't happen or put it together again.

Tonight, the l'orangerie looks… unreal. String lights hang above the long table like a constellation. Thick handmade candles flicker in hurricane glass. The air smells of salt and herbs, and of something sweet caramelizing in the kitchen.

The guests are a mix of island locals and out-of-towners who keep saying things like, "We just love the way this is curated," which makes me want to both thank them and run into the ocean.

Samuel is supposed to arrive at seven, and he does—not a second later—which is either a sign of good character or proof he is OCD.

He's dressed simply: dark jeans, navy sweater, coat slung over one shoulder like he's trying not to look like the guest of honor. Which is, of course, exactly how the guest of honor looks when he'd rather be literally anywhere else than the center of a room.

He finds me by the kitchen door, eyes scanning the table like he's doing a headcount for anxiety.

"You made it," I say.

"I'm contractually obligated," he murmurs. "Also, I heard there would be food—by you."

"You're the reason there's food."

He winces. "That seems… excessive."

I open my mouth to tease him, but his publicist materializes behind him like she's been summoned by the scent of humility. She's sleek and efficient in a way that makes me suspect she has a color-coded calendar for every emotion Samuel has ever tried not to express.

"Everyone!" she announces, tapping a glass with a spoon. "If I could have your attention."

Samuel's shoulders tighten like he's bracing for impact.

His publicist beams. "We're here tonight to celebrate Samuel's new novel, *Cassandra*, which is already doing incredibly well—" she pauses, savoring it, "—and I am thrilled to announce it has been nominated for the most prestigious prize in literature. Yes, the one that begins with a 'P.'"

The garden goes quiet for half a second and then erupts.

People clap. Someone whoops. Someone else says, "Oh my God," as if Samuel had personally cured a disease.

Samuel, meanwhile, looks like a man who has just realized he's the guest of honor at a party he didn't know he was attending.

He makes a pained face. "There's still time for them to discover they've made an administrative error."

I laugh—loud, delighted—and something in Samuel's expression softens, as if my amusement is the only part of this he trusts.

The dinner goes beautifully. People eat. People drink. People lean across the table to tell strangers their life stories, because apparently that's what happens when you feed them properly.

Samuel does his part: smiling when spoken to, answering questions, looking like he'd rather be subjected to a root canal than talk about himself for more than thirty seconds at a time.

And then, at the end of the night, when the guests drift out, glowing and full …

Samuel stays.

He rolls up his sleeves and starts stacking plates like a man who's been drafted into the army.

I stare at him. "You know you're the guest of honor, right?"

He glances over. "That's why I'm helping. If I don't make myself useful, I'll have to stand around while people tell me the book made them cry and then look at me like I'm responsible for their feelings."

"But that's sort of what you do."

He points a spoon at me. "Don't say that. You make it sound like I have power."

"You do," I say. "You make people feel things they didn't agree to."

"That's your department," he says.

He reaches for a stack of wine glasses, and I suddenly remember washing dishes at this very sink with Gavin. Samuel's sleeve slides back just enough to show a small tattoo near his inner forearm. A dark, clean symbol that looks vaguely like something from *Twin Peaks*. It's the first time I've seen it, and it makes him feel less polished somehow. More rooted. Like there are woods in him. Like there is a past he doesn't advertise.

He catches me looking and clears his throat. "If I didn't know better," he says, "I'd think you were admiring my extremely pretentious tattoo."

"It's... charming," I manage.

"*Oof.* That is *not* what I was going for."

I snort, and he smiles like he's proud of the sound.

We clean together. He doesn't act like it's beneath him. He doesn't act like he's doing me a favor. He just does it.

It's absurd, set against the backdrop of the night—this critically-acclaimed novelist drying forks like a camp counselor—and for some reason, it makes my chest ache.

When we finish, I lean back against the counter.

"Thank you," I say.

"For what?" he asks.

"For... being a person who stays."

His gaze flicks to mine and holds for a beat too long. Then, gently: "Do you want to get coffee tomorrow?"

"Are you asking me on a date?"

He makes a face. "Coffee can't be a date. Coffee is a beverage aware of its own limitations."

"Samuel."

He sighs. "Fine. Yes. I'm asking you on a date. A very low-risk, low-commitment date that can be aborted at any point if you decide you hate me."

"I don't hate you."

"That's how it starts," he says solemnly. "Everyone says that."

THE COFFEE DATE is easy. And then the second coffee date is easier.

He knows where to sit in the Westside Kitchen café to avoid the draft from the door. He knows which pastry sells out first at Olga Rising. He knows who to nod at and who to pretend not to see because they'll trap you in a twenty-minute conversation about a local tax levy. He is exceptionally good at island life. Like he's made a home out of routine and quiet and people who show up.

And I find myself looking forward to him in a way that alarms me. It's not lightning. It's steadiness. It's the kind of attraction that doesn't need drama to feel real.

Tonight is date three, and it's not coffee.

Samuel steers us into the restaurant Houlme. The name suits it. Soft around the edges, deliberate without trying too hard. It glows from the inside out: warm light, woodsmoke, the low murmur of people who don't have anywhere else they need to be.

The door opens on a gust of cold air and a pause, the small room taking inventory. Not suspicion. Just attention.

It's the island in winter: fewer faces, fewer distractions. Everyone knows everyone, and if they don't, they notice.

Paintings by an islander named Indigo line the walls, moody surrealist pieces that tilt the room toward dream. They don't fill space so much as set it.

Behind the bar, Jocelyn—co-owner—looks up. Micro bangs, luminous skin, tattoos climbing her arms. When she spots Samuel, her face shifts into something that's half greeting, half assessment.

"Look what the tide brought in," she says. Then her eyes slide to me. "And you brought a friend."

Samuel's hand rests at the small of my back, light, almost polite, but it sends a ridiculous little shiver up my spine anyway, and I wonder if this is what I need to finally let go of Gavin.

"This is Ava," he says.

"Welcome," she says, and it somehow sounds like a challenge and a gift at the same time.

Chef Jay is visible in the open kitchen, working with the calm focus of someone who has earned seven James Beard nominations but doesn't need to prove anything to anyone. He glances up once—Samuel, then me—and gives a brief nod before returning to the fire.

Jocelyn leads us to a nook in the dim corner, buffered by plants and candlelight, where the world softens at the edges. She sets down a drink menu.

"What are you feeling?" she asks.

"Phony Negroni," I say automatically, because my mouth apparently knows what it wants before my brain does.

Her smile turns quick and private, like I've said the right password. "Good answer."

She disappears toward the bar, not bothering to take Samuel's order—apparently, she already knows what he wants.

Samuel reaches for the water pitcher, then leans closer to pour water into our glasses. Close enough that his shoulder brushes mine, close enough to feel the heat from him. "You come here a lot?" I ask, voice low.

"Enough to have opinions," he says. "And to know to trust the chef."

His gaze drops to my mouth for a beat—brief, unhurried—then lifts again.

Jocelyn returns, sets the drink down in front of me, and I take a sip. Bitter, sweet, bright. Something in my chest loosens.

Jay sends out food without anyone ordering it. A sourdough wood-fired pizza with blistered edges and winter produce arranged like it's been placed by instinct, not instruction. A skewer of grilled carrot coins with yogurt and something sharp and herbal that keeps pulling you back. Then Jocelyn sets down a small plate with two hot dogs, which would be unremarkable anywhere else, except these are not.

The bun is perfectly toasted. The sausage smells like smoke, spice, and umami.

"Is that a frizzled kale chiffonade on top?" I ask because I'm still me.

"Jay's in a mood," Jocelyn says, dry.

Samuel's laugh is quiet, close to my ear. "You're going to like it here," he says, as if he's already certain.

I should tell him not to talk like that. I should not enjoy the certainty of his words. Instead, I pick up the hot dog and take a bite.

I actually make a noise. Out loud. An embarrassing, involuntary moan of pleasure.

Samuel's eyes flick to mine, amused. "That good?"

"I can't talk about it yet," I say, chewing, trying to recover my dignity. "I need a minute to process."

Jocelyn watches me with the faintest smirk, then, like she's remembering something, she retrieves a folded piece of paper from her apron and slides it onto the table toward Samuel.

"For you," she says lightly, and moves away again, leaving the gesture behind like it's nothing.

He doesn't open it right away. He runs a thumb along the crease, as if checking a pulse.

"You get poems?" I ask because I can't help it.

He glances up. Something in him softens, then shutters. "Jocelyn writes," he says. "I read." There's pride under the restraint. And something else: a quiet protectiveness.

He opens the paper and reads once, fast. Then again, slower.

The room goes a little quieter around us, or maybe that's just my attention narrowing.

It moves me more than it should—the idea that this young woman, bold and unmistakably herself, trusts him with her words. With something tender. That he receives it without making a performance of it.

"So *this* is why you come," I say softly.

He folds the poem back along the original line. "It's part of it," he admits.

His hand finds mine under the table. The touch is soft, steady.

I take another sip of my drink because it gives me something to do with my mouth that isn't reckless.

"Still okay?" he asks, quiet enough that it feels like it belongs only to us.

I look at the leftover pizza, the last bite of the ridiculously good hot dog, the poem folded in his hand. Indigo's paintings holding the room in their strange, watchful grip. The warmth, the woodsmoke, the sense that the world has narrowed to this corner table, and the feel of Samuel's hand on mine.

"Yeah," I say, and realize I mean it. "I'm okay."

His mouth curves, not quite a smile, more like satisfaction. "Good," he says. "Because I'm not ready to let you leave yet."

I should make a joke. I should remind him I'm a woman with agency and a bedtime and unresolved problems.

Instead, I hear myself ask, "Is there dessert?"

His eyes shift—quick, assessing—and something bright sparks there. His gaze drops to my mouth again, slower this time. Under the table, his thumb traces small, deliberate circles on my wrist.

Jocelyn reappears as if summoned. "Dessert?" she asks, one brow lifting.

"Whatever Jay feels like," Samuel says.

He turns to me. "Should we take it to go?" His voice is a shade rougher than it was a minute ago.

"Yes," I say too fast. And when his hand tightens, just slightly, it feels less like a question and more like an answer.

Back at his place, a modest beachfront home in the hamlet of Olga, we finish a bottle of wine. Samuel comes up behind me as I stand at the window, watching the waves, and wraps his arms around my waist.

"You always smell so good," he murmurs. "Like vanilla and mint and your garden."

His mouth is so close I can feel his breath on my skin. I guide his hand to my breast, and he exhales a low sound that sends a shiver through me. I tip my head back, and he kisses the place where my neck meets my shoulder.

In his room, I lie back on his bed with the kind of nervous bravery that makes my skin hum. His mouth traces careful paths—down my chest, my stomach—and my body responds, eager and real.

And then my mind does the thing I wish it wouldn't: it goes somewhere else.

Suddenly, I'm remembering Gavin's mouth, Gavin's hands—memory laying itself over the present like a double exposure. I'm still moving, still breathing, but now there's a hitch in it. A split. A feeling I can't quite outrun.

When I hear the sound of him opening the drawer, I finally stop.

"Samuel," I say, pushing myself up on my elbows. "I'm thinking about someone else."

He considers this for half a second. Then, choosing humor as a kindness, he teases: "If it helps, I can think about someone else, too."

"But ..."

"Really," he says. "It's okay, Ava. The last time I did it—months and months ago, mind you—I thought of Alexa Chung."

"The model?"

"Actually," he says, deadpan, "she's a writer now, too."

"Oh, well, then …"

"*Well then*, we can have sex?" he asks, like a man proposing a perfectly reasonable solution.

"No," I say, then immediately ruin it by adding, "I meant: well, then she's good enough for you if she's not just a model without a brain."

He laughs softly, like he can't help it, and kisses me again.

It does feel good.

But Gavin's face pops into my head again like a cruel party trick.

"It's not fair to you that I think of someone else."

"If it means I get to have sex with you, it's more than fair. Plus, half of America fantasizes about someone else when they make love."

"But we're not in love."

His shoulders slump, ever so slightly, so subtly I almost convince myself I imagined it.

"I wasn't so sure of that, actually," he says quietly.

"Oh, God," I whisper. "I'm sorry."

He looks at me for a long second. Then he exhales and softens.

"You deserve a woman who wants you more than anyone else in the world," I tell him.

"Damn it, Ava," he mutters. "I knew when I met you that you were a romantic."

He sits up, studying me with amused resignation and something gentler underneath.

"Are you at least going to tell me who this guy is who just ruined a perfectly good date?" he asks. "I'll write him into my next book and take creative liberties."

I pour us another glass of wine and proceed to tell him everything about Gavin.

How I used to hate him. About the time he changed place cards at a Thanksgiving dinner just so he wouldn't have to sit next to me. Not being invited to his engagement party, then working for him and becoming his friend, then falling madly, deeply in love with him even though I knew it was foolish, then sending him away to Olivia.

"He was your blind spot," Samuel says finally.

"Blind spot?"

"You know when you're driving along and suddenly you see a car come up on your side," he says. "Even though you were checking your rear-view mirror and your side mirrors, maybe you even looked over your shoulder if you're a cautious person, but there that car is, it just appears."

He sips his wine, choosing words carefully.

"Sometimes it's frightening," he continues, "sometimes it's surreal, like they came out of nowhere. Almost shocks you that you could have missed something like that."

He looks at me.

"But the truth is they were there all along," he says quietly. "And they could probably see you long before they blindsided you."

His voice goes softer.

"Gavin Jones is definitely your blind spot."

CHAPTER 44

Hello, So Long.

HOBOKEN IN APRIL is all false starts and small miracles. Trees bristling with new buds, flowers pushing their way up and out of window boxes, the whole street pretending spring is a sure thing.

The Jones brownstone is still a steady beacon on the block, the porch light pooling on the steps, grapevines webbing up the facade in dark green veins. As Samuel and I climb the brick steps, a murmur of voices and laughter reaches us, as if it's slipping through the seams of the old front door. I know I'm wanted in that house—the easy warmth waiting just beyond the door. Once, that warmth was unquestioned. The kind you walk into without knocking, without wondering if you still belong there.

I hesitate on the top step. The house hasn't changed—but the shape of my place inside it has. Because I've learned the hard way that new beginnings don't guarantee safety. Sometimes they just teach you how easily hope can grow roots in a place that might not keep you.

Samuel shifts beside me on the step, close enough that I feel the warmth of him through his jacket.

Somehow, in the months since everything fell apart and reassembled into something quieter, Samuel and I decided to be friends. Real friends. Late-night texts, smart jokes, long talks that make my loneliness feel, well, less lonely. When I mentioned I didn't have a date for Jared's engagement party, he didn't hesitate. He said he was in New York for a literary panel anyway. And he showed up. Like that was normal.

As we reach the stoop, the scent hits.

Chocolate. Butter. A bright flare of bourbon under the sweetness. *If Pigs Could Fly* Chocolate Croissant Bread Pudding.

For a second, the memory is warm. *Patricia in her kitchen, a towel over her shoulder, humming as she pulls croissant bread pudding from the oven at Christmas.* And then the scent tilts, and … *I'm back in Gavin's kitchen on Orcas Island, all those months ago, the air heavy with sugar and possibility. Gavin's hands on my waist, his mouth against mine, the bread pudding cooling in the background like it knew it didn't stand a chance.*

"I don't know if I'm ready," I murmur.

I glance over. Samuel's adjusting his collar. "Then we'll pretend you are until it's true."

I nod, trying not to fidget. The dress is emerald-green silk, cut low in the back—a little riskier than I usually go for. If I'm being totally honest, I didn't dress for Gavin, but maybe I wouldn't mind if he noticed. The air's cool against my skin, and I can't decide if I feel beautiful or just exposed.

Samuel looks unfairly handsome. Black wool peacoat, blonde hair curling at his collar, his tattoo hiding just under the cuff of his sleeve, black ink on olive skin.

It shouldn't do anything to me, but it does.

He catches me looking and his mouth tilts, amused. "If you're about to say something nice," he warns, "I don't do well with compliments."

"You're a literary thirst trap," I say.

He exhales a laugh. "That's either the worst compliment I've ever received or the best insult."

I laugh, and it loosens something in my ribs.

Samuel tips his head toward the door. "I'm happy to be your emotional support person. But you do have to actually enter the building at some point."

Before I can answer, the door opens.

Patricia is there, cheeks flushed, hair pinned back in a way that always makes her look younger than she has any right to look. She takes one look at me, and her whole face transforms: warmth first, then relief, then the particular brightness she gets when she's decided someone she loves is safe.

"Ava," she says, pulling me in before I can say anything, arms firm around my shoulders, the scent of flowers and citrus comforting me.

"I'm so glad you're here," she whispers.

"I'm early," I say. "I came to help."

"That's my girl," she murmurs, kissing my temple the way she did when I was twenty-two and crying in her kitchen.

Then Patricia's attention slides to Samuel, her smile blooming into delighted mischief.

"And this must be the writer everyone keeps gossiping about."

Samuel tips his head down politely. "Only regionally scandalous, I promise."

Patricia's eyes brighten. "Liam told me you were just nominated for not one, but two literary prizes."

Samuel's face does that quiet, attractive thing, half wince, half humility. "I'm still waiting for the follow-up emails that start with 'Apologies—wrong Samuel.'"

Patricia laughs like she's already decided she likes him. "Come in, both of you—I want a minute before everyone else gets to you."

The hallway is exactly as I remember it, framed photographs running up the walls like a timeline you can touch. Jared's gap-toothed grins. Him blowing out candles on a birthday cake. School photos where he's trying to look serious and failing. Then Gavin: shoulders already squared, a serious expression, as if he's been appointed guardian of each moment. Cari everywhere, glittering even in childhood, caught mid-laugh, mid-dance, mid-something loud and joyful. Patricia and Liam thread through it all in different seasons of their lives: holidays, vacations, ordinary days made worth saving, and on their first road trip in the Beetle.

I stop, my breath catching on something small and ridiculous. There I am, scattered in the margins: an arm slung around Jared, a blurry New Year's kiss on Cari's cheek, my face tilted toward the camera like I'm surprised to be included. A family photo of all of us in Mexico grinning. Except Gavin who stands off to the side with a scowl.

They didn't remove me from the family wall.

Samuel's gaze flicks over the photos once, then he turns his attention elsewhere, giving me the moment without asking me to explain it.

When my breath turns shaky, he's there again, close enough to steady me, not so close I have to perform okayness.

He's the type of man who knows when to stand beside you and when to pretend not to notice you're breaking.

His being here with me tonight—showing up like this, steady as a pulse—does something to my body that my brain did not approve.

It makes me wonder: *What if the easy choice is the right choice?*

Patricia touches my elbow, sensing the shift. "Come on," she says, voice brisk but kind. "Before I put you to work, I want you to see something."

She leads us into the open plan dining and living room. The furniture has been rearranged for flow, a long wooden table set up with linens and candles. A few of the culinary crew, two women in black aprons and a man with a chef's knife who looks like he could fillet a salmon with his eyes closed, move in and out of the space under Patricia's quiet command.

"Jared and John wanted their engagement party here. In the house. Not some venue." She smiles. "They said this is where they learned what family looks like."

My eyes sting.

"And," she adds, softer, "they said they wanted you in the room when they started theirs."

I swallow the ache down like a horse-pill-sized multivitamin. It's good for me, but it doesn't go down easy.

"I'm here," I say.

"I know," Patricia says, and squeezes my hand like she's proud of me for simply existing.

Cari barrels into the room, eyes alight, dress glittering, mouth already in motion.

"You made it!" she squeals, pulling me into a hug. "Oh my God, you look like Ava 2.0."

Max follows—tall, soft-eyed, steady in that way that makes you trust him with sharp objects and secrets.

He spots Samuel and his face brightens with genuine, nerdy delight. "Samuel Gailey," he says, offering a hand. "Okay, I've read all your books. I force-fed *Deep Winter* to my freshmen class."

Samuel's face shifts, genuinely pleased, a little embarrassed.

"Then I owe you hazard pay, and your students, my condolences."

Max laughs and lifts his glass. "To being the plus ones tonight."

Samuel clinks back, easy, amused. "Ready and willing to be humbled," he says. "And fully prepared to be outshined."

As they drift into easy conversation, Cari hooks her arm through mine, tugging me toward the kitchen.

"Just us girls for a second," she says.

She waits until we're away from them before dropping her voice.

"How are you," she asks, "*actually*?"

I try for light. "I'm upright."

"Ava," she says, and the way she says my name is a gentle threat.

I exhale. "I'm doing my best not to throw up on your mother's antique runner."

Cari's mouth twists, sympathy and humor colliding. "Okay. Valid."

Then her eyes sharpen. "I know I'm not supposed to mention his name, but Gavin's here."

"I assumed," I say. "He's family and the best man."

Cari watches my face as she grabs an olive from a grazing board. "Do you want me to run interference?"

"No," I say too quickly.

She raises an eyebrow.

"Maybe," I admit. "I don't know."

She squeezes my hand. "You don't have to be brave."

Patricia claps once. Soft, not sharp, but it quiets the room anyway. "Okay," she says, scanning. "I need Ava here in the kitchen with me, and I need Jared's sister, to stop flirting with the grazing board."

"I wasn't flirting," Cari says, mock-offended.

"You were," Max says.

"I need you," Patricia tells her, "to find Jared and John and make sure they eat something that isn't champagne."

"Yes, Chef," she salutes and drags Max away with purpose.

The kitchen smells like butter and citrus and sugar and that bread pudding—rich and intimate.

I take my post at the counter and start prepping crudités, because it's easier to be useful than to be emotional.

Samuel slides in beside me and rolls his sleeves, the Twin Peaks ink peeking again. His elbow brushes mine, accidental, and my body reacts like it's been waiting for a reason.

He leans in, voice low. "You okay?"

"If I start crying, you're allowed to pretend you don't know me."

"I can do that," he says. "I have an extremely believable face."

"And if I start punching someone?"

"Then I'll write about it later," he replies, "with great tenderness and minimal legal exposure."

A laugh breaks out of me. Then the air changes.

Gavin stands in the doorway. He looks painfully himself, familiar enough to make my stomach drop. His gaze flicks to Samuel's rolled sleeves, the tattoo, the calm confidence. Something sharp flashes across his face, and his jaw flexes like he's bitten down on something bitter.

His eyes find mine.

"Ava," he says.

It's just my name, but he says it like it still belongs to him. My body agrees before my brain gets a vote.

Samuel straightens slightly, polite. "Gavin."

They shake hands. Civil. Tight.

A woman enters the kitchen like the dramatic reveal in a prestige miniseries. Flawless, glossy, perfectly lit by accident on purpose.

"There you are," she says, sliding a hand onto Gavin's arm like she's placing herself in the frame. Now, *I* feel something sharp.

Where is Olivia? It would be just like her to be too busy for a family event that doesn't revolve around her. *Or has this woman replaced her?*

Her eyes land on Samuel, and her smile turns deliberate. She looks to Gavin for an introduction.

"Celia, Samuel Gailey." It's gruff at best.

"Samuel Gailey," she says, like she's tasted his name before. "I loved your latest book."

Samuel's expression remains pleasant, but it doesn't open.

"That's kind of you," he says.

Celia tilts her head. "Are you here alone?" A flirtation disguised as curiosity. Or maybe the other way around.

Samuel doesn't look at her first.

He looks at me.

Just a quick check-in, a question with no pressure: *Do you want me to handle this? Do you want an out?*

Gavin sees it too. His gaze sharpens.

My pulse skitters.

"I'm here with Ava," he says simply.

Not possessive. Not loud.

Just true.

Celia's smile wobbles, then resets. "Lucky Ava."

Samuel's mouth quirks. "She is, generally."

The dodge is deliberate. The refusal is kind.

Gavin's mouth tightens. "Can we talk?" He's only looking at me.

Samuel shifts closer, not blocking me, just steady, and murmurs, "Take your time. I've got you."

And, I know he does.

Gavin narrows his eyes and something in his face tightens again—not anger, exactly. Jealousy. The realization that someone else is being careful with me.

I nod, because if I don't, I'll spend the rest of the night feeling him like a bruise.

Gavin leads me down the hall to Liam's study.

The door clicks shut behind us.

His eyes flick down to my mouth, then back up like he's forcing himself to behave.

He opens his mouth, closes it.

"I thought—" he starts. Then stops. "You blocked my emails and my calls," he says.

I flinch. Because he's right.

Because I did.

Because I was too chicken to say the thing that has lived inside my chest like a second heartbeat.

"I don't get you," he says. "You show up with him, but you look at me like—"

"Like what?"

He rubs the back of his neck.

"Ava, we need to talk. The last time I saw you—"

"The last time we saw each other. You said you still loved Olivia."

He looks frustrated and confused.

We hear Cari calling from down the hall. "Toast time!"

"I need to tell you—"

I don't wait for him to finish before I escape into the hallway.

Because suddenly the room feels too small.

Because my pulse has climbed straight into my throat.

If I stay another second, he'll see it—the way my breath keeps catching, the way some part of me still leans toward him.

And I refuse—absolutely refuse—to let Gavin Jones see that.

The party fills the house the way the tide fills a shoreline, gradual until it isn't. Jackets pile up. Glasses clink. Laughter climbs the staircase and settles into the corners. Everyone looks sharpened for the occasion: men in dark suits and polished shoes, women in velvet and satin and sequins that catch the candlelight at every turn. Perfume and champagne and rosemary drift through the rooms in overlapping, invisible clouds.

I search for Samuel.

I find him in the living room, near the fireplace, a half circle of people around him. He's smiling too brightly, leaning in a little too close. Someone laughs with their hand on his forearm. Someone else is asking a question with the intensity of a graduate seminar. Samuel is polite, attentive, giving them his best public version.

But his eyes aren't on them.

His gaze lifts, finds me across the room, and steadies there—quiet, unshowy, like he's checking that I'm still breathing.

Then he looks away, returns to the conversation, and lets the circle close back in.

And somehow that—the choice to keep watch without claiming—lands harder than any flirtation.

The room hushes as Liam raises a glass.

"There's someone here who's known Jared longer than almost anyone. Who's stood by him through the best and worst, and tonight, gets to speak as his Maid of Honor, and as family. Ava."

All eyes turn to me.

I feel Gavin's gaze.

I do not look at him.

I focus on the rim of my champagne glass as I raise it, my hand suddenly unfamiliar.

"Hi," I begin, and a little laugh ripples because I sound like I'm about to confess to a crime. "I've known Jared since we were nineteen, which means I've had the privilege of watching him evolve from a boy who thought a fedora counted as a personality—"

Jared groans. The room laughs.

"—into a man who is somehow still dramatic," I continue, smiling at him, "but now he's dramatic with purpose."

More laughter, softer this time.

My eyes lift automatically, searching for something neutral to land on.

Instead, they find Gavin.

Of course they do.

Just for a second.

He narrows his eyes, like he knows what I'm up to.

My grip tightens on the stem of my glass.

"I met Jared when I thought I knew who I was," I continue, letting the humor settle into something real, my voice only slightly thinner than it was a second ago. "He's the person who showed me I was more than I had been led to believe. He's been my first real home, my first heartbreak, my best friend, and my fiercest advocate."

I pause, swallowing around the lump.

"When my own family was gone," I say, finding Patricia and Liam, "he gave me this one. And when I forgot how to belong, he reminded me I never stopped."

The room goes quiet in that way that feels like love holding its breath.

"And John," I add, turning toward him, "you should know something: Jared doesn't do anything halfway. Not love. Not loyalty. Not holidays. Especially not grudges."

A few affectionate laughs.

"So the fact that you're the first man he has ever loved like this—openly, honestly—" My voice tightens. "That matters."

Jared's eyes shine. John's hand tightens around his.

"Because it isn't always easy to be the first," I say, voice steadying. "The first can be brave and terrifying and messy. The first asks you to step into a world that doesn't always make space for you."

I look at them, at the way they hold each other like it's both a choice and a promise.

"But you did," I say. "Both of you did."

I breathe in.

"Jared is capable of so many kinds of love," I continue. "And you both deserve all of them." I smile through the burn behind my eyes. "John, you see all of him. You love all of him. And you make him steadier without dimming him."

John puts his hand on his heart as he mouths "thank you."

I lift my glass.

"To Jared and John," I say. "May you keep choosing each other, loudly, softly, always."

Applause breaks out. Warm. Real.

I step back, pulse roaring.

Samuel appears at my side like he's been there the whole time.

"You were incredible," he murmurs. No flirtation, just recognition and respect.

Then, softer, wry: "Also, this friend group is terrifyingly literary and functional."

A shaky laugh escapes me.

His gaze flicks past me to Gavin, watching us from across the room like he's holding himself together by force.

Samuel's lips press together, almost imperceptibly.

And then he does something that lands in my body like a touch:

he stays close anyway. Not claiming. Not crowding. Just… there. Choosing to stand beside me when he could step away.

I hand off my glass and move toward the foyer. I need air. I need cold. I need anything that isn't Gavin's eyes on my skin.

I almost make it to the door.

"Ava."

His voice is behind me. Close.

"I can't do this," I say, reaching for my coat.

Gavin's hand catches my wrist. His touch is gentle, familiar, devastating. "Talk to me."

"I can't be around you," I whisper. "It hurts."

His voice drops. "Why?"

"Because I'm not a one-night-or-two-night-stand kind of girl, Gavin. And thanks to you, I can't even say that literally."

Pain crosses his face. Real and immediate.

"I didn't mean—"

"I know," I cut in. "That's the worst part. You weren't cruel. You were just… not brave."

He shuts his eyes for a beat like he's taking the hit.

Then he asks, voice stripped bare: "Are you in love?"

My lungs lock.

Because the truth is right there, pressing against my chest. The truth I sent him away for. The truth I've been too scared to name because naming it makes it real, and real things can leave.

I could tell him.

I could finally say it out loud.

That I never stopped loving him. That he's still so present, I can't seem to love anyone else, no matter how perfect they are.

But the foster kid in me—the girl that learned to survive by never putting all the pieces of her heart on the table—chooses the safer thing.

"I need to know, Ava. Are you in love?"

The thing that isn't fully a lie; it's just not about who he thinks it is about.

"Yes," I say.

The word lands between us, heavy and final.

For a second, he just looks at me, like the world tilted and he's still trying to find his footing.

I add, softer, not unkind, just done: "If you ever really cared about me, you'll let me go."

His gaze slides past me, toward the living room, toward Samuel, sleeves rolled, speaking quietly with Patricia, the kind of man who would hold a woman gently and never make her beg for clarity.

Gavin swallows.

His hand releases, and he steps back from me like he's been hit.

And I walk out into the cold without looking back.

Not because I'm not tempted to stay.

But because if I do, I won't want to leave.

CHAPTER 45

Quiet Commitments

THE WOODPECKER HAS returned. He lands with authority on the north side of the roof and hammers out his morning rhythm like he's auditioning for a woodland percussion band. I don't groan anymore. He's become my unofficial alarm clock, and honestly, he saves me a fortune in batteries. It's July, after all. The island is drenched in bloom, and I have things to do.

Outside the window, Eastsound's Fishing Bay is smooth as glass except for the V-shaped ripples behind a family of otters making their morning commute. A great blue heron stands on the shore like a sentinel. The same bird, I think, that keeps showing up every Friday when I have my coffee on the porch. My spiritual wingman, just vibing in the shallows while I reset.

The pigeons of New York City are a distant memory. Here, I get Bald Eagles, Cormorants, and the occasional Barn Owl overhead.

This is my life now: winged creatures, meals built from whatever the garden throws at me, and fresh butter I churn myself. Sunday night suppers with friends. Two book clubs—one serious, one scandalous. I garden once a week with the girls, all of whom have strong opinions about soil acidity and the sourdough pastries at Seabird Bakeshop.

Hungry Love is booked solid. We serve three days a week, have a waitlist a mile long, and we could open seven days, but why? We like the space between the days. The breathing room. The way the island insists we slow down.

When I first arrived, the plan was to stay for the summer. Now I can't imagine leaving at all. This place has rewired my nervous system. New York felt like a test I was always failing or a rash I couldn't get rid of. Orcas Island is a salve. A daily reminder that life can be beautiful, simpler, even if it's inconvenient as hell.

Patricia and Liam moved to the island full-time this month, and there is a steadiness in having them nearby. I didn't realize how much I needed parents within shouting distance until they were here: Patricia in the garden tending to peonies and dahlias, Liam quietly fixing whatever leans too far or squeaks too loudly.

The only thing we don't talk about is Gavin.

They understood right away that I couldn't handle it, so we leave that space alone.

Planning a wedding menu on a remote island? Wildly challenging. But I'm loving it.

Jared and John are getting married next month. They want a menu that feels like the island, untamed but elegant. I'm thinking Dungeness crab bisque with charred garlic scapes, followed by cedar-planked salmon with blackberry miso glaze and a wild greens salad scattered with edible flowers. Dessert will be shell-shaped Earl Grey madeleines with dark-chocolate pots de crème, served in mismatched teacups we found at the Orcas Senior Center's "Granny's Attic" annual rummage sale.

Patricia hired her favorite local couture florist, Ms. Morgan, to build the altar from driftwood, fir boughs, and wildflowers. The Olga Symphony will greet guests. The Crow Valley String Band will bring their fiddles and harmonies to the dance floor. Later, Bad Dads will play a punk set on the old boat dock. It will feel like a life you chose on purpose.

I finish my tea and throw on a jacket and a hat for ROAM, the town's annual art walk.

Summer is glorious here. After a winter that sharpened every edge and an April that stayed stubbornly brisk, the island has exploded. Fruit trees flaunt their tiny promises. Salal is already swelling in the understory, and huckleberries are beginning their slow work, turning sunlight into something you can eat. It's the kind of natural abundance that doesn't ask you to pay for it.

Half the island is out, sauntering between art pop-ups with cups of coffee. I wave to Tom, the ex-lawyer turned beekeeper, and pause at a booth where Susan Singleton's botanicals bloom across sheets of antique paper. One of the quiet miracles of island life is realizing the people you volunteer beside at beach cleanups or school fundraisers are also making museum-worthy work in their spare time.

Then I see them.

Samuel is standing beside a woman with wavy blonde hair and a stunning smile. She's pretty in a natural, indie way. They're marveling at a charcoal, mixed-media piece called *Shroud*. It's my favorite piece on the island by my friend Kate Geddes, who, at 83, is still making her fiercest, most fearless work.

Kate created the life-size charcoal figure after she came home from the hospital after an illness—still fragile—wrapping herself protectively, turning survival into shape. The gold rice paper enveloping the figure isn't decoration; it's the shroud, the self-made shelter. I used to think shelter meant walls. Turns out it can be paper-thin and still save you.

Samuel gestures to the painting, and his date leans into his shoulder. She doesn't just look. She tracks the edges of the rice paper with her eyes like she's reading braille. "It's not hiding," I hear her say quietly. "It's holding."

Samuel glances at her—quick, bright—like he's been waiting for someone to say the right thing. And when she does, something in him eases.

And the thing is, I'm happy for him, happier than I expected to be.

If I had truly been in love with Samuel, this moment would sting, but it doesn't. It settles over me softly, affirming what I already knew: I could never give Samuel my full heart because it still belonged to someone else.

He sees me before I can slip away. "Ava!"

I cross the street, smile already forming. "Hey, stranger."

"This is Kara," he says. "She teaches ceramics and jewelry-making in Olga."

Kara holds out a hand, dried clay on her wrists. "I've heard all about you. Samuel says you're the kind of person who saves people and then disappears before they can say thank you."

I laugh, a little startled. "That sounds dramatic."

Samuel shrugs. "You saved me from myself. And from putting crab on pizza."

We talk for a while about art and the best places to pick berries in town, Kara insisting the sweetest blackberries are always the ones you have to bleed for.

I find myself laughing, which surprises me.

When I excuse myself to head to Ray's General Store, Kara hugs me. Not a quick, polite one. A real one, like we've known each other longer than five minutes.

Seeing them makes me wonder if Gavin is happy. And if I'll ever be happy with anyone but him.

LATER, I SIT on the deck with a bowl of Tatsuta age and sunomono, watching the heron stalk the shallows. The sky is painted in layers of apricot and lavender, and the water catches it all like a mirror. I don't know what's next. But for now, it's enough.

Inside, Kiki is sketching out a chalkboard menu for the wedding. I poke my head in. "I was thinking we could offer Gavin a monthly rental for the apartment and garden. It doesn't feel right to just live here indefinitely without paying. And I'm not leaving the island."

Kiki looks up, one brow raised. "Oh, you're really *staying* staying?"

"Yeah." I smile. "There's no way I'm giving up our garden. Even if that woodpecker thinks he owns the place."

"Thank God," she says. "The deer aren't going to slow-drive past themselves."

She sets down her chalk. "You know, we have a waitlist for a year, Ava. We're not just surviving; we've really built something."

For a second, she contemplates the words like she can't believe she gets to say them out loud.

"So, we're really doing this," she says.

"We already are."

We sit on the deck, watching the day end. The summer light lingers as the island unspools into quiet.

I think of the people I left behind. My parents, first. Because they're the original ache, the absence that taught me I could keep going. Then the living: Jared, who never let distance turn into disappearance, still sending me songs at odd hours like he's apprenticing me in other words for love.

And then I think of *him*. The one I might still run into.

Even if I see him again. Even if it hurts.

I'm not going anywhere.

CHAPTER 46

Rehearsals

THE NIGHT BEFORE the wedding, we all gather in the l'orangerie, tucked into the garden, the way a heart tucks its most fragile things behind bone.

Flowering dogwood stems are laced through the rafters. Candles flicker in mismatched jars. The air is warm and sweet with the scent of tomato vines and late-summer basil, the kind of perfume you can't buy because it only exists when something has been loved into growing.

It's just the Jones family and me.

Kiki runs the logistics like she's hosting a global summit. Jay from Houlme has taken command of our wood-fired oven with the calm authority of someone who believes in heat and patience. Platters come out in waves: blistered pizzas with squash blossoms, a little char at the edges; tender-leafed salads topped with shavings of cured hen eggs that look like something you'd find in a magazine spread.

Negronis are flowing, some real, some pretend, and no one seems to mind which is which. Patricia has already decided the phony negroni is "darling," the way she politely describes dishes she'll later reverse engineer in her own kitchen.

The playlist was curated by Gavin.

I know because it sounds like our road trip to Vancouver. Now, all of the songs sound like they hide secrets. Chords that rise unexpectedly, like a hand on your back when you weren't braced for touch.

I've been seated opposite him at the long table. That distance feels deliberate. A choice. Discipline.

He laughs with Patricia, gestures toward Jared, says something sarcastic to Cari. But every now and then, his gaze flicks toward me. It lands, stays, moves away. Like his eyes are doing their own rehearsal. Practice looking. Practice not reaching.

Olivia isn't here tonight. Neither is Samuel.

I do everything I can to avoid his gaze, but my body remembers my time with him. Not in a romantic, tasteful way. In a cellular way.

His hands.

The shape of them on my ribs. The way his thumb used to draw slow circles at my hip as if my body was a map he'd already memorized. The way he could make me feel safe and wrecked at the same time.

It rushes back in unexpected waves. Months apart, and I haven't untangled a single thread. It's like he moved in, quietly, and my cells refused to let him leave.

When a server passes a platter down the table, Gavin reaches for it at the same time I do.

Our fingers brush. A shared accident.

My whole nervous system lights up like a match.

He stills. I still. The platter wobbles.

Patricia laughs at something Liam says, and the moment is swallowed by noise, but my skin won't forget.

We don't speak.

But the tension is so present, it has elbows and sharp corners.

Later, when I step outside for air, it's as if the garden is breathing in the dark. Thyme and rosemary and the faint, wild sweetness of strawberries and huckleberries. I can hear the distant hush of Fishing Bay across the road.

Gavin's shadow appears in the doorway, but he doesn't join me.

He just stands there, like he's waiting for me to decide something.

My foster-kid instincts snap awake: don't ask for love out loud. Don't put your whole heart on the table. Don't hand someone something they can use against you.

So I walk away first.

And I tell myself it's the safer choice.

CHAPTER 47

96 Words for Love

THE WEDDING DAY arrives like a long-held breath released.

August on Orcas Island is the one month you can count on not being betrayed by the sky. It's all blue above us—clear and unapologetic—and the late-summer light is soft enough to make everything look forgiven.

The garden, our improbable, unruly Eden we coaxed into bloom, is a cathedral of color and scent. Wild hollyhock rises along the fence line, tall and bright, their pink cups opening to the sun. Blackberries bristle on the brambles, still a week from peak ripeness, a promise that everyone can see coming.

It smells and looks like joy.

Guests drift in carrying cocktails, shoes sinking softly into the gravel walkways. The Olga Symphony tunes up under the arbor: Gordon—who takes French class with me at the chocolate shop—plucking at his banjo; his partner, Anita, drawing eerie magic from an ordinary wood and metal saw that makes the air shimmer when she plucks it.

Tara runs the bar. Salmonberry lemonade over pebble ice. Shrubs and sangria made from fresh garden herbs. Mixed drinks in glasses that sweat in the heat. Warm pidé made by Isabel in baskets on nearby tables.

There is mussel smoke in the air, éclade de moules roasting over pine needles the way they do it in France, shells blackening and hissing open. People cluster around it, delighted by the drama of food that announces itself.

I'm reaching for a glass of sangria when I see them.

Quinn drifts toward the bar, where Kiki is already holding court in a pair of sequined sandals that definitely weren't meant for sand. He doesn't see me. Not yet.

"Still not having sex?" he asks, grinning like the question is a sport.

Kiki doesn't even blink. "I'm sure you're having enough for everyone. Have you considered donating the excess to science?"

Quinn laughs—full-bodied, delighted—and for a second, he looks at her like she's the only person on the island.

I don't know what's happening between them. But I wonder—not for the first time—if sometimes the people who confuse you most are the ones meant to make you braver.

Then Olivia steps into view. Sun catches the gold in her hair. The same careful smile. It's like watching the villain of an old story walk calmly through the background of a new one.

For a second, I can't move. Not from jealousy, but the whiplash of memory. The punch of seeing a past version of yourself reflected back through someone else's choices. It should scramble me. Instead, it lands like a door clicking shut.

She crosses the gravel toward the bar. Toward Quinn. She slides next to him and takes his hand.

Cari leans in when she sees me stiffen.

"Gavin forgave them. We grew up with Quinn. He didn't want to lose their friendship," she says. "Honestly, I think he was relieved."

"But he and Olivia. The Save the Date cards," I whisper.

"Gavin didn't call you?" she asks, surprised.

I remember him trying to tell me something in Hoboken—before I lied to him.

"I blocked his number. His emails."

That admission lands harder than I expected. I wasn't just protecting myself. I was choosing silence.

It's time to take my place at the altar as the band cues guests to take their seats. Jared and John stand beneath the driftwood arch strung with the palest of flowers—white and blush—and hanging moss.

And then I feel it, that shift in the air. The heat that happens when someone steps a little too close.

The best man.

Gavin stands next to me. Opposite us, John stands with his sister and best friend. I hold my bouquet so tightly I can feel the stems bruise in my palm.

Gavin shifts subtly. Not obvious, not inappropriate, just enough that our arms brush. Hands nearly touching, but not quite. The restraint is almost indecent.

I don't look at him. But I feel everything.

I can't help it; I look at his hands.

They're folded in front of him. Calm. Controlled.

I remember them differently.

I remember them as gentle but insistent. As the thing that made me believe I belonged with him before my mind could.

He catches my eye.

But it isn't just a look.

It's everything sharp and unfinished between us made visible.

Jared begins his vows, and his voice catches on the first sentence. John steadies him with a smile that says, *always*. I blink hard, like I can keep the tears inside by force.

Gavin keeps his eyes on Jared and John, but his body leans, slightly, imperceptibly, toward me.

I feel it like a touch.

And something in me cracks.

Because this moment, this altar, this garden—it exists because Gavin gave me room. He gave me time. Most of all, he never asked me to leave, even when I did everything I could to make him leave.

He chose me in actions. Just never in words.

And that kid in me, the one that learned love could evaporate if you named it too loudly, whispers: *Don't. Don't ask. Don't hope.*

But the Ava that is me now needs to know.

The vows end. The rings go on. The music swells. The crowd cheers.

John and Jared kiss.

And it's beautiful.

And it hurts.

Because it reminds me how simple love can be when people are brave.

After the ceremony, the lawn becomes a living painting. Family photos, congratulations, more photos, laughter skipping across the grass like thrown stones. Female guests hijack Gavin for pictures and selfies. For conversation. For the kind of flirtation that gathers at weddings like bees to honey.

Jared pulls me in for a photo, one arm warm around my shoulders. "Hey," he murmurs under the noise of the crowd. I glance up. His eyes flick past me—to Gavin—then back again. "You know he still looks at you like that, right?"

"Like what?" I ask.

Jared's smile softens. "Like he never stopped hoping."

I watch Gavin smile with relatives. He's polite with everyone.

But his eyes keep finding me.

Not in a possessive way.

In a searching way.

Like he's asking: *Are we doing this again? The running?*

I tell myself I'm fine.

Then I go to the kitchen.

In the kitchen, I have a team I trust with the food, but I stay hands-on anyway. Partly because it's my menu. Mostly because it's easier to be a machine than a woman in love.

The crab bisque course was a hit. The salmon is glazed, seared perfectly, skin crisp. The risotto is rich with chanterelles and matsutakes I foraged myself at Doe Bay, mushrooms that smell like forest and rain and the kind of wild you can't buy.

Wildflower salads go out like bouquets in the hands of servers. I wipe the edges of plates. Taste sauces. Adjust salt.

Service has a rhythm.

It lets me breathe.

Focus.

Not feel.

Then I hear someone announce Gavin's name. Through the doorway to the garden, I see him walk toward the stage.

Patricia said he's been invisible for weeks. Now he steps under the arbor with his guitar, caught in that honeyed golden hour light like the universe decided to be generous.

The song is an original, which means he's been using the studio. The one I helped paint and patch and fill with furniture and better faith. Because I believed he had something in him that deserved a place to create.

He doesn't say who the song is for.

Everyone assumes it's for Jared and John.

I know better.

//Loving is so short// Forgetting is so long//

Every lyric peels me open.

And still—beneath the ache—something warmer curls in my chest. Pride. Not because I helped him get there. But because he let himself arrive.

When it's over, Gavin is handed a glass of champagne, and the toasts begin.

He doesn't do speeches, which is how I know he means every word.

"Jared," he says. "My whole life, I've watched you seek joy even when it scared you. That's your best instinct. And a kind of bravery. You're the baby brother, but when it comes to love, I've watched you choose, at every turn, to love more, not less, to keep the important people in your life even when it's hard."

There's a pause. A swallow.

"I didn't always understand it," he adds. "But I do now."

He laughs once, tight, controlled. "Also, I'd like to formally apologize to everyone for any emotional constipation I've brought into group settings over the years."

The crowd laughs.

I don't.

Because then he says, quietly, almost like he's not sure he's allowed to—

"And Ava… thank you. For feeding us. For building this place. For staying."

My name, in his mouth, lands like his hand at my waist.

I go cold.

Then hot.

Then I can't breathe.

I don't even hear the end of the toast.

Then the cake—lemon and elderflower—is being sliced. Pale, perfect layers, and the scent is suddenly a memory of being twelve and finding a rare dessert at a foster home, something sweet that didn't belong to me, something I was told to take only a small piece of, because I wasn't allowed to want too much.

Sweetness has always been conditional.

Joy has always come with fine print. Even now, my body waits for the catch.

I grab a piece of cake and lift a forkful to my mouth.

It blooms on my tongue—soft, bright, sweet.

And something in me collapses.

Because it's not just cake.

It's proof.

Proof that I built a life that can taste like this.

Proof that I'm still terrified it will be taken away. *But why?*

I cry.

Not the elegant kind.

The full-body kind that makes you grip the counter, shoulders shaking, breath snagging like you've been running.

Kiki is there in seconds.

She doesn't speak.

She just hands me a kitchen towel and rubs my back in slow circles like she's smoothing out a panic attack.

"I love him," I gasp.

Kiki leans in, eyes sharp, voice gentle. "Then tell him. Not because you're guaranteed the ending. Because you deserve to stop swallowing your own heart."

My throat burns, and the girl in me panics.

But the woman I've become stands up anyway.

Through the swinging kitchen door, a cheer rises, the scrape of chairs, the sudden rush of feet.

Kiki stills, listening, then meets my eyes.

"Family dance," she says softly, like she's offering me a hand. "That means you."

My hands shake, but my feet still find the floor.

Jared and John made room for me on purpose, leaving a space as if it were always mine. Now all I have to do is be brave enough to step into it.

The song starts.

True Love Will Find You in the End.

The song Gavin once sang for me in this very garden, back when I pretended I had nothing left to give.

As I push through the café doors and re-enter the garden, he appears beside me.

He offers a hand.

I stare at it for half a second too long.

Then I take it.

We move together.

His palm is warm. Familiar.

He guides me onto the dance floor with the rest of the family. Jared and John swaying together under the string lights, Patricia tucked into Liam, Cari laughing softly as Max spins her close, everyone moving like a single, steady breath.

Gavin draws me in, and there's no more pretending; my body goes sweetly, mortifyingly honest against his.

I don't look up.

Not yet.

"You're crying," he says softly.

"I—" My voice catches. "It's the cake."

"Ava."

He says my name like a plea.

Like an apology.

Like a door.

I lift my gaze.

And there he is.

The man who gave me room to root.

The man I sent away.

The man I wouldn't let reach me.

The man my body never stopped choosing.

I can feel the words pushing at my ribs, demanding to be born.

And the fear—God, the fear.

Because saying it makes it real.

And real things can leave.

"I love you," I say anyway, voice shaking. "I didn't say it before because I was scared that if I did—and you didn't say it back—I'd disappear. Like I used to."

His face changes.

Something unguarded, almost painful.

"You could never disappear," he says. Then he swallows hard. "You stay. Even when it hurts."

I blink. Another tear escapes.

He catches it with his thumb.

"I love you," he says. It's plain. Not poetic. Just true. "In the beginning, I didn't say it because I thought I'd betray Jared. And then, because I thought you weren't ready to hear it. I kept thinking if I said it out loud, I'd ruin everything we built here, everything and everyone I was trying to protect."

His breath shudders.

"Turns out silence made it worse. It ruined me instead."

My heart breaks open.

He leans his forehead to mine.

"I've loved you since the day I met you," he whispers. "I just wasn't brave enough to wait while you figured it out."

I exhale, shaking. "I'm here."

"So am I."

We kiss. His hands slide warm along my cheeks, drawing me closer.

And it tastes like summer fruit and salt air—and every word I've been starving myself of.

LATER, THE SKY goes indigo, and the stars bloom overhead.

Down on the shoreline, Bad Dads wail a punk version of *Stand by Me*—guitars shrieking, tenderness stubbornly alive underneath—as Jared and John step onto the sailboat at the dock, waves catching moonlight like sequins.

When the song ends, the crowd lights sparklers and cheers until their throats go raw as the boat drifts away, Jared and John wrapped around each other on the bow.

I stand beside Gavin, sparklers hissing down to wire in our fists, their gold light flickering across his face and mine.

I think of all the words for love and, for once, I ask the only thing that matters.

"What happens now?"

"I never let you go again," he says. "And someday people will stand right here, watching us sail off into the night."

I believe him. It took us a long time to get here. But we're here.

This time, when he reaches for my hand, I tuck into his side, and I don't let go.

MORE TO SAVOR

Thanks for reading *Hungry Love*. This next section is your invitation to stay a little longer—like when the night's winding down, but no one wants to leave the table just yet.

You'll find Ava & Gavin's playlist, book club questions, an author interview, my rom-com love list, and a few heartfelt thank-yous. Basically: the afterparty.

LOVE NOTES

THE HUNGRY LOVE PLAYLIST
AVA
GAVIN
SCAN ME!
TO LISTEN TO THE MUSIC
ON SPOTIFY

The Hungry Love Playlist

Ava, Gavin, and Jared's shared mixtapes, surprise serenades, and emotionally reckless song recs. Scan the QR code to listen.

New Partner — Spink
The perfect breakup song—because it still remembers the love. Played on repeat after Jared and Ava ended, but didn't quite let go. Originally by Will Oldham, reimagined and sung here by the real-life man who inspired Jared's character.

Let Your Song — The Ellis Court
The feeling Ava has after discovering the island and the garden. Another song from Jared's real-life muse. Because not all love stories end in regret.

Poison Cup — M. Ward
Gavin and Ava's eventual friendship—coded, basically. Because a little bit of love won't do.

Heart of Glass — Coeur de Verre (after Blondie)
Gavin's obsession with French cover songs starts here.

Mean Something — Miel
A song about wanting something to matter and not knowing if it should. Miel is island-connected and Henri Bardot-adjacent.

Make You Love Me — Henri Bardot
The song in Gavin's head as he slips his jacket over Ava's shoulders at Doe Bay. He just wrecked her with a song—this says the rest. Singer Bardot is the brother of Miel, also with Orcas roots.

Shelter from the Storm — Bob Dylan
It's on everyone's playlist. Ava's. Gavin's. Jared's. It deserves to be.

I Want You To Want Me — Cheap Trick
Gavin, sweaty and loud, sings this when Ava shows up with Kiki and absolutely no one is prepared for the hot rockstar version of him.

I'm on Fire — Cassandra Violet (after Springsteen)
For Ava's post–Doe Bay spiral. Same song. Different ache.

I Don't Like the Man I Am — Pete Molinari
Gavin sings this at Doe Bay when Ava connects the dots.

My Love Mine All Mine — Mitski
Inspired by Kiki's quiet, asexual coming out.

All the Time — Bahamas
The song that reminds Gavin and Ava that one of them had all the time in the world. The other couldn't wait.

You Never Can Tell — Chuck Berry
The song Gavin dances to with Patricia, and the moment Ava realizes he's the one.

Into My Arms — Nick Cave & The Bad Seeds
Gavin plays this onstage, in the garden, when he saves the day—and maybe Ava, too.

I'm Gonna Be (500 Miles) — The Proclaimers
Ava (5,000 miles) and Gavin (500) argue over the lyrics on their first road trip. Neither of them was entirely right—or entirely wrong.

Tower of Song — Leonard Cohen
Ava and Gavin's Vancouver concert date, where Leonard plays third wheel.

Hallelujah — Brandi Carlile / Jeff Buckley / Leonard Cohen
Ava and Gavin hear this song, sung by Leonard Cohen, together in Vancouver. There's no wrong version. There's just the one that ruins you.

Magic in the Air — Badly Drawn Boy
Ava plays this during THE backyard dinner cooked to console Gavin.

Wild Horses — The Rolling Stones
It's the song Gavin plays when he's thinking of Ava.

Death of the Phone Call — Whatever, Dad
For no other reason than: it's cool.

The Times They Are A-Changin' — Goth Babe
Gavin plays this cover of Dylan's song for Ava. Moody and, yeah, it's definitely on the nose, but in the best way possible.

The Night We Met — Lord Huron feat. Phoebe Bridgers
After they had it all and lost it. Ava's late-night reach. Maybe Gavin's too.

When the Lights Go Out — Cry Baby
Moody, slow, and exactly what Gavin sings to himself when Ava is gone.

Exile — Taylor Swift (feat. Bon Iver)
The beautiful and bruised doom track to Ava's fears, and how she feels when Gavin goes back to Olivia.

I Know — The Ellis Court
For when Ava has to love Gavin from far away, but he feels close anyway.

True Love Will Find You in the End — Headless Heroes
True Love Will Find You in the End — Daniel Johnston
You get both. Some love songs don't land until the second time.

Stand by Me — Pennywise (explicit)
Bad Dads, a favorite island band, tear into this punk version at Jared and John's wedding while sparklers flare, guests croon along, and Ava and Gavin quietly imagine the day they'll be the ones sailing off together.

At Last — Etta James
The song that Gavin and Ava dance to at Jared & John's wedding. For the ones who take the long way. At last.

Acknowledgments

Thank you for reading *Hungry Love*. Truly. If this story made you laugh, cry, crave carbs, or text someone you miss, I'm so grateful you spent your time here.

If you feel inclined to leave a review—wherever you like to leave such things—please know that it means more to authors than we can properly express. Stories don't travel very far without readers carrying them. And if you ever share a post or review, I'd love to see it. You can tag #hungrylovenovel #tomikodiaz.

This book was written in many beloved corners of the world, including the Encinitas Public Library, the Carlsbad City Library, the West Hollywood Library, the Anacortes Public Library, and the Mount Vernon Library. A special shout-out—inside voice—to the Orcas Island Public Library, which offered not only daily warmth and Wi-Fi but the quiet magic that only libraries can. I wrote surrounded by people who believe in stories, and in the radical idea that books should be available to everyone. Libraries have always been lifelines. This one was a lighthouse, too.

Gratitude to the staff at Darvill's, Orcas Island's one and only indie bookstore, and quite possibly one of the most charming places on the planet.

Deep thanks to readers Ashley Westbrook, Sara Farish, and Tara Anderson, and especially to Melissa Rodriguez for her enthusiastic deep dives into the steamy bits (your dedication did not go unnoticed), and to Kiki Luna for her extra support and inspiration. Your insights and excitement made this book better.

To Jen Robinson Arellano, Frances Carrillo, Shannon Bindler, Margalit Ward, and Linda Goldstein Knowlton. You read an entirely different version of this book over fourteen years ago in Los Angeles, before life (and detours) took over. The story may have changed completely, but my gratitude to you hasn't.

To my island writers group: Theresa Marl, Angela Saxe, Guy Woods, Jeff Henigson, and especially Samuel Gailey and Joe Thoron—thank you for reading rough drafts, asking smart questions, and being the kind of humans who show up.

To Gray Gailey, who happens to be not only my eagle-eyed editor but also my brilliant daughter. I trust your instincts, your notes, and your heart. Collaborating with you on this book has been one of the great joys of my creative life.

To the real-life Samuel Gailey—thank you for your steady love, your wit, and for living so patiently alongside a rotating cast of imaginary people. You inspired one of my favorite characters in this book, but more than that, you helped make the writing of it possible.

To the Orcas Island community—thank you for welcoming me with such open arms. It's a rare and beautiful thing to find a creative and compassionate community. Special thanks to Martha Farish, Sara Farish, and Joe Cohen. Your steady encouragement and support have made it possible for me to show up, create, and make an impact—especially in the literary and visual arts space on Orcas.

While *Hungry Love* is fiction, it's grounded in a truth I've lived. So, thank you to Tim Halloran, who provided much of the real-life inspiration for Jared. Our story—and the way we navigated your coming out, our never-ending friendship, and our creative connection—shaped not just Jared's character, but the emotional core of this book. Thank you for letting me draw from it.

And finally, to my mom. It's a gut punch that you didn't live long enough to read this book. But there would be no book without you. You taught me how reading can carry you through hard times and open doors to other worlds. You read books—especially mystery romances—to get through motherhood, menopause, and divorce, with your sense of optimism intact. And your passion for food, your belief in its power to heal, and your way of making nourishment about more than just what's on the plate—that's all in here, too.

Thank you, always.

READER'S GUIDE

"For fans of Emily Henry and Abby Jimenez, a deliciously funny debut rom-com about ambition, appetite, and the kind of slow-burn chemistry that refuses to stay on the back burner."

-Darvill's Bookstore

HUNGRY

a novel

Playlist + Recipes Inside

TOMIKO DIAZ

10 Questions for Readers

1. Let's talk about Ava and Jared. How did you feel about the way Ava navigated their relationship? Have you ever had a romantic partner evolve into someone you didn't expect?
2. Author Michael Pollan says, "*All cooking is transformation.*" Ava uses food to soothe, process, and express heartbreak. Have you ever used food—making it, eating it, sharing it—to transform a situation or emotion?
3. Unrequited love. Brooding men with secret feelings (*Mr. Darcy, anyone?*). Why do we keep falling for this dynamic on the page? What's the enduring appeal?
4. One of the novel's quieter themes is the art of slowing down, of *choosing* a life, not just reacting to one. Ava trades in a fast-paced, unsustainable city life for a remote rural island. Have you ever dreamed of (or actually made) a big life pivot to simplify?
5. Ava lost both parents at a young age. How do you think that early grief shaped her expectations in relationships—both romantic and platonic?
6. Gavin Jones is clearly the main love interest—but then along come Nico (the musician) and Samuel (the writer), throwing a little delicious uncertainty into Ava's romantic arc. How did these other potential connections impact your reading experience? Did they make the story feel more layered, more real, or more complicated in the best/worst ways?

7. Kiki comes out as asexual in the novel—something that surprises even her. Were you familiar with asexuality before reading? Did Kiki's story change your understanding of what intimacy can look like? And what does it say about Ava that Kiki feels safe enough to share this with her?
8. Music plays a quiet but powerful role in *Hungry Love*, especially for Gavin, who gave it up to support his family. Have you ever put aside a dream or passion to care for someone you loved? Do you still think about going back to it?
9. Be honest: which recipe made your stomach growl? Is there a dish from the book you'd love to cook—or be cooked *for*?
10. If you could sit at Ava and Gavin's kitchen table—wine poured, food simmering—what would you want to ask them? What would you want *them* to ask *you*?

Q&A with the Author

What made you want to write this book?

When I was 27, my boyfriend Tim told me he was attracted to men. It cracked open my understanding of love, identity, and the quiet bravery it takes to tell the truth. In the end, it was heartbreaking, disorienting, and unexpectedly beautiful. We're still best friends decades later. I thought the experience was fertile emotional ground for a novel. It actually ended up inspiring material for a literary novel, too, which I've been working on for a decade. However, after beta readers read the first draft of the rom-com version, the focus shifted. They wanted the heart of the story to belong to Ava and Gavin. It meant a lot of "killing your darlings," but I saved some of those original scenes with Jared. If you want to see how they met, you can read that and other bonus scenes at tomikodiaz.com.

Why did you set the story on Orcas Island?

Originally, the book was set in Summerland, California, a small coastal town near Santa Barbara where I used to escape for romantic getaways. Then I moved to Orcas Island, a quiet, remote island in the Pacific Northwest that feels like it exists slightly outside of time. I wrote a piece about taking the ferry to Orcas for *Kinfolk's* slow travel coffee table book, and it reminded me how special this place is—the ritual of the ferry, the mist lifting off the water, the sense that you've arrived somewhere you're meant to pay attention to. And the characters here? Just as colorful and meddling and big-hearted as any small-town trope novel I've ever devoured—except they're real.

Do the businesses in the book actually exist?

The bookstore—and pretty much every business I mention—does exist on the island. We have only a handful of restaurants, and zero chain stores, and you get to know the shopkeepers well enough that they ask about your mom's hip surgery and mean it. That intimacy felt essential to Ava's story. When you live somewhere small, you can't hide. (Which is both the problem and the point.)

Cooking is important to Ava's character. Do you have a cooking background?

My mom owned two Japanese restaurants in San Diego, California—Tomiko in Encinitas and Nobu in Solana Beach—and a fish store in El Cajon. So I grew up in kitchens. I can clean squid and shrimp like a pro, run a deep fryer without fear, prep for a dinner rush, and plate like a queen. Also, in my generation, when you grew up Taiwanese or Mexican—especially as the eldest—you were cooking by eight. Food wasn't a hobby. It was language. It was responsibility. It was love.

Tell us the story behind your pen name.

Tomiko Diaz was born out of freedom. I've long been at work on a very different novel—more literary, darker in tone, and headed down a traditional publishing path. But I didn't want to wait years to share this side of my writing: the romantic, funny, tender stories that had been quietly insisting on their own space. In publishing, different genres are often treated as different lanes. Tomiko gave me a way to fully claim this one. My mom's Japanese nickname was Tomiko. She died a few months before I finished this book, but I feel like she lives on in this name, in the food she taught me to cook (some of which made its way into these pages), and in her love of books. Diaz honors my Indigenous Mexican heritage on my father's side.

Why did you initially release the book exclusively through indie bookstores?

I have a thing for indie bookstores. They are the beating hearts of literary communities. They hand-sell books. They remember your name. They host your awkward first readings. If we want indie bookstores to survive, we can't just *say* we love them—we have to structure our launches in ways that support them. I wanted to give them a head start. I also wanted to make a small, stubborn statement about where I believe stories belong.

Is this your first foray into rom-com?

Not exactly. I wrote *Sex Y LA*, a humorous relationship column about biracial relationships in L.A., and a memoir-*ish* book entitled *Pornology* about my experiences with men and sex. In 2020, it was adapted into the rom-com film *A Nice Girl Like You* starring Lucy Hale, Mindy Cohn, and Jackie Cruz. I'm also working on a rom-com screenplay and a serialized

Substack novel with actor Bradley James. But this is my first time building a fully fictional romantic world from scratch—and letting myself lean into the joy of that.

Your characters are multiracial. How does your own identity shape that choice?

I'm Taiwanese, Mexican, and Karankawa. My daughter is all that plus Scottish-Irish from her dad's side. Thinking of people—and characters—as multiracial is simply how I see the world. Gavin is part Lummi because I wanted to honor the Indigenous roots of Orcas Island. We live on the ancestral lands of the Lummi (Lhaq'temish) and other Coast Salish peoples who have lived here and stewarded these lands and the sea since time immemorial. Representation isn't a trend for me. It's reality.

Kiki is such a fun, unique character. What was the inspiration behind her?

A lot of Kiki is inspired by my real-life Orcas Island friend named Kiki—her fabulous fashion sense, enormous heart, wicked sense of humor, and instinct to stand up for justice. (Real-life Kiki is not asexual or gender-fluid, but she is gloriously open-minded.) I made fictional Kiki asexual because I've been exploring the many ways people experience intimacy. While developing a TV project, I began thinking about the delicious challenge of writing a character who does not desire traditional sex but falls in love with the most hypersexual person in their orbit. Conflict. Tenderness. Rewriting assumptions about what love looks like. That's catnip to a novelist—and the driving force behind book two. You can read a scene between Kiki & Quinn at tomikodiaz.com

For the last decade, you've mostly been an editor and ghostwriter. What made you decide it was finally time to focus on your own writing?

I got serious during COVID. After years of editing and ghostwriting for brands and other writers—helping them earn critical acclaim and land on *The New York Times* bestseller list—I realized life was not slowing down. If I didn't make space for my own dreams, no one else would. This is also my debut in fiction. Until now, I've only published nonfiction—memoir, essays, personal work rooted in fact. Stepping into a fully imagined world felt both terrifying and electric, but I didn't want to keep waiting for permission to try. The other turning point was being accepted to Hedgebrook, a coveted writing residency on Whidbey Island. I went there to work on my literary novel and spent three weeks alone in a cabin in the woods—no WiFi, fresh organic meals cooked by farmers, and the kind of radical hospitality that makes creative work feel not indulgent, but essential. I wrote in the same cabins where Gloria Steinem worked on her memoir, and where writers like Ruth Ozeki and Ursula K. Le Guin shaped their novels. There is something wildly clarifying about sitting at a desk knowing literary giants once stared out at the same trees. I wrote more in three weeks than I had in three years. It proved that focus wasn't selfish. It was possible, necessary, and nurturing.

What scene was the hardest to write—and why?

Honestly? The first almost-sex scene with Gavin in the hotel in Vancouver. I came at it a hundred different ways. In one version, they kissed. In another, they almost did more. I kept circling the tension between my own more prudish real-life instincts and what readers might recognize as emotionally authentic and satisfying. Writing intimacy isn't just about bodies—it's about pacing, vulnerability, and earned desire. I didn't want to rush it. I didn't want it to feel like the characters were performing it. I wanted it to feel inevitable. But what was even harder than creating new scenes, at first, was cutting scenes between Jared and Ava that showed just how painful it was for them to let each other go. I felt a deep responsibility not to gloss over the complexity of coming out within a long-term relationship. Love doesn't evaporate just because its form changes. I needed readers to believe that walking away cost them something. Otherwise, the new love story wouldn't feel hard-won.

Will there be a book two?

I've always imagined *Hungry Love* as a series, with book two following Kiki & Quinn's love story and book three revisiting Ava & Gavin fifteen years later. I would be thrilled to keep going. So if you loved this novel, leaving a review wherever you read books is one of the most powerful ways to support it. Reviews help books reach more readers—and they can make all the difference in turning hoped-for sequels into real ones.

The Rom-Com Love List

If I ever sounded even remotely confident writing a rom-com, it's because these ten books went first and made it look not only possible, but irresistible. ***Bet Me*** (Jennifer Crusie) was the gateway drug to my rom-com addiction and taught me that chemistry can feel like an argument you're thrilled to lose; ***Book Lovers*** (Emily Henry) proved you can be sharp, tender, and laugh-out-loud funny on the same page; ***The Happily Ever After Playlist*** (Abby Jimenez) reminded me that heartbreak and hope can share a scene without canceling each other out; ***How to End a Love Story*** (Yulin Kuang) made me believe in emotional honesty with a serious pulse; ***Just Last Night*** (Mhairi McFarlane) showed me how to punch straight through the jokes into the softest parts; ***The Kiss Quotient*** (Helen Hoang) showed me that sexy isn't one-size-fits-all—it can live anywhere on the spectrum; ***Wild Love*** (Elsie Silver) was my first audiobook and the moment I learned billionaires aren't boring when the heroine is strong enough to set the story on fire; ***The Hating Game*** (Sally Thorne) is a masterclass in tension and exposes the thin line between hate and love; ***Not in Love*** (Ali Hazelwood) made me want to write intelligent characters who insist they're fine right up until they absolutely aren't; And of course, ***Pride & Prejudice***, the blueprint for enemies-to-lovers by Jane Austen, the patron saint of longing, the OG rom-com influencer, still reminding us 200 years later that the most romantic thing on earth isn't the spark—it's respect earned the hard way. Consider this my thank you note to the writers who ruined my ability to enjoy "normal" love stories—and I mean that as the highest compliment.

STILL HUNGRY?

THE HUNGRY LOVE RECIPES 

AT TOMIKODIAZ.COM 

Recipes

You didn't think I'd leave you without the recipes, did you? Here's an easy Phony Negroni, a recipe for my favorite noodles, and a QR code to more recipes in the book—just in case inspiration (or heartbreak hunger) strikes. Apron optional.

Phony Negroni

A shrub brings the tang and sweetness. The Pathfinder brings the brooding, rooty depth. Together, they make an NA Negroni that might just outshine the classic.

Ingredients

2 oz The Pathfinder Hemp & Root Spirit
2 dashes All The Bitter Aromatic Bitters or Giffard Aperitif NA Bitters
1 oz Girl Meets Dirt Rhubarb Shrub
Large orange peel, for garnish
1 large ice cube

Instructions

Add The Pathfinder, bitters, and shrub to a mixing glass with ice. Stir until chilled, 20 to 30 seconds. Strain into a rocks glass over a large cube. Express the orange peel over the drink and drop it in. For a less sweet drink, add a squeeze of lime or a splash of seltzer.

Five-Minute Forever Noodles For Two

These five-minute garlic noodles are savory, a little spicy, and easy to fall for. They started as the midnight snack my mom made when I was growing up; in my twenties, they inspired a steady stream of marriage proposals from guy friends, which tells you almost everything you need to know.

Ingredients

8 oz somen noodles
3 garlic cloves, finely chopped
1 tablespoon toasted sesame oil
1/2 teaspoon chili oil, plus more to taste (optional)
4 scallions, finely chopped
1 teaspoon avocado or canola oil
6 tablespoons low-sodium tamari or soy sauce
1 star anise (optional)*
Chopped serrano, jalapeño, or Fresno chile pepper (optional)

Instructions

In a large bowl, stir together the garlic, sesame oil, chili oil, scallions, avocado oil, tamari, star anise, and fresh peppers if using.

Bring a pot of water to a boil. Add the noodles and cook until tender but still springy, about 2 minutes. Using tongs, transfer the noodles directly to the sauce and toss until evenly coated and glossy. The noodles should turn a light brown throughout. Taste and add more tamari, soy sauce, or chili oil as needed.

Note

I learned this recipe by sight and taste from my mom, not from a written recipe, so trust your instincts and adjust as you go.

Optional upgrade*

My mom made a dish we called dee-kah, similar to hong shao rou, aka red-braised pork. If you happen to have a little of that broth—or a bit of the pork—on hand, adding some here makes these noodles especially good. Omit the star anise if you add this.

Recipes from the book can be found at www.tomikodiaz.com.

ABOUT THE AUTHOR

Tomiko Diaz is the rom-com pen name of writer Ayn Gailey and editor Gray Gailey. Ayn is also the co-creator of *Wannabe*, a serial rom-com on Substack written with Bradley James. Her writing has appeared in *Cosmo* (Germany), *Elle* (UK), *Latina*, and *Kinfolk*, and her memoir *Pornology* was adapted into the film *A Nice Girl Like You*. Originally from Los Angeles, Ayn now lives on Orcas Island, where she curates the Love & Relationships book club at Darvill's bookstore.

Follow Tomiko at @tomikodiaz_romcoms and visit tomikodiaz.com

www.ingramcontent.com/pod-product-compliance
Lightning Source LLC
LaVergne TN
LVHW091248150826
845673LV00006B/1355